DORA BIRTLES

was born in Wickham, New South Wales, in 1903, and educated at The Women's College, Sydney, and Sydney University. Fascinated by the sea and a keen sailor from an early age, in 1932 she joined the crew of the cutter *Skaga* on an eight-month voyage from Newcastle to Singapore — the first such journey to include women from Australia, and one keenly followed by the press at the time. She and the other women on board wrote regularly for various newspapers throughout the voyage as a means of financing the venture. *North-West by North*, her account of shipboard life, was published in 1935.

When *Skaga's* journey ended in Singapore, Dora Birtles spent several years abroad with her journalist husband. She continued to write articles and was active on the Women's Committee Against War and Fascism in London before the Second World War. She then returned to Australia and was closely involved in the making of the wartime Ealing film, *The Overlanders*, which inspired her novel, published in 1946. A year later, she published *Australia in Colour* and has also published two novels for children. Dora Birtles still lives in Sydney with her husband. She has two sons and is now a grandmother.

VIRAGO
MODERN
CLASSIC

NUMBER
271

THE
OVERLANDERS

DORA BIRTLES

WITH A NEW AFTERWORD
BY THE AUTHOR

Published by VIRAGO PRESS Limited 1987
41 William IV Street, London WC2N 4DB

First published in Great Britain by Shakespeare Head 1947
Copyright Dora Birtles 1947
Afterword Copyright © Dora Birtles 1987

British Library Cataloguing in Publication Data

Birtles, Dora
The overlanders.——(Virago modern classics)
I. Title
823'.914[F]   PR6003.I8/

ISBN 0-86068-808-9

Printed in Great Britain by
Cox and Wyman Ltd, Reading, Berks

This book was inspired by the Ealing Studios film of
the same name, which was written and directed by
HARRY WATT.
All characters are fictional and there is no intended
reference to any living person.

THE OVERLANDERS

CHAPTER I

HELEN PARSONS came panting uphill through the tall grass, tugging the unwilling skewbald pony behind. The grass was sappy still and where she and the pony had pushed through, a grey track, like a wind-eddy on deep water, marked the greenness. Helen had been getting some calves out of a water-hole and her boots and jodhpurs were muddied; the skewbald was mud to the belly, too. He had one blue and one white eye, and it gave him a rancid expression as if his disposition could never be entirely relied on.

"He's got the makings of a rogue in him," Bill Parsons, Helen's father, had once admitted to himself, but it suited him to have Helen ride the skewbald and he had said nothing of his fears. Instead, he kept his eye on the skewbald and hoped for the best. He was proud of his little daughter's riding and he wasn't going to have Ma alarmed when there wasn't a better mount for the child available. He made a policy always to praise the pony up. "He's a goer, that one. Just train him a bit and he'd win the Melbourne Cup." For a while Helen took him seriously. She was only eleven.

As she climbed she talked to the pony. "Com'mon you. Put your best foot foremost. Ups-a-daisy over that one. C'mon. Don't be a lazy on it, Rusty."

The skewbald looked maliciously out of its white eye over its white eyelashes at the little girl with her relentless upward tug on the bridle. It mumbled at the bit and shook the flies off its head. A patch of sweat had spread down round the saddle-cloth. "C'mon, Rusty."

With a "Hurrup" that was an exclamation of disgust, the pony made the steep and treacherous grade. "I knew you'd see it my way," said Helen. She noticed a couple more calves with their mothers and added them to her tally. "Fifty-nine. Not bad at all, fifty-nine. Another one and I make another knot." For each twenty calves she made a knot in a piece of dirty-brown native string that she carried. Her pockets always held an accumulation of very ungirlish trifles, waterproof matches and bits of string, gum resin, fish hooks embedded in bits of cork, a surgical needle and some catgut, the end of a broken spur, a patent screw-on gadget of Condy's crystals, a super clasp knife with all the trimmings. Sometimes when Ma turned out these pockets she felt very wistful that Helen hadn't been a boy. The only boy Ma had had, had died at birth—and that was quite a long, sad story, the sort of story familiar enough among women of the outback.

"When it comes to counting cattle," Bill had said, "never trust your memory. Always make a knot or a notch. Keep it in twenties. That's a score. That's what you call keeping a score, my girl. And settling old scores is just another way of saying that someone didn't count his cattle right the first time and it led to a fight. . . ." Bill was always one for a bit of moralising. Of course, he never knotted or notched himself, trusting to his own memory and an eye that, though perpetually bloodshot, was as keen as a hawk's when it came to a strict count. He had sent Helen round three or four of the gullies beyond the white gums to get an idea how many calves there were tucked in there and if the mud round the waterholes was bad. The mothers like to hide the calves away.

"Fifty-nine," said Helen to herself, "And what's that over there? Another one. Gee, Dad will be pleased."

The Parsons's holding was small, as holdings go in that territory—just a few thousand acres on the far edge of the Kimberleys where the gullies are short and rough, and the timber heavy enough to make the cattle nimble and very wild.

Bill Parsons depended on his two daughters, Mary and Helen, and two aboriginal stockmen and their dependants to work the place. Now and again, at mustering, drafting and branding, he got casual white help when it was available. When he had a mob ready he either took it himself to Wyndham, if he could spare the time, or else, if it paid him better, he sent it with a contracting drover, who happened to be taking a mob along at a time that suited him. He wasn't, however, in a big enough way habitually to employ a contracting drover. He liked taking his cattle down himself. He kept them in better condition that way, slowly moving them on wherever the stock route feed was good. There weren't many legitimate points about the game that anyone could teach Bill, but he had had terribly bad luck—bad seasons when prices were right and other times with plenty of prime beasts but prices dead low. He had had more than his share of accidents and calamities—flood, fire or disease in the stock—and he had had several dealings with men who were crooked and cheated him—partners and agents who acted in their own interests and not Bill's. Bill had had to learn that a chap who looked and talked and acted like a decent cove could do the dirty on him. It was hard learning, and learning it the hard way had given Bill a crustiness in his approach that younger men resented. He had a reputation for being short-tempered as well as short in the pocket. But there wasn't a better man with cattle in the Territory. Even his enemies—and he had plenty —gave him that in. The trouble with Bill was that he was too honest in an undeveloped area where the smartie often got rich quickest. It is curious how many men like to stand in well with a clever chap instead of standing by an honest one. At fifty-two Bill still found this hard to take. He ought to have got used to it long ago and started fighting back with their weapons: the downright lie, the quick grab, and the underhand agreement, "You do this for me and I'll do that for you." But he never did.

Ma was glad he never did. She knew, better than anyone, that Old Man Parsons' bark was worse than his bite, but she didn't want to change him. There were men who had got on in the North, who were nothing to start with—gaolbirds and derelicts and rouseabouts round the shanties—and who now hobnobbed with the politicians, the civil servants, and the big station owners and managers. Ma wouldn't have had Bill like them—smooth as oil on the tongue and sharp as vinegar in the gullet.

"You need never take any insults about your Dad," she had told the elder daughter, Mary, the time Mary went down south to boarding school. "He's a better man than most, even though he doesn't have a Rolls Royce station waggon."

Ma was so used to protecting Pa that she even took the rough side of her tongue to Mary if she thought Mary needed it. Mary had been uppity to Dad about Dad not wearing a tie the last time they were in Wyndham together. The cream

Rolls station waggon belonged to the publican's missus two hundred miles down the track and was the love of Mary's heart. When the Parsons family travelled they went in the four-wheeled, eight-horsed light waggon that they called "The Shay." The shay was a thoroughbrace waggon all the way from the days of Cobb and Co. There was more history than paint to it. It could do in a day—with luck— what the cream station waggon could do in an hour on the rough Territory roads. Admittedly it was a handy vehicle for following the cattle on a drove, but a bit of an anachronism on the King's highway.

Helen loved the shay. She would have loved the cream station waggon if Pa Parsons had owned it and, no doubt, would have sneaked a chance of driving that the way she had sneaked into driving the shay with a couple of polers, but she didn't hanker after it or any other car. Horses were enough for Helen—as they had been for Mary until she'd got a sense of shame that her Dad didn't even own a motor car.

"That old Parsons' shay," Mary had heard the publican's daughter say with scorn, and ever since Mary had been uncomfortable about it on their annual trips down to Wyndham with the fats. To her the shay was the symbol of Pa Parsons' lack of success after a lifetime of effort. It put him forever, in the eyes of the world, she thought, in the droving, not the station-owning class.

Ma could be cruel to Mary when she day-dreamed about such things, but she could also be very understanding. Not a woman who went in for a lot of talk, she could often get to the heart of a situation in a few sentences.

"That pub-keeper's girl down at the Eighty Mile," she said, "she's got glitter and six evening dresses and rides round in her old man's Rolls Royce, but she can't sit a horse like you can and she doesn't know 'B' from a bull's foot when it comes to knowing how a lady behaves or what a sentence in a book really means. Never forget that your education cost nearly as much as that Rolls Royce and at a time when money was a darn sight harder to come by. And in the long run it's worth a great deal more. That's what your father and I thought, at any rate." At that Mary had raised her eyes to her mother with a shamefaced tenderness and Ma had added: "Maybe in another season we can get a good truck or even a smart utility."

Mary had laughed with the happiness of something to hope for again. She was nineteen and a utility would make all the difference to her life. Getting anywhere with an eight-horse shay was like organising an expedition.

"But don't let your father know I said it," warned Ma. "He'll have to think of it himself or it'll be no go. Remember the shay is a lot more convenient in this country and a darn sight cheaper to run. . . ."

Helen, counting calves with her pony, Rusty, and taking a look at a couple of the waterholes for her dad, knew all this in the back of her mind, as she knew everything that went on round the homestead, but she didn't feel it. The difference between eleven and nineteen is a lot more than eight years: it is the difference betwen childhood and womanhood. Sharp as a needle about anything to do with the cattle or horses, the lie of the land or the flight of birds or the little idiosyncrasies of the few people who came her way, Helen was yet very young for her age, still a child rather than a girl, her body slim and quite sexless, her mind pure and innocent as her profile.

It was a funny thing about both the Parsons girls' bringing up; the way they'd been exposed to all sorts of gruelling physical risks and at the same time the way they'd been protected and cherished on the mental and emotional sides. It was something rare and hard to beat, something that you only find in the bush and outback these days. Pa Parsons would let his daughter Mary throw a steer, but he wouldn't let a man swear in front of her. He wouldn't swear himself. He was an old-fashioned, clean-mouthed fellow who would call a man a wretch or a begger, and rant and rave in anger, but never in obscenity.

Ma would let Helen ride all day alone over practically trackless country and never worry about it, but the same Ma kept her ears cocked for anything unsuitable being mentioned in front of the child, and she kept Helen, who hated book-work, up to the mark in spelling and writing and reading.

She made her learn poetry by heart and she taught her French seams, run and fells, top-sewing, drawn-thread, and all the fancywork stitches, small, neat and beautiful, just as she had been taught in her own girlhood.

Ma was very methodical, and she had a great respect for things of the spirit. Her father had been the first bush minister in the Territory, a formidable old saver of souls who would have been an explorer if he hadn't been a missionary. In a way he was an explorer, because he went first and fearlessly where other white men had never ventured. There were still many of the old-timers here and there throughout the North and North-West who loved and remembered him. "A gentleman and a Christian," was the way they always spoke about him, and invariably they added, "and pretty good with his mits too." More than once he had taken off his clerical collar to fight for the right with his fists. There were lots of stories still circulating about Helen's grandfather. Ma still thought tenderly—when she had time to think tenderly about anything, because she wasn't normally one to waste time sentimentalizing—of the jokes on her wedding day. "Had to keep a Parson in the family some way. . . ." and all the rest of them.

"A God-fearing young man. . . ." was how the toastmakers had described Bill Parsons at that wedding twenty years before. Maybe it was his early training that kept his mouth clean now, but his late father-in-law would have been very caustic if he had ever sat in at the Parsons' dinner table through the last depression. "A belly-aching and not a practising Christian," would have been the old gentleman's comment. He was a great one for saying, "The Lord helps those who help themselves." Bill often thought privately that Ma took after her father a lot. He respected her for it, but in the depression he had left off saying family grace.

Helen had taken over that little duty. "Thank the Lord for this food; for Christ's sake, Amen," her mother had taught her to say, until Helen, knowing a lot more directly how the beef came to be on the plate in front of her, had added firmly, "and Daddy, too."

Now she left Rusty, the pony, free to pick, first taking her lunch out of the saddlebag and removing the waterbag from round the pony's neck. She drank the water out of her quart pot but didn't bother to make tea. Grace, she muttered to herself, not out of religion, but out of habit. She had a little superstition about it really: she thought the day mightn't go well, the next meal not arrive, if she didn't go through the ceremonial of thanks. A child can't live in a black man's country without absorbing the atmosphere of magic. If her tribal taboo was to say grace, then she said grace. She would never have explained it that way, but that's how it was. "For luck," she would have said. She would also throw a pinch of spilt salt or a cast horseshoe over her left shoulder for luck— unless the horseshoe was still serviceable, when she would have carried it home. An anthropologist, working on Helen, would have found a wonderful mixture of Scotch and aboriginal beliefs tucked inside the well-shaped skull under the neat blonde plaits of hair. Pa Parsons' mother had been strong Scotch, and there was more than a trace of the old lady in Helen. Actually, the lunch Helen was eating was something old Mrs. Parsons had taught Ma Parsons to make—bannocks, a sort of thin triangular oatmeal cake, mixed with flour and water and a little fat and done in the oven, or, more usually, on a dry frying pan. They were very sustaining things and a few could keep Helen going a whole day. To-day she had some strips of smoked beef and a handful of sultanas as well. The sultanas had a few grubs in them, but Helen picked these off. You can't live long in the tropics without getting a bit blasé about weevils. The smoked beef was a speciality of Mrs. Parsons, a change from the usual salted beef they had most of the time. She had a bough smoke-house built, where she cured some of the beef they killed. If she hadn't salted and smoked the beef there would have been a lot of wastage in killing a beast. Neither she nor Pa liked wasting anything. Life was much too hard for that. Maybe there was a bit of superstition in it too. The Lord giveth and the Lord taketh away. The food on the plate, the life-giving water, the infant son, the natural increase of cattle. On the elders, too, the influence of the aborigines was strong. The aborigines never waste tucker. The Parsons family had been two full generations in this outback. They didn't like to waste tucker either. The smoked beef kept well enough in the Dry, but in the Wet it was apt to go mildew. Ma Parsons' method of preserving it was a primitive sort of dehydration.

Helen lay back against a sun-warmed stone chewing a little

frayed-out piece of stick to get her teeth clean. "I wonder if we really will go South," she thought.

Pa had ridden down the township track two days before, ostensibly to get mail and on important homestead business, but really to see how the war was going. The Parsons had no wireless set. They were too far out to make charging the batteries practicable, and a crystal set, even if Pa had been the sort of man to play round with it, which he wasn't, wouldn't have been strong enough or reliable enough. They got news every fortnight, riding down thirty odd miles to the boundary track, where a supply truck passed pretty regularly on its way to their neighbour seventy miles distant; but the war situation, since the fall of Singapore, was so tense that Pa couldn't wait so long. He reckoned that the Japs would make for the North of Australia and guessed there was nothing much to stop them. They were mopping up the East Indies already.

The Indies lie like a pagoda'd bridge between Asia and Australia, like a fertile golden sickle, the point tipping daintily on Singapore and the handle resting between the tip of Cape York and the blunt, clenched fingers of Arnhem Land. The Japanese were loop-landing along the bridge, marching, an army with menace.

The old-timers in the Territory knew it was the natural path for the invasion of the Australian continent. "Make a few landings in strength, well-supported from sea and air, take as much territory as they can easily—and that will be plenty. Police it with troops and strong bases, use guerilla tactics on the inland perimeter, keep up the pressure from the sea on the south, and send the meat home to Nippon!" That was how the men talked, riding in to the Parsons homestead. There were more callers these days. The military were out buying beef and there were survey and observer groups in the field and commando units doing training. The Parsons were enrolled as aircraft spotters and they were waiting for diagrams to come of what they were to spot. There was talk of establishing a signal-station on the property and much more talk of evacuating women and children south.

Helen didn't really think they would move south. They would never leave this property. It was all they had. Pa couldn't work it on his own; he couldn't spare the girls. He

wouldn't send them south. Maybe he would try to send her,
but he wouldn't send Mary. Mary had had her turn down
south. Helen knew that some time or other in the future she
would be sent south to mix with other girls and learn a bit
more than she could in the bush, but it was always in the
remote future. She didn't want to hurry it at all. Mary had
told her that the girls down south had a very tame time of
it. You soon got tired of picture shows every week, and even
the zoo was only worth going to a few times. "The animals
up in the Territory are much more interesting. An old-man
buffalo, savage and alone, out to kill, is really much more
exciting than a cage full of monkeys."

There was a pair of polished buffalo horns up at the homestead four feet nine inches from tip to tip. Pa had shot the
buffalo long before he was married. Helen had the theory
that there was a lone old buffalo feeding along the chain of
waterholes on the property. It was not real buffalo country,
but now and then an odd one came through. The blacks had
said they'd seen buffalo tracks. That track she'd seen down
at the Weeping waterhole this morning was certainly buffalo,
even though it had been partly trodden over by other cattle
coming and going.

From where she sat over the crest of the ridge, scanning the
gullies for any sign of cattle, she saw a thin column of smoke
rise, no more importantly than a casually-lit cigarette. "Must
be old Wattlebunge and his crowd from the coast," she told
the pony. "Sid-the-Chopper's Lily said they were coming.
'Japs no good to Wattlebunge,' Lily said. As if the Japs would
bother about old Wattlebunge!" She picked up her quart
pot, the water and saddlebags and fastened them on the pony,
which she led downhill again. "Wonder how many there are
with Wattlebunge this time," she thought. Last year when he
had come over they had made a corroboree with the homestead blacks. This year Lily said the old men said they were
going to cook up something special to bring back the bandi-
coots. There used to be plenty feller bandicoot round here in
the old days and now bandicoot all gone. "Cattle come,
bandicoot go," Lily said. Lily was Helen's closest acquaintance
down at the blacks' camp. When Helen had time for it they
went tracking together.

Suddenly, at the bottom of a red soil ridge with open timber along it, in a patch of dense brushwood and scrub, Helen saw the unmistakeable signs and tracks of pigs. Mounting the pony, she followed as rapidly as possible, skirting the bushes. Clattering along, she roused an old sow, a couple of young tuskers and a small litter. She tried to ride down a tusker, but he got away, perhaps fortunately, and the old sow ran grunting ahead, the piglets squealing behind her. In the confusion Rusty put his foot in a hole and nearly threw Helen. She dismounted, chasing the sow, which twisted and turned, its black ears flopping, its teats swinging like a loose undercarriage, the thin, rather delicate legs carrying it along at a great rate out of Helen's view and hearing. But not so the piglets. Helen swooped with her hat on one and fell on the other, winding it. When she got up, puffing, she had one, nearly all black, kicking and twisting in one hand, and the other, black with large white spots, limp but still alive in the other.

She was very pleased with herself. Ma would see that the pigs were looked after. Maybe Sid-the-Chopper's Lily would look after them, and the day would come when sucking pig would be on the menu. They were quite old enough, she decided, to leave their mother. She would get back home before the old sow came back hunting for her babies, bringing maybe reinforcements. Helen had no wish to meet an outraged grandfather boar in that scrub. She cradled the piglets in an arm and rode a mile or so that way, but it was very trying. Then she tied their hind legs together with one string and their front legs with the hemmed piece of chintz that she wore as a hair ribbon. She put both piglets in her long-suffering hat, tied the other hair ribbon round it to make a sort of basket, and passed her plaited kangaroo-hide belt round the lot. It formed a sling, comfortable enough for the journey home.

Often enough she had seen the lubras carry little nanny goats like that in their coolamons.

"A coolamon might be quite a handy receptacle to carry round," she thought, but finally decided that it would be impractical to carry a coolamon along with her other horse gear.

She had about seven miles to go home, but Rusty was travelling well. A light breeze had come up, making the journey pleasant. It was late afternoon. From the second of the four ridges she had to cross she looked back, but the smoke from the blacks' fire was gone. She sat for a few minutes giving Rusty a spell and enjoying the prospect of the lightly-timbered country, with bright greens along the bottoms and the red soil starred with a spiky heath whose pink blossoms had come out after the rains. Moving out of the gully where she had caught the pigs was a little procession. She strained her eyes to see. One, two, three figures, the front one carrying something, a bunch of spears, and the other two—? What in the world had they got? Something slung between them on a pole. Not a kangaroo. Must be the sow—they must have got the sow she missed! That was a wonderful piece of luck for them, her driving it down to them like that! Just as well she'd decided to bring the piglets with her; they wouldn't have lasted long in the scrub without their mother.

It was at this moment that the plane droned over from a little to the south of east. A silvery wasp of a thing with a high note like a circular saw heard from a distance. It was flying towards her and into the sun at a height of a few thousand feet. It came fast, a pretty thing, like a spear of sunshine thrown by a giant hand from a long way off. Helen waved her arms. It was something they always did for the planes passing over, a greeting and a farewell. Seen from the plane, through glasses, the airman could have distinguished a figure on a horse, for the skewbald stood out prominently against the cinnabar of the long range. This was a new type of country, well-wooded, with steep gullies and gulches, and surface water lying like broken pieces of mirror scattered here and there on the rough terrain. Now and then there were breaks in the timber and the red earth showed through, regular and level as jungle landing strips, with outcrops of dark rock, smooth and bare, broken up in unusual shapes like the camouflage effects of the early war period, which were all surrealist and away from nature. The "pound" where Helen had been looking for calves was one of these natural clearings, and where she had found the pigs was just on the edge of it. The natives walking so close carrying their burden must have given an effect of considerable activity in a landscape over which a plane can pass for hundreds of miles and the occupants not see a human being.

The plane turned, making a half-circle off to the north-west, and as it turned there, Helen could see, for a brief instant, the glittering turret as it banked. Then it went on, over to the north-west. But even as it did so, there was a loud thump, a boom like thunder but shorter than thunder, without the roll and echo of thunder. "Funny!" thought Helen, but Rusty played up at the same time. He reared and plunged and almost threw her. Helen dropped a piglet. She got down, feeling a sting like a wasp bite in the back of her hand, and annoyed with Rusty. "This is twice in one day," she thought, "He's getting really naughty." But when she had picked up the piglet she found that Rusty was trembling all over, that sweat had broken out all over him, that he moved and stamped his feet and had his ears back and his teeth showing as if to bite. "Don't be frightened, Rusty," she said, patting him and talking to him to give him confidence. Blood welled out from a small gash in the back of her right hand. It looked deep, but didn't hurt. "Some new sort of insect," she thought. Insect bites don't bleed as a rule. Whatever it was it must have frightened Rusty too. She couldn't see any marks on him, however. She put the pig down and tied up her hand with her handkerchief, which was very soiled, what with falling over on the pig, and eating sultanas and smoked meat on a hot day. To draw the knot tight she used her teeth, worrying the handkerchief into a bandage. She did this not so much to stop the bleeding as to keep the flies off.

Then she collected the piglets. The black one was trying to get away, making funny little bounds with its tied trotters, the other was rolling on its back, waving its feet in the air and squealing like an indignant and very angry human infant. She put both piglets firmly in her hat again, made Rusty stand still long enough to get into the saddle, and went for home, singing as she went: "To market, to market, to buy a fat pig; home again, home again, jiggerty jig."

It soothed Rusty and it pleased her. She sang it over and over, the way blacks do at a corroboree, for the fun of saying what was true and boasting at the same time. Not a bad day's work. Fifty-nine—no sixty—calves, two pigs, and the news of seeing old Wattlebunge on the track. "To market, to market— C'mon Rusty. . . ." Rusty lengthened his steps, knowing he was turned for home.

CHAPTER II

TEA, the evening meal at the Glenrichard homestead, was the important meal of the day, even if sometimes it wasn't the heaviest. Ma saw that all of them came fresh and clean to it and that it - .arked the end of the day's labours for all of them. She liked the girls to get into dresses for it, and there were a whole sets of shirts, high slippers, and several old-fashioned but serviceable alpaca linen and tussore suits kept for Pa to change into. "My evening clothes," he always called them.

Once, a visitor, a government official, on a data-gathering trip from Darwin, heard Pa bellow, after the brisk shower, "Where's my evening clothes, Ma?" and heard Ma's pattering steps and the quiet rejoinder, "Sorry, Bill, I forgot to lay them out." The visitor sneaked back to his bedroom and emerged later in all the glory of formal whites and black bow tie. Ma had retrieved the situation by shushing Mary off to dress in the prettiest dress she had, a dress originally bought for the end-of-term party that finished her school education. She had grown taller since then, but the fashions had made skirts shorter; she looked lovely in it and knew it. She had it on to-night. Though not her most recent, it was still her favourite dress, blue and soft, with amusing little pleated frills. To-night there were no visitors, even Pa was still away, but there was a large and glowing moon. One long cloud lay like a high-water mark of silver, half-way across the sky. Mary reacted quickly to beauty. She had a sudden desire to do something crazy, to saddle a horse and go galloping on and on over a white sandy track under the black boughs of trees, galloping, never looking back, away from the homestead and her mother's perpetual guard and the tediousness of doing the same things day after day.

The mood passed. She saw her mother dishing up the meal, carrying it across on a tray from the kitchen, which was a separate building from the bedrooms and living room, to the vine-shadowed verandah, where they ate most of their meals. The verandah was fly-screened. Moths battered in flight against the fine-meshed wire, drawn by the glow of the kerosene table lamp which stood in the centre of the table. Mary had put red salvia and white oleander in float bowls on either side of the lamp. The flowers were like flags saying: "This is a home, not a cattle camp." She went to help her mother with the tea-things.

"Helen's late," she said.

"She'll be here in a minute," said the mother. "She caught a couple of little pigs and had to take them over to Sid-the-Chopper's Lily to look after. Sid's going to build a little run for them to-morrow. She saw old Wattlebunge's people on the track. They're early this year. Lily says they're frightened of the Japs landing. I think that's nonsense. . . ."

"Don't you think the Japs will land, Mother?"

"Don't ask me. I think it's nonsense that Wattlebunge is frightened of them. I think Lily is frightened and she puts it on to Wattlebunge. I wish I knew who's been terrifying the camp with these yarns of Japs."

Helen came by, still in her riding clothes.

"You've got two minutes," said her mother, warningly, "and I'm not keeping anything hot."

"Mercy!" said Helen, and scuttled.

"That'll make another night when she doesn't do her hair before tea," said Ma.

"I wouldn't either, if I had her hair to cope with," said Mary. Helen's hair was fair, a natural platinum blonde, and so fine that it was like combing out cobwebs if it got tangled. She wore it in two tight plaits, the ends firmly secured. Until she was two years old she had photographed quite bald, her head covered by a silky down. Now she was eleven it was just the same, except that the down had grown longer. Lily-the-Chopper used to beg combings of it—such hair, the black women said, was magic. They used to put a strand or two into the fine twisted string that they used in bird snares. They said the glittering hair attracted the birds better. Ma Parsons put a stop to it when she found Helen, at the age of nine, cutting long hunks out of her hair to give away to her admiring friends for the gifts of feathers, strings of bean beads, and little parrakeets that they kept bringing her. She made Helen burn the combings, having a rather odd feeling herself about the wisdom of letting anything so personal as one's hair, even one's dead hair, into the tribal possession. Helen didn't really care—except that she felt it spoiled a good trade.

Mary turned on the old gramophone that stood on the side table with a nephthelenthum fern in a pot beside it. "Begin . . . the beguine . . ." made the moonlight suddenly more sensuous than ever. She danced a few steps holding a plate of cut bread in her hand. "I wish Dad were home," she said, "I don't know how it is, but I've missed him more this time than ever I did before."

"So have I," said Ma, "and that's saying something." Pa had been away with the cattle the dreadful night when her only son Richard had been born and died. This homestead, far away from that other one, had been called Glenrichard after that boy who had not lived long enough to have been christened.

A big tabby cat with an immaculate white shirt front came in from the darkness, cleverly swinging open the shut screen door with his soft, exactly-patting paw. "Hullo, Snookums," said Mary, "did the music bring you in?" Under the table a little half-mongrel cattle pup gave a low whine, flicking his tail.

As a matter of fact, the animals did like music. Sometimes they had to turn off the gramophone because a collection of half-wild native cats would congregate in the trees, out in the garden and yearn out their miaowing accompaniments, the moon and the music too much for them. The cats, however, kept the snakes and the centipedes down, and if they, in their turn, got too numerous, a hint to the natives and the pussy cats made a meal in their turn. There were no rabbits so far north. They had not worked their way up from the south yet. Perhaps the grass was too rank and the damp, warm climate not suitable to such cold-country fur-bearers.

Helen came in, her hair wet on either side of the parting, ribbon bows on the ends of her plaits, her short·checked skirt well above her knees, her skinny, long legs bare and a pair of sandals on her thin brown feet. "What's for tea, Mum? I could eat a horse."

"It's goat, dear," said Ma, without thinking. Mary burst into laughter. "I mean lamb," Ma went on without a blush. Goat always came to the Parsons' table under the name of lamb. "Fricasseed lamb and little quandong tarts to come afterwards. Betty Black-eye brought me some quandongs and I thought they'd be rather nice with sultanas and spice."

"Those sultanas did need using up," said Helen. She and her mother understood each other perfectly. Ma Parsons gave her a little look that meant, "Don't go into that now." Mary could be a bit choicey about food since she came from down south the last time.

"Say grace, Helen," said Ma. The evening meal began. Helen was full of talk about the calves, the pigs, Wattlebunge and the aeroplane. "Might have been some of your friends from Darwin," said Helen to Mary.

"They don't usually fly so far south."

"Did they dip their wing or anything?" asked Ma. "I was lying down. I didn't see it."

"I was down by the dam," said Mary. "I could hardly see it at all from there. I thought it might have crashed for a second because I heard a kind of big bump and felt a sort of vibration."

"I heard that, too," said Helen, "and Rusty felt the vibration." To Ma she said: "They made a half turn but they didn't circle or anything like that."

"Mightn't have had time," said Mary. "I heard the new C.O. was down on stunting."

"Might have been some sort of a signal," said Ma, "but in that case you would have thought they'd come right over the homestead."

"Might have been just to say 'Hullo'—let me know they'd seen me," said Helen. "You know what they are—let fly a kerosene tin just to let us know they'd be dropping in for Sunday dinner soon. You know those R.A.A.F. boys. Anyway, all they did was to frighten Rusty."

"Sometimes they're very thoughtless," said Ma. "We'll have to ask old Wattlebunge if he noticed anything special about the plane and then get them told off."

"Oh, Ma," said the girls, disapprovingly.

"Why not?" asked Ma. "Helen could have been badly thrown. There are enough natural risks without making any more. What did you do to your hand, dear?"

"Some sort of insect," said Helen. "It bled quite a bit. I put iodine on it just now. It's starting to hurt and throb."

"Let me see," said Ma. She put down the plates and got her reading glasses from the side table. "It looks very bruised. More like a bang than a bite. You're sure you really didn't take a tumble off Rusty?"

"Positive," said Helen, virtuously. "I didn't see what stung me. It happened just after that thump Mary heard too. I dropped the pigs. But I looked Rusty over to make sure and I didn't see any sort of a horse fly or anything on him."

"I think there's something in it," said Ma, squeezing and feeling. Helen winced away. "It hurts," she said.

"Mary," called Ma. Mary had taken the dinner plates away and was bringing in the little pies. "Fetch me the first-aid kit and sterilise the basin. There's plenty of boiling water in the iron kettle. Might as well get it over with," she said to Helen, "then you can enjoy your pie afterwards. I want the probe," she called to Mary.

Ma did most of the cooking at the homestead. She only got the lubras to help with the rough work and the laundry, a little each day in the mornings, to keep things going. There were only a few natives on the homestead, and, as Pa had to have their help, she liked the lubras to be down with their picanninies and the old women as much as possible, ready to wait on their lords and masters when they came home. The bucks liked it that way. They drew their rations and what Ma could spare beside, for she liked the picanninies to glow with good food and care, but she didn't like too many blacks close about the place.

She thought it made them lose all their independence and native ways, which were good ways. The natives here still obeyed tribal laws largely—they were not like the compound natives of the closer settlements. In any case, the Parsons could not have afforded to keep a large native establishment going.

Mary gave a little squeal from the kitchen door. "You frightened me, Sid-the-Chopper," she said. "What's the matter?"

Sid-the-Chopper had run panting up from the camp. "Missus, Wattlebunge's fellas all got big time belly-ache. You come bring 'em medcin. Them fellas close-up dead. Saymore dead finish. Big hole in ground. Plane makem big hole. That be Jap plane, missus?"

"Helen," said Ma, sharply, "what sort of a plane was that?"

"Silver," replied Helen, "with blue along the sides, just like sunlight in the sky. A very beautiful plane with a blunt nose and four engines and fast, much faster than anything I've ever seen before. And a sort of window in the top— I could almost swear I saw someone looking out and giving a wave, but of course they couldn't have been—and I don't know. I waved, and it was only there, coming and going and taking a turn over me, just about forty seconds, no more."

"You sit down outside, Sid," said Ma firmly. "Eatem tucker. Missus think what to do."

Mary had put the lint, bandages, forceps and probe on a sheet of clean linen on the table. "Get Sid-the-Chopper something to eat," ordered Ma. "First, you," she said to Helen. She worked gently, murmuring quick reassurements to Helen, who sat still, though the probing hurt. Presently she worked out of the wound a thin sliver of stone about three-eighths of an inch long. It was not a pebble, but a three-sided fragment, and when dipped in water, its razor sharp edges looked to have been freshly chipped off the parent stone. Ma laid it on the linen cloth and stared at it. Then she put antiseptic on the wound, which was bleeding again, and padded it and bound it up. "It must have hit with some force," she said, "because of the bruising. Lucky it wasn't your eye or your temple. As it is, a little bit more and it would have gone right through. It's really just as dangerous as a bullet. More so, because it's sharper." Like a spent bullet, she thought.

She went out to Sid-the-Chopper and questioned him. His account, second-hand from the native who had brought the news from Wattlebunge, tallied in some respects with Helen's tale. Ma sent for the boy and through Sid learnt that old Saymore, the wiseman-witchdoctor-rainmaker of the tribe, had been smitten by something invisible from the silver plane. There was no mark on his body but he was dead. Sure-enough dead, no gammon. Not far from where the other blacks had found him was a big hole blasted out of the rocky ground. "All same big-fellow bandicoot him dig, him dig."

Saymore had swallowed the magic from the plane and had saved his people. They could tell he had swallowed it because his insides were all pulled up, his tongue so—the native demonstrated—the tongue swollen, held out and puffing. Two little boys, nephews to Wattlebunge and nearest to Saymore when the thunder fell, were sick-fellow bad. They were lying down and crying, crying, all the time crying, and sick-fellow (vomiting). Wattlebunge had felt it, too. He had felt the magic pulling him up, turning his bingy upside down, his ears hurt, and he kept on with what Ma reckoned was dry retching—a prolonged sense of foul nausea. "Spillem all same grass," said Sid.

The tale was detailed enough to be true, Ma thought, and not exaggerated. She could get no details about the hole in the ground. They had all run away from it as fast as they could. "Big fellow debbil-debbil camp along there, Missus."

It must, Ma thought, have been one of our planes skylarking with bombs, or a Jap plane. The chip of stone that had hit Helen had evidently been from rock hit by a bomb fragment ricochetting. If she had been closer or struck by a direct splinter it would have probably killed her.

"A Jap plane!" exclaimed Helen.

"You can thank your Maker you're still alive," said Ma fiercely. Her knees were knocking now in sheer terror of the danger past. "Get to bed. Mary, help her to bed. Give her a couple of aspirin."

"I don't need aspirin," said Helen.

"Come on," said Mary, "You don't get bombed by a Jap every day."

"I want you to have a good sleep, dear," said Ma. "I might need you very early in the morning. I'll come in and say good-night to you in a minute."

Helen went, looking white, but not so shaken that she didn't remember her pie. She sent Mary out to the kitchen for it and ate it sitting up in bed. Seeing her eat the pie comforted Ma a lot. She kissed the little girl in her nightgown, and said automatically, "Mind you clean your teeth."

"Missus come fetch him medicine?" inquired Sid.

"Just a minute, Sid." Ma went inside and got a couple of bush blankets that the station issued to the stock boys and a couple of her home-made eiderdowns that she kept for this sort of emergency. They were roughly-quilted, clean sugar bags, split and joined up in large diamond shapes, each diamond filled with clean down and breast feathers from poultry, wild pigeons, or brush turkeys used on the homestead. Sugar bags, flour bags, salt and grain bags: nothing was ever wasted in Glenrichard. Ma rolled the swag up neatly, wondering how she might best help the blacks. She had a certain prestige among the camp blacks for her treatment of sores, inflammations, bad eyes, and infant disorders, but if anything went wrong with Wattlebunge's group she would get the blame; if anything went right the medicine man next in office would get the credit.

She called Sid to the door and made quite certain for the second time that none of the natives had been wounded.

"Then it must be shock or blast that's up with them," she said to Mary.

"You're not going to try to get to old Wattlebunge's camp at this hour, are you Mum? It's too far to walk, and you couldn't ride."

"I wish your father were here."

"I'll ride down."

"Indeed you won't. That's one thing I know he wouldn't want." Finally, Ma got a billy-can of hot soup, fortunately in the stock-pot, some tea and sugar, the custard from dinner, a loaf of bread and some warm cornflour sauce made with plenty of sugar and good goat's milk.

For morale she put in tobacco. For medicine she measured out chlorodyne and diluted it. For warmth she put in two old stone gin bottles, well stoppered, and filled them with boiling water. They had flannel covers and would retain heat for hours. She showed Sid how to fill them. "Sick fella keep warm, plenty warm," said Ma. "These (the custard, corn-flour) for picanniny; good tucker. This fella medicine curem quick bad bellyache belong Wattlebunge. In morning Missus come look see. Not better then this fella castor oil." She held up the well-known bottle. "Cleanem out bingy, all right?"

"All right, missus," said Sid. He took the swag, and the rest of the stuff in a sugar bag, and carefully mounted. Ma handed him up the billy-cans. He set off for the camp with the boy. But there was one thing he wanted to know before he went: "Jap—him come back?"

"No," said Ma, with mock bravery, "too much moon." It was the very reason why they might come, but Ma worked it out that wherever the blacks were they'd have to take a chance that night, like anybody else, and that the moon was there anyway, comforting and visible like a great lantern. As he rode along, it would reassure Sid, who had seen so many other full moons, bright and ordinary.

"Big fellow debbil belong hole, Missus?"

"Myall talk, Sid. Wild blackfellow nonsense. Good-night. See you in the morning."

"Good-night, missus."

She was far from reassured herself. She didn't think our boys, however high-spirited, would risk injuring anybody. Whoever had dropped the bomb had definitely seen the blacks and Helen and, if they hadn't done it on purpose, had taken a risk that none of our airmen in his senses would ever have done. It must have been a Jap plane. Next morning she must get word, as soon as possible, to the authorities.

"Let me ride down to the first gate to meet Dad," begged Mary. "I've got the feeling he'll be coming home to-night."

"He said he'd try to be back by to-night," said Ma, "but it's not like him to travel so late. He'd more likely camp and come on in the morning."

"Let me go, Mum."

Ma knew how the girl must feel, seething with restlessness and the desire to do something—swing into action one way or another.

"Hero is in the top paddock. I could saddle him in a minute."

"All right," said Ma, "but stick to the track. I don't want to go out chasing you—with a broken ankle." Ma often predicted the worst to make the girls more careful. "You can take risks yourselves," she used to say, "but for goodness' sake remember the people who have to come out to get you."

While Mary changed out of her blue dress Ma watched her, talking: "They could have shot Helen, I've no doubt, quite easily."

"Not from that height," said Mary.

"They could have flown right over the homestead and bombed us to bits. I wonder why they didn't?"

"What would be the good of burning us up?" asked Mary. "We look what we are, a homestead."

"If they thought of taking those hills they'd want all the shelter they could get," said Ma. "That would account for them not bombing us, but why waste a bomb on a child, a horse, and a few blacks, and blow up a big hole in the bush?"

"It couldn't have been a bombing raid," said Mary, "or there'd have been more of them. It must have been reconnaissance and they thought they saw something too good to miss and took a pot shot."

"To stir the sitting bird. Perhaps they thought there was an aerodrome near here. There was talk, you know, a while back, of putting down airstrips all over the north. Perhaps . . . If they're going to come in then they must know where the aerodromes and the ammunition dumps are—"

"That pound where Helen was, it might look like an airstrip from above. Those big rocks near Iron Knoll—they might think they were sheds, or hangars—"

"We'll never know," said Ma. Mary was ready now, changed into riding pants and a white blouse. "If you do meet your father you can tell him what's happened. He may feel like riding down at once with the news. If he does, tell him we're all right. We're not frightened and we can manage and I'm going to get things ready to-night in case we're ordered suddenly to get out."

"All right," said Mary. She kissed her mother, who walked down to the paddock with her.

Mary cantered smoothly along the track. She wouldn't gallop until she was quite sure she was out of Ma's hearing. The moonlight gave the air a chalky milkiness, something warm and at the same time semi-solid, like feathers. The belt of air above the earth was still rising, emanating the heat of the day and the honey-sweetness of the flowering shrubs that had blossomed after the rain. On the hilltops, however, a cooler air came sweeping in, but there was no wind, only these lazy local movements like cool pools under the bank of a sun-kissed river—just odd currents and not a regular flowing.

Mary's galloping left her face still burning. She hated to reason things out as Ma did. If she ever had to make up her mind she went for a gallop, and when she came back, some-how—she didn't know how herself—her mind was made up.

Japs over the property! She was mad to rush out and tell her father, give him the news. She would have liked to have shouldered a rifle and set off herself, along with the army, to be right in the front when the Japs tried to land. All sorts of glorious images of herself in action went through her mind like shadows in the out-of-doors cinemas they sometimes saw. The moonlight and the trees rising and passing her by and the movement of the horse under her all somehow had that phantasmagorial quality of action in two dimensions associated in her mind with the cinema. Those who have sat, patiently watching the flowing of an action on a white screen in a darkened area, with cigarettes glowing like stars in the darkness and real stars and a moon overhead, with real trees, and maybe a windmill turning its vanes round and round, high above the hoarding walls, know the kind of un-reality that seizes the watchers, so that they hardly know which shadows are substantial—their own or the miming shades on the unrolling drama in front of their eyes.

Mary, like every girl of quality, had at one time hated her destiny of being a girl.

She had always been aware of the quiet but deep disap-pointment of her father in having no sons. The death of the infant Richard had been, in a way, more of a tragedy to the father than to the mother, especially as he always, in his heart of hearts, blamed himself for the catastrophe. "I ought to have made her go. I ought to have foreseen better how it would be," he used to blame himself.

In spite of not be. .g a boy, however, she knew that she stood in a peculiar relation with him. She was his girl, always the eldest, his little sweetheart.

Love for the mother sometimes flowers again, as delicate as the original passion, chivalrous, quixotic and intimate, between the father and his chosen daughter. He had at first tried to bring her up as a little boy, giving her her first stockwhip, her first saddle, taking a delight in her short-cut hair, her splendid balance, her neat straight legs in their long dungareed pants. The old grandfather, the missionary, had stopped that. "She's a girl," he had said, "and to please God you'll keep her one, and none of these half-creatures about her."

Ma, sensitive in spite of her habit of plain talk, had always kept that attitude. "A womanly woman," she had willed Mary to be, in spite of the cattle-mustering, the steer-throwing, the life in the saddle. And Mary was that. Her breasts, her shape, the curve of her thighs and the coquetry of her glance were all woman, but her hands were the hands of a boy, and her knowledge, the light and shade of her feelings, when she was with her father, were those of a boy, too.

The years between fifteen and seventeen had been her bitterest years of rebellion against her sex. Now she had only anticipation of the stranger who should come galloping into her life, perhaps on a night like this.

The moon was higher now, the air calmer, cooler, less curdled with the milk of light. The horse had begun to sweat, the smell of leather and horse rising in a little cloud to her nostrils. She steadied her pace, letting him work it out quietly so that he shouldn't suddenly chill. At the same time a decision came to her. She knew that she would be glad to leave the homestead and travel south again, that if there were any choosing for her to do, she would not choose to stay. Life at the homestead was useful, exhausting, interesting, but it was not her life. It was her father's life. Her future lay ahead, somewhere where she didn't just sit beside the track and wait for someone "suitable" to come calling in his best clothes, with his stockyards and his cattle twenty or a thousand paddocks away.

The big horse settled into its long walk. Here the timber grew thickly beside the track, arching overhead. The air was heavy with the honey-scent of blossom. She pulled down a white flower that glistened in a tree and stuck it in her hair.

At that moment, when her mind was miles away, full of moon-shadows, Hero tripped on the stretched rope and as she jolted forward, arms caught her from behind, twisted her wrists behind her back, tumbled her out of the saddle hard on the sand of the track, noosed her ankles and her wrists with rawhide, leaving her helpless, trussed in the same way as Helen's little piglets.

CHAPTER III

ALONG the pagoda'd bridge of the Indies, between Asia and Australia, the Japs were loop-landing. First they came sky-seeing, then they bombed, then they landed, then they possessed and enjoyed—all the Indies. But the last island, the closest island, the biggest island in the world was New Guinea. There the little brown ants found their way blocked at last, in the desperate jungle, by tired men, Australians, holding the last ridge before the invasion of their country. So, because of the struggle in New Guinea, the mainland had respite. Ultimately, many things occurring, the invasion never came. But it was close enough, and the reconnoitring, the bombing, the softening up, were just as terrifying in their preliminaries as if the invasion really occurred as it had been scheduled.

*　　*　　*　　*

The moon which Ma had falsely told Sid-the-Chopper would prevent the Japs coming again was really the giant searchlight speeding them on their way. Now, knowing opposition from inland to be non-existent, they came in fast flights, like night-stinging wasps, over the unprotected little town.

Wyndham lay flat under the moonlight, its main street, its corrugated iron roofs, its mud flats by the mangrove edges, drawn in main relief, in highlight and dark shadow like the strong, rough contrast in a lino-cut, white and black. The salt-pans glittered sharp as ice. It was not without beauty in its starkness. The hill behind the town loomed spine-backed and bald, the great meatworks on the other side behind it a temple to the industry of the whole hinterland. Once Wyndham had lived on pearls, the fleets like white butterflies sailing in and out, but now it lived on meat, the solid stockyards of the holding paddocks striping with blackness the lino-cut of the moonlit land. As a target the meatworks could not be missed, but the bombers did not aim at it.

Up the dry, wide, ancient river valley they flew, over the pot-holey road out past the Six Mile to the aerodrome. Bang! Up went the hangars. Rat-tat-tat-tat ran the bullets through the corrugated iron. The hills beyond, beyond the valley, seemed to shrink back at the sound. The road skirting the contours of the riverbed hid itself behind corners. Over the town again. The post office, the pub, the meatworks jetty high on its crane-like legs over the mud, the small ships by the old town jetty, cowered defenceless against the aerial blows. The little engine that pulled the train that went to the meatworks cowered in its shunting shed. The Chinese and the aborigines and the half-bloods and the whites in the shops and dwellings beside the country-town road, the sprawling road that led, so it seemed, from nowhere to nowhere again, cowered, too.

Then the Japs flew off. The town was wounded for the duration, but not vitally. The meatworks stood, the houses stood, the burning aerodrome could be cleaned up, the jetty was still serviceable. The Six Mile was bombed, but the Wyndham pub, with its picketed palisade round the balcony and its long, high line of posts, still stood, askew but conval-escent—a drunken driver did it more harm really than the bombing, going smack, smack, smack against the verandah posts.

The Japs got the ships and the stores at Darwin. They got the last Dutch planes flying out of Java to Broome. They had the sky and they nearly had the sea, but they never had the land.

The order came up from the south: "Evacuate the civilians. Women and children first. First line of defence forward." First line of defence!—such as it was!

*　　*　　*　　*

The bully beef from the meatworks at Wyndham goes all over the world. Slabs of the solid, life-giving stuff. Good quality stuff, wonderful stuff to get on a little boat, starving, out at sea. Good meat to chew on the cold range of the Pindus in the starving, cold, highlands of Greece. Good meat to heat up and put a sauce on in cold, blitz-bombed cellars. Good meat for the Indies and China, for India, Siberia, the meat-hungry East, and the country of the ants, Japan.

The Japs saved the meatworks for themselves. They thought it might come in handy later on. The meatworks was the reason of the town's existence. It was the lifeblood and the heart and the body of the town, the economic motive, in some way or another, of all the men, life and chance had gathered there.

The Australians, whose life and lifeblood and living it was, were prepared to sabotage the meatworks themselves rather than let the Japs get it. They were willing to kill the cattle, whose existence they had so carefully nurtured there. Behind the cattle being there at all was two generations of effort. In a continent like Australia and in a place like Wyndham an industry is not established like running up a factory of bricks and steel anywhere else. In Northern Australia an industry is pioneered. The pioneering takes sweat and discouragement, hardship and long waiting for success, a lifetime of battling. The pioneers were willing to sabotage their own efforts, the joint labours of all their lives. The danger was great and the means to avoid it must be violent.

*　　*　　*　　*

Bill Parsons was one of the pioneers who knew what had to be done. He rode home without waiting for the official say-so. He had an implacable bitterness in his mouth, a feeling as substantial as if he had chewed the rind of the tamarind. His mood was black with bile, his despondency beyond danger. Anger was to come later.

For the third time in his life he was on the threshold of success and for the third time he was going to see the years of his effort going for nothing, wasted. Glenrichard was getting to be now the homestead he had seen in his mind's eye from the beginning. The homestead itself cream-washed, neat, compact; the outbuildings well placed, the stockyards all that stockyards ought to be, well-built, durable, in good order. The dam finished—and what a work that had been! The two waterholes fenced and the creek still running most of the time; the main paddock, the home paddock and the paddock for the weaners all securely fenced, well grassed. The experimental cultivation plot looking as if it was going to be a success, the stockboys now thoroughly trained and pretty dependable fellows, the girls enjoying the life, Ma satisfied with her garden and her home and the wide view from the verandah over the timbered hills, the cleared pastures, the thickets of scrub and jungle; the liabilities getting less and the assets accruing; the cattle still wild and rangy, but improving with the two bulls he had bought last year. . . . He went over what he had done and how he had worked to make the place out of the wilderness.

He was never a man to take up another man's property—inheriting all his mistakes. He liked to tackle virgin country. "These blokes from the south," he used to say, "they overstock, eat the heart out of a place just to get big profits quick. They've no idea of using the land so it'll be a better place when they leave it." The work Bill put into starting a place would have broken many another man's heart. And he had done it three times!

The first time the little fella and the near death of Ma. The melancholy of all that meant that ultimately neither of them liked the place the way they had in the beginning—and it was a poor man's selection anyway; a lot of natural obstacles to overcome. The second time it had been the droughts and the fires and the floods and the banks. He was working on too big an overdraft. The third time it had been Glenrichard—the work of their hands. And now the Japs.

Himself he would have stuck it, but there were Ma and the girls. He might send them south and get along as best he

could on his own. Join some defence force, some bushman's
guerilla squad, and do what he could. The Pastoralists'
Organisation was already caching food, getting ready. Bill
had been a lighthorseman with Allenby in the last war. That's
what he would do if he could persuade them: act as a guide
and guerilla. How he could keep the women down south was
another problem. Helen could go to school, but Mary—
Ridiculous even to imagine her behind a counter or a type-
writer. Ma— He wouldn't have Ma work for other people.
At her age it was unthinkable. He ought, after the work of
a lifetime, to be able to keep his family. They could live on
their capital for a while. But most of the capital was in the
land, and if the Japs took the land? The surveyor he had met
on the track, who had told him of the devastation in Wyndham, had said it was next door to impossible that the Japs
wouldn't land in the next month—maybe the next week.
There was talk of dismantling the meatworks. There were
seven 500lb. bombs under the wharf and bombs planted under
the powerhouse, the refrigerating plant, and the machine
sheds. Things must be bad if they could think of doing that!

Over and over Bill Parsons thought of these things and all
the ramifications of them. If the Japs came they must leave
the furniture. Or would they? It was impossible to get it
out. It would be valueless anyhow. The only value it had
was the value of distance. An armchair in the store in Adelaide might be worth £5, but in Glenrichard it was worth £20
if money could buy it. Transport was three-quarters of its
value. It was twenty-five hundred miles to Fremantle, longer
by sea, but near-enough, that was it. Twenty-five hundred
miles to replace an armchair—unless you made it yourself, as
Ma had made so many things around the homestead. Twenty-
five hundred miles—further—for a sheet of corrugated iron.

Tools, indispensable stores, new blood for the stock, luxuries, clothing, medicines—they all had to come that minimum
distance from civilisation. The stores at Wyndham were only
changing houses. Money for goods, goods for money.

He rode along, his horse going tiredly uphill. He would
make home, he reckoned, about two in the morning. If the
Japs were coming he would have to burn his home, destroy
the water tanks.

CHAPTER IV

MA moved restlessly through the house, putting this and that to rights. If it had been some of the homestead natives ill and wanting her she would have been down to the camp doing what she could, but it would have been neither wise, customary, nor practicable to go off ten miles to Wattlebunge's camp. By the morning she knew they would be either all right or all wrong.

The shock of Helen's escape still numbed her. Undoubtedly with things like this going on the girls would have to travel south.

Send the girls to their aunt in Melbourne? Stay on here with Bill looking after the place? There were hardships and risks whichever way. She had never really thought the war would come so close. If they were to go they had best go quickly. She began to prepare things. Some clothes they could take. Stores? She went to the storehouse, taking the key and a light with her. Bill would have to decide about stores. It was fortunate the half-year's supply hadn't come up yet. It was due, but it could be cut. If Bill went south, was Sid reliable enough to leave in charge of the stores? Hardly. The store shed was always kept locked and the key in its special place inside. She wished they had had a half-caste overseer.

She thought of the Japs she had known in Darwin and Broome, and Thursday Island; the Jap lugger owners, secret and clean and aloof; the Jap dentist, smiling and evasive and competent enough; the Jap barber who was also a blood-letter; the Jap pearl-buyers, with their expensive clothes and jewellery and their thick-lensed bargaining eyes. These were the representatives of a race she had grown up with in the north. Some of the Christian Japs had been, as it were, parishioners of her father. They had given her presents as a little girl. They had given Helen a different sort of present. How was it possible for them to have done such a thing? Was that war, or hadn't she really known what they were like all along? On the night when they walked out and carried lanterns they had given her a lantern and a kimono and a flower and a sash. They had given her a doll too. A Japanese girl-

doll with a black fringe. She could still remember that doll.
Mary had played with it when she was a little girl. They
were such very smiling, amiable people, the Japs.

She shivered.

The things they couldn't take with them and what would
be in Pa's way if he stayed on alone, she could pack up in the
teak and camphorwood boxes. The spare bed linen, the
photographs and vases, a lot of books. The sewing machine she
would oil and lock up. It was the first sewing machine ever
to come to the Kimberleys. Pa might have occasion to use
it. He could teach Sid-the-Chopper's Lily. She had already
seen Helen learning. The cane chairs ought to be painted over
with kerosene, the joists done again with creosote. She would
do what she could to protect her furniture from the ravages
of white ants and borers, mildew, damp, and all the rot that
attacks wood in the tropics. The unbleached calico curtains
didn't matter. They could rot and be replaced. She got out
and dusted some old hampers from the storeroom. The
droving chests caught her eye. The tucker-box and the
groundsheets for the swags. Pa would want all those. They
would need them themselves when they went in in the shay.
Say four or five camps. A week if they called in on the Taylors on the way down.

It was past midnight, but she still kept packing and sorting.
Whatever news Pa might bring she still thought the girls
ought to go south. Pa would probably insist that she go with
them. Perhaps she could return to him—if he stayed on—if
the Japs didn't land. She ravelled and unravelled all the
possibilities, her face drawn with the worry of it, haggard at
the prospect of losing, for the third time, the home she had
built up out of the wilderness.

*   *   *   *

Wattlebunge's camp was on a small flat. Big boulders behind the camp were still warm on their western faces from
the sunshine of the day. Dung on one of the little fires kept
off mosquitoes and sandflies. Though there was scarcely a
breath of wind, a slanting shelter of bushes leant over where
Wattlebunge was lying, wrapped in the blanket Ma Parsons
had sent. A couple of lubras were sing-songing over two

children who had been nearest when Saymore was magicked.
They shielded the children's faces from the moonlight and
from time to time bent down, listening to their breathing.
They had been very ill, and crying, unable to talk properly,
but afterwards the pains had gone and now they were asleep.
Old Wattlebunge was still ill, cramps taking him in the
stomach every half hour or so. There was a howling of dogs
and old women over the corpse of Saymore the medicineman.
A more emaciated frame it was hardly possible to imagine.
In death, the cadaver had fallen already into the grim outline
of the skeleton. It wouldn't take much to clean the flesh off
those bones, which is the custom of the blacks in the north.
The blacks were already saying that Saymore had swallowed
the magic from the sky to save his people. His chest and
tongue had swollen from the magic. They were cutting themselves with knives and sharp stones, and rubbing themselves
with grease and ashes, grieving loudly. In the morning the
grief would all be over. Saymore's life would be accomplished,
his end turned to a story to explain how his shade, reborn,
would be stronger than ever from the power of the poison
he had swallowed.

In the meantime, Wattlebunge groaned under his bough
shelter that kept off the moon and later would keep off the
dew. He took the chlorodyne only because Sid said he had
to. Sid took a dose himself to help things along—a sort of
sympathetic magic that did Wattlebunge a lot of good. Afterwards he ate some of the custard sauce and a mess of the
cornflour. Clasped to his broad stomach were several parcels
of hot ash and ant-bed clay wrapped up in moistened leaves
—a primitive sort of poultice that his two wives, who waited
on him, kept changing. Others were drinking tea, strong and
sweet enough for a spoon to stand up in it as bushmen say.
The tea and tobacco together were great morale builders.

Old Nebnezzer—younger than Saymore but with a beard
and a patriarchal look—was beating with two boomerangs in
the dust and singing a long chant that started and stopped and
started again, over and over again—singing Wattlebunge back
to health, singing all the night through. If Saymore had been
alive he would have been doing the singing. Nebnezzer, his
name a corruption of Nebuchadnezzer, born a mission boy,

was taking over the office of medicineman. It was a big moment, a night often to be talked about again. His voice was fresh and vigorous; he only stopped often enough to get breath; Wattlebunge would be restored to health from the very energy of his song. Wattlebunge himself felt this because he didn't behave with the despair of a man who sees no road but the road of death before him—he didn't behave, although under the circumstances he might have, like a native lying down to die.

Sid-the-Chopper, his stockman's hat pulled down well over his face, sat drinking tea out of the billycan by the fire. If Wattlebunge lasted till dawn he would get better. It looked as if he would get better.

There was a didgeree-do now in the wailing over the corpse of Saymore. Its booming notes, like a savage bull frog in full voice, seemed specially designed to trouble the soul of man, black or white. "Boom, boom, boom . . ." the resonant, deep notes blurted out like immense globules of purple blood breaking in waves of sound through the darkness of the night lit by the moon and the shooting stars. "Blup, blup, blup eroo . . ." The note was cradled in the barrel of the wood the way a great singer uses his chest. The wailing of the women rose tremolo over the undertones still vibrating.

*　　*　　*　　*

"A hell of a hullabulloo," thought Pa Parsons, catching an earful of it at a long distance. "Somebody's dead." He listened again, thinking which of the old grannies up at the homestead camp was likely to die. "Not at home," he decided. "More beyond the Iron Knoll, over towards the Weeping Water-hole."

He got down to undo the first gate on his property. He thought he might walk a little way, deciding as he went how best to break the news to Ma of the abandonment of the homestead. Fifty yards along something drew his attention to the track. He got out some matches, struck a light, and saw the heavy treads of a truck going off to the left over the underbush.

There is nothing like action to make a man forget his worries. Pa sneaked along the track, now and then lighting a match to make sure he was still on it. His tired horse trod softly after him, aware of his master's new need. There wasn't a jingle from stirrup, spur or bit. It took Pa, in a moment, back to the days of patrol work in Syria in the Great War. There hadn't been so much cover there.

Who was camping secretly on his land? What had they come for? A man doesn't sit down on another man's land just to admire the scenery. Pa went on with caution, but hoping he'd meet trouble. He just felt like knocking some-body down. The problems of his life seemed to concentrate in the anticipation of the wonderful relief such a knockdown blow would be to him. It never entered his head that he was single-handed and might be knocked down himself. These intruders were on his property without permission, and that stirs up a very ancient impulse in a man.

About thirty yards off he saw a blurred light. It was under a small, thick, dark tent, and the illumination wasn't strong. He dropped the reins, the horse stood still, Pa crept on.

Then he heard Mary's voice and laughter. Without any preliminaries he barged in.

"Hullo, look who's here! More company. Never rains but it pours. Come in, Mr. Parsons, and have a seat. That box there, Sandy."

They were three soldiers in the most jungly get-up Pa had ever seen. Enormous men. They had a tiny spirit lamp on a box and an opened tin of coffee with milk and some enamel pannikins stood beside it. There was also the smell of rum in the air. Mary was bright-eyed and evidently enjoying herself. Her hair was a little untidy and had a white flower drooping in it. There was a big smear of dirt right across the back and shoulder of her white blouse and another smear from her cheek across the left side of her forehead.

"Have a cup of coffee, Mr. Parsons? We've also got a little something to keep the cold out."

Pa knew the speaker, Bart Wells, whose father owned Podmore and Wickham and Linwood properties and who used to own Merryfields. One of the cattle barons. This young chap Bart had been sent to England for his schooling. He was six feet two, with a bright blue eye, broad shoulders, a smooth tongue, and hair and beard a bright desert red. "Firestick," the natives called him. He was about thirty and unmarried though if reports about him were true he ought to have been married or in the divorce court a dozen times. He was still the catch of the north for an unmarried girl and knew it. It was as clear as water in a moment to Pa that he was now in the mind to fascinate Mary.

"It's not so cold to-night," said Pa, stalling for time, "but I will have a cup of coffee if you've got it handy." He sat down.

They relit the spirit stove and washed out the pannikins for another cup all round. Pa disapproved of the spirit stove. Why couldn't they have had a fire like honest men? Call themselves bushmen and carry round a contraption like that! It just showed what Australians were coming to.

Bart must have read his thoughts; he said: "I suppose you're wondering what we're doing on your land, Mr. Parsons. We were going to come up and see you to-morrow. We only got in late to-night. We're a kind of defence group organising a signals lay-out. Observer Corps, they call us. We reckon this would be a good spot for a signals sub-base. It's easily picked up from the air by our chaps who know it's here, it's got a marvellous look-see area in front of it, and it's under good cover without the bush being too thick for the truck and the signals." Trust Bart, son of old Pagan Wells, to have all the answers ready. Everything he said was true enough. "You'll have to excuse this," said Bart, indicating the spirit lamp. "We're under orders not to light fires except when necessary."

A lot of tomfoolery that, thought Pa. Aloud he said, "What about the light in the tent?"

"Aha," said Bart, "we couldn't entertain Mary in the dark now, could we? Much as we'd like to."

"The scallywag," thought Pa. He watched the blush travel like a bushfire with the wind behind it over Mary's face. Bart watched it too. He saw that it coloured even the deep "V" in the front of her open-necked blouse. It gave him quite a sensation to see that.

"We were in the dark till she happened along," said Bart.

Mary began to talk, very fast, about how she had fallen across a trip-rope they had rigged up across the track just ahead of this camp and how they had tipped her up, man-handling her until they found out she was a girl.

"And supposing," said Pa, "It had been me or the missus come riding along our own track in the dark? Or supposing she had broken a shoulder or killed herself falling off her horse like that? Whom did you reckon to catch, anyway?"

"Just military precaution, Mr. Parsons," said Bart, airily. "Routine. Of course, we hadn't the faintest intention of trapping you or any of your family. We took a risk, no doubt, not supposing that any of you would be out riding over the property at night like this. But the Jap aero that travelled over from the east this afternoon was seen to dive down into one of the valleys around here and we were warned by radio code to be on our guard against parachutists. They thought it quite likely a few had been set down here. We've got trip ropes all round about. We were really lucky to catch her, the scrub's not exactly thick round here. We never expected to catch anyone—least of all a—"

"I was dreaming," Mary interrupted, "just mooning along."

"And you mean to tell me," said Pa, "that you kept that girl gossiping there with parachutists all around. That you didn't try to get her home!" "Call yourself a gentleman!" was what the implication in his words said. The impulse to punch anybody—this cocksure redhead or anybody—that had been balked by Bart's friendly palaver, urged itself again through him so that he shut his fists.

Bart stood up. There wasn't enough headroom for him in the little tent and he moved outside the entrance, holding himself at his full height of six feet two. He spoke quietly, very firmly, and yet not deliberately enough to annoy. "You'll appreciate, Mr. Parsons, that she might be a darn sight safer with the three of us here than back at the homestead with only the dogs watching the doorstep."

That gave Pa pause, but Bart didn't let up. "As a matter of fact we wouldn't have dreamed of letting her go back un-escorted, but she was waiting for you. It was her idea in the first place that you would be coming home to-night. That's why she came down here, to meet you. We thought we'd hear you on the track—we didn't dream you'd catch us as you did." His tone altered to one of warm admiration, flattery, laughter: "Trust an old soldier! Wait till we've been through this. Coffee's ready now."

One of the others poured out the coffee. Pa took a cup. He felt all right about Bart now. He had swallowed the flattery with the coffee. "First I knew about a Jap aero," he said, "It's new to me. Where did you come from?"

"Over on the crossroads up to Taylor's."

"You must have passed me on the track when I took that short cut down by the sandy-bottoms there?"

"Must have," said Bart. The way these old-timers always wanted to work out where they passed whom, was quite out of date with groups of men being given war jobs all over the North and the Japs with their white-socked toes stuck out ready to land on the continent.

"Did the Jap plane pass over home?" Pa asked Mary.

"About ten miles off, we guessed," said Mary. "I only saw it come fast and dip down and rise again and buzz off to the north-west. I didn't get a good view. We didn't know it was a Jap plane, either. We thought it was a new one of ours. It passed right over Helen, though. She was out at the Weeping Waterhole looking to see how the calves were going. She said there's about sixty in three little pounds. The Japs saw her, too, Dad."

Pa looked at Mary in fear, his eyes holding hers, knowing all the implications at once—"The Japs saw her, too, Dad."

"Did they get her?" Fear clutched at Pa's throat. He choked, unable to swallow, in a dreadful constriction.

"No, more by good luck than good management. It never even entered her head it was a Jap plane. She thought it was some of the boys from Darwin skylarking."

"Good God!" Pa Parsons never took the name of God lightly. For a moment it seemed to him that he could feel the Angel of Death, like a black owl, silently brushing its wings against his child, the second child.

"Sid-the-Chopper brought news that old Wattlebunge's crowd got caught. They're pretty bad he said. Mother sent down some hot soup, but we really couldn't do much about it. That's why I came down to meet you," she concluded, "to give you the news to send to headquarters."

"Some of them must have died," said Pa. "I heard a bit of the wailing while I was coming up the rise back there." He rose in the little tent. "Come on, Mary, I'll have to go down there as soon as it's daylight. Good-night all. Glad to know you're around. Thanks for the coffee."

"I'll get word down, Mr. Parsons," said Bart. "It's only confirmation of what we already knew. What we didn't know was that they'd laid an egg. The parachutist report came from much farther west, if it's any comfort to you, but we were told to keep our eyes skinned here just in case."

The little group broke up with subdued good-byes. One of the boys brought Mary's horse round. Pa caught his own. Pa and Mary rode along the track together. "I'll be seeing you," said Bart to Mary, softly, "in Wyndham three weeks from to-morrow." Then, aloud, "Remember, we're cousins."

Mary's laugh was nice to hear.

"How does he work it out that you're cousins?" asked Pa when they had ridden on a little.

"Grandfather's sister married his grandfather," said Mary.

"The second marriage," said Pa, "and there were no children. Don't you fall for that line of talk, Mary."

"No, Dad," she said. She knew, too, that Bart Wells had been all out to impress her. Knowing it didn't make it less sweet, less of a triumph either.

"A show-off," said Pa.

"Oh, rather," said Mary. She remembered the astonishment when he half-dragged, half-caught her, falling from the saddle, his knee on her chest in the dust, his hands holding her striking arms while the boys tied her feet; the grin that came into his voice when he said, "Let her up boys, we've caught us a nice little yellow-girl lubra, what-ho!" The hand on the bosom, at once. Afterwards, all the time afterwards when she had had her say, the quiet way he had worked to retrieve that first bad impression. And, when she had smiled, the way he had stopped calling her Miss Parsons and called her Mary!

"There's Wells in the Territory under every rosewood," said Pa, struggling with a couple of images. "Not any of them got married yet that somebody didn't have to take a shot gun along."

"Did grandfather have to take one to old Mr. Wells, Pa?" asked Mary, very quick.

"Well hardly—" said Pa, and then added softly, "Not that I ever heard of."

He laughed and smacked his horse. She was his own daughter after all, not one likely to be taken in by the flash talk of any Bart Wells. For a moment or so it had been nasty, finding her in the tent with three men. It was the first time since she was grown up that she'd been out like that—alone, on her own feet. If she'd been a boy he could have talked more openly to her. Anyway, she'd be going down south.

"We must get off by three o'clock this afternoon," he said, looking hard at the sky. About two o'clock now, he reckoned. Through the trees, a long way off, he could see the light of the homestead. Ma hadn't thought to black out. Always, when one of the family was out at night, the light was there to guide them safely home again.

CHAPTER V

THE waggon, with its eight horses, was ready outside the neat pickets of the whitewashed fence round Ma's flower garden. The eight horses made a flamboyant bit of driving anywhere. Ma sat on the box seat holding the reins in her hand. She would have been still putting things in even better order, giving the geraniums a last drink of water and sweeping the crumbs from the table where it was set with the last pot of tea they had had, if Pa hadn't bustled her into the waggon.

He had loaded the shay himself with only the necessities of a long journey. These lay piled up high under a stout covering of tarpaulin. If he had told Ma of what was in his mind, she would have wanted to bring all sorts of treasures along.

It was a pity, but that was how it had to be. No treasures.

It had pained him seeing her so carefully locking this old cupboard and that ancient chiffonier drawer, folding and putting away every old garment they weren't taking, leaving every much-used utensil shining in its right place—just as if waiting for some other tenant to take over. There would be no other tenant. No yellow-bellies or anybody else.

He went in for a last look around the kitchen, opening the shallow drawer at the far end of the white-scrubbed kitchen table. Ma's cookery books lay in it. He took one out, the mottled-covered, thick exercise book in which she had written out every special recipe ever since they were married, with the donor's name on the top of every recipe. It was like a garland of Ma's friendships through the years: Rosa's sago plum pudding and Miss Woodget's special orange cake. From the drawer at the other end of the table he took a handful of kitchen implements: a ball-bearing egg-beater, its composition handle looking like old ivory from the years of pressure of Ma's hand; the carving knife that he had sharpened for every joint he had carved for many years back—it had been a wedding present; the knife that was always called "the sharp knife"; the worn, old, silver spoon with the crest half obliter-ated that they always stirred porridge and gravy with—these things he folded in a cloth and put in a little gunny sack that he tucked in under a corner of the load on the waggon. It was his only concession to sentiment—not so much sentiment either, because he didn't know how long they would be on the track. Ma thought a week, but he had his own anticipa-tions, and knives and such were hard to pick up along the track.

"There's a cup of tea I left for you on the table, Bill," said Ma.

"Tea!" snorted Bill. He was going to murder their past in this place and Ma talked about tea!

He took an axe and slashed into the thousand gallon tank beside the homestead. The pumping plant he had already dismantled and hidden the parts where the Japs would never find them. The water leaped from the tank in a jagged gush.

Such a waste. Taking a drum of kerosene three parts full he walked through the house and kitchen splashing it everywhere on everything that was burnable. As he walked out again he threw a match down. The next moment he was up on the waggon seat with Ma, driving away. "The Japs will get nothing from me," he said.

Mary sat on her horse watching her home burn down. Smoke poured from the dwelling, almost seeming to lift the roof off with the uprush. The whitewashed walls of hand-made burnt clay brick crumbled and fell in. The verandah posts were catching now, the plants Ma had been watering half an hour earlier were withered and black.

Little Helen, from the back of the shay, watched in consternation. Ma couldn't speak, her heart pounding in her throat. Somehow, though she had expected catastrophe, she hadn't thought of it coming this way.

"I'm sorry, Ma," said Bill. His elbow touched her side with the reassurance of sympathy. Did an abo, he wondered, knocking a piccaninny on the head, tell the mother first? He thought not.

Ma didn't cry. The tears were all behind her eyes, in her mind.

"We'll never get it so nice again," she thought, "never."

Bill touched up the offside leader with a lot of sound in the whip.

"He's too old to take on another new place now," Ma thought. "He's too old for the hard yacker of it. And so am I," she thought. Now the tears pricked at the back of her eye-balls. She moved her hand to pull down her hat further over her eyes. There was a gutter ahead across a dip in the road and the waggon had to go over it. "Hang on, Helen," she called, "Here's a big bump."

It was her first instruction. She was taking up her new life. It was really an instruction to herself: "Hang on, Ma. Hang on over this big bump. There are plenty more houses, plenty more homes to be built. At least, we're all alive, all together. That's more than many poor homeless wretches are in this world to-day." Her hand clutching the low iron rail at the side of the box seat relaxed, her feet, braced against the footboard, shifted to a better position.

"She's over it," thought Bill Parsons. "She's over the worst of it." He swallowed himself. It had been like knocking a loved one down and then watching the first stirring to consciousness of the prostrate beloved. "She's over it."

The track swung on a half-turn. He could see smoke still hanging in the sky. "Better that way, Ma, than to let the Japs use it." He had spent most of the morning potting off a lot of his cattle till the slaughter sickened him. After that the homestead was not so bad. Just an ultimate loss. The wedge-tailed hawks rose up in rings, feasting.

"Come on. Git up," he bellowed to the horses, the reins spread carefully through his fingers like through the slats of a fan. "Get a move on will you." They were in good condition, a bit fresh. They got a move on.

CHAPTER VI

IT was full tide and a double gang was working. The s.s. "Toowoomba" leaned in towards the Wyndham jetty like a dirty blonde half tight and tilted on stilt heels leaning over the shoulder of her little clutched dancing partner. "Dammit, dammit," shouted Mr. Johnstone, the mate. He ran down ladders all the way from the bridge, shouting and calling out names. These fellows loading were so damned stupid they couldn't understand what he said if they did hear it. He had a megaphone that nobody listened to. They called themeslves a wharf gang and they had no notion of stowing stuff. A word from him and they'd walk off. For two pins they'd walk off, Japs or no Japs. "What do you think you're handling?" shouted Mr. Johnstone. "Dynamite? Pianos?" He almost danced with anger. "Meat. Nothing but bloody canned meat. Shove it on board. Look out you. Why can't you stow that over there? That's where it ought to go. Anyone with half an eye . . . She's down to port as it is and you stick all the heavy stuff there. Wait till she rolls. Wait till she turns turtle. You're travelling on her yourself. You'll have a long swim ashore—" He leaned over the hold and his voice could not be heard. The donkeyman at the winch rolled a cigarette.

On the foredeck, leaning over the rail, was a young sailor, a Scotsman, about twenty. He had fair hair with a wave

in the front and a stocky body with a deep chest. His forehead was dripping with perspiration and there were several
big red blotches from mosquitoes on his cheeks and his hands
and arms. He had a narrow waist and his pants were cut
tightly. He was suffering from the heat and all his visible
flesh was deep pink, more startling because everyone else
on the ship and wharf was sunburnt, brown, sallow, yellow,
copper-coloured, or the greyish green mauve that is the aboriginal tint. The sailor was watching an old aborigine on the
wharf fishing. In the midst of the obscenity, the confusion,
the shouting, the rattling of the crane and the bumping down
of the crates of canned meat, the old aborigine sat with the
stillness of a tree stump, one brown arm, like a branch, now
and then moving, as it were at haphazard, the hook through
the water. The old aborigine fished with a mother-of-pearl
hook, double-barbed and unbaited. He had filed down the
hook himself. It seemed incredible to the young Scotsman
that he would ever, from the whirlpool of this hubbub, draw
forth a fish.

He looked down into the eyes of a young native, a nephew
of the old fisher. The young aborigine smiled with the sudden
warmth of soul that is so likeable, so easy. "Him silly," he
said to the Scotsman, and giggled at the old man over his
shoulder.

"What for you fish?" he asked the old man—to show him
off to the fair-head as a child makes a cicada shrill by
shaking it. "Jap bomb make plenty dead fish."

"Me no want Jap fish," grumbled the old man.

The Scots sailor turned away. Even an abo, even a
darkie, knew what this bloody war was all about. He felt
sad and restless and unsettled. After last night he couldn't
count on himself any more. He thought he'd forgotten it
and he hadn't. The bombing. He couldn't stand another
bombing. After last night he'd had it. The picture of the
rubble that had been his home on the Clyde was clear in the
heat. It was still a picture that came and went at odd
moments. It was weeks since he'd thought of it, and here
it was again, just when he thought he'd got over it.

He went up to the mate, who had the gangs working again.
"Mr. Johnstone," he asked timidly. He knew it wasn't a good

moment, but if he waited for a good moment the ship would be at sea again. Mr. Johnstone was only good-tempered at sea. In port he had too much to do to stay civil to his crew. "Could I have shore leave to-day?"

"Shore leave? What in blazes do you want shore leave in a dump like this for? Save it till Perth. There's nothing to do in Wyndham. Nothing that a young fellow like you ought to do anyway. Nobody takes shore leave in Wyndham."

The sailor was confused by the natural megaphone of the mate's loud voice. He felt that all the ship heard what he was asking and knew why—that he couldn't take it.

"I want to walk around a bit. Want to stretch my legs a bit. Want to see the cattle, see the wild horses."

"Oh, a sightseeing trip. O.K., O.K. Don't worry me about it any more. And leave the wild women alone will you. The Sergeant up here's very particular. And some of the husbands are particular. You might get a wild waddy on the back of your neck or a wild 'gator snap you up in a wild creek if you go swimming. He was not as bad as he sounded, this man. Cheered by his own wit, he was almost jovial. "If you go over to the meatworks you might get a nice cold beer. Some of the boys are having a break-up out there. They're having a wild party." Still grinning at his joke, he shouted down the hold, "Leave plenty of room for the big stuff. They're putting a bullock team on it now—the tractors couldn't take it." He turned to the boy starting down the gangway, "Remember shore leave ends at midnight. We sail on the full tide."

"O.K."

"Where's he getting off to?" asked the Third, jealous, coming up just then.

"Shore leave."

The Third spat over the side. "You'll never see him again. The kid got the jitters bad last night."

"So would you," said the mate, "if you'd had what he's had."

They both knew what the boy had had. His home bombed, his people killed, his call up for the merchant navy and on his first trip the torpedo off Greenland. Nineteen days in an open boat and frostbite. One toe lost and two others not much use to him. Dive-bombed and sunk in the Channel and now, after all that, the Japs. No safety anywhere.

"He's got the wind up now properly," said the Third. It was just a spectacle to him, seeing the boy suffer.

"Well he can't go far from here," said the mate.

"If he doesn't show up at midnight you'll cop it."

"Mind your own business. He'll show up. He won't like it, but he'll show up."

"Poor little Kiltie." Sarcastic.

"If I were a doctor, I'd write him out a nice long certificate and never let him go to sea again."

"I'll bet you ten bob he won't sail this trip."

"Done," said the mate. All the time he had his eye on what was going down the hold. Suddenly he sprang forward again, shouting. The exasperation of dealing with blockheads made the blood run to his head, his anger racing like a fever as if someone had twisted him violently upside down.

"Liver," thought the Third. "Apoplexy." He thought of promotion and of quick ways of getting up the ladder of rank.

Chapter VII

Dan McAlpine, the drover, was sitting under the shade of a big turpentine tree about sixty yards off the gate into the main holding paddock. The mob of 1,000 head he had brought down from the inner Kimberleys were about three miles off, held by his stockboys and the four cattlemen with him. They were no trouble to hold because the grass was still good enough, but they had to be watched. Two months before they'd made a bit of a rush every night—they'd hardly been handled in their lives before, except for branding. Dan had travelled them slowly and very gently. They'd actually picked up a bit of condition on the way. They were prime fats. Dan was pleased about that. He was a good contracting drover. Owners liked to get him to handle their mobs because he spared the beasts, kept the losses and strays down to a minimum, and made the fastest time consistent with water and feed conditions. It paid them to take a little longer time on the track and keep the beasts prime.

Dan fussed over each mob he looked after, the way a conscientious school teacher fusses over each class he handles. "There's a lot of psychology in the way you handle cattle," was one of Dan's favourite themes. He was an unerring spotter of the natural leaders in a mob. He had pets, the way any good teacher has pets—not that they got any better treatment than the rest, but he just liked them. "That baldy brute with the black eye," he'd say affectionately, and flick his whip, with a crack, round its rump. One of his grumbles was that he just got a mob educated to the point when it was no trouble at all to handle, when he had to turn them over. Actually, he loved the mental and physical sense of mastery that breaking in a new mob meant. The mob that was out on the Three Mile now he hadn't had long enough to get tired of. It was like a particularly fractious and unruly class of highly individual pupils that a master gets fond of, just because they are so wild and unpredictable, so high-spirited and charged with electricity. He liked these cattle because they were wild, rangy, big-horned beasts, bred in the remote hills and gullies of the Kimberleys, sure-footed to climb and with enough stamina to run hard and fast. They were very suspicious of everybody and everything that came near them. Nervous types and not aristocrats.

They were like himself.

Dan couldn't stand towns, and he'd never settled down.

There was a wildness in his breeding that showed itself physically. He was six feet six tall. His height gave him a perpetual sense of loneliness, like the clouds that only clear from Mont Blanc at sunset. It made him a laconic but not a melancholy man. Often silent, he was never unfriendly. When he relaxed he was wildly hilarious, indulging in the most freakish pranks of the imagination, his inhibitions lifted by alcohol. More often he felt the need to be alone. He couldn't suffer fools for too long at a time. His mates always spoke well of him, but no mate was indispensable to him. This was something strange in the outback, where two mates often grow so close they are like the self and the reflection of the self in a glass; like the upper and lower half on a playing card, inseparable, of identical value.

He had known women, but was no womaniser. Where
other drovers carry a dirty picture postcard or puzzle trick,
he carried a detective yarn. He always had a paper-backed
book with him and always a different one. He liked detective
stories and digests and was a confirmed reader whenever he
got the chance. He liked playing patience better than poker.
What he read he thought about deeply, but he didn't go out
of his way to provide himself with philosophical literature. He
read whatever came along. The only magazine he subscribed
to was the "Bulletin," and that because it was such a good
swapping medium. The vogue for paper-backed Penguins,
Pandas, Albatrosses and short story collections was a god-
send to him. He always had one in his pocket and a few in his
pack. He was as near to being an intellectual as a man who
spends most of his life in the saddle can be. That means that
ideas and words mattered to him, that he had a natural pre-
dilection for chewing things over the way a ruminant animal
chews its cud. If he ever got into an argument he had a
bitter ferocity that made him stubbornly tenacious, unwilling
to let the slightest point pass. He was like a bull ant that
rears up, its fangs biting, its front antennae weaving like a
trained boxer, its narrow insect length a venemous lance with
grappling hooks. The only fights Dan had ever been in were
fights about ideas. What the bull ant must be among ants,
Dan was among men—they respected him and let him alone.

Now, his back propped against the turpentine tree, he was
chewing a long stem of grass while he thought things over.
His horse, its reins trailing, picked at the tufty grass a little
way off, some part of its attention always on the man. If Dan
had clicked his tongue it would have stood still, its ears
pricked, and let Dan come up and catch him. Not so any
stranger. Dan was waiting for a message from the manager
of the meat works to bring the cattle in. The planes and the
bombing the night before hadn't worried the cattle much.
The horses had felt it much worse. They were still nervous.

Dan had heard of the fall of Singapore to the Japs weeks
after the event. He knew that when he handed over the
mob he would have to do something about it. He was thirty-
three, able-bodied, and single. He'd tried to enlist in the
phoney war period and the sergeant down at Hall's Creek

had refused to take him. "You're more use where you are, and in any case you've got flat feet."

Dan's feet weren't flat, but he did have trouble with them. They were thin-arched feet, and his shoes and riding boots were made specially by a Chinese saddler up in Darwin of soft, hand-cured leather. For his height his feet were disproportionately small.

"I wasn't aiming to go as a foot slogger," Dan had said. "The Light Horse for me."

"And before you know where you are," the sergeant had replied, "you'll be sitting inside a tank like a sardine in a tin. They're mechanising the Light Horse."

Anything more incongruous than a six-foot-sixer, without any mechanical sense, sitting in any of the half dozen light tanks that Australia then owned couldn't be imagined. Dan had to grin himself.

"I'd try for the Air Force," he said, "but I'm too old for a pilot and I've not enough book knowledge for anything else. I only had eight months' schooling in my life and that was in half a dozen different schools. You don't need to pass exams to navigate cattle." Dan's father had been prospector, dingo trapper, shearer, fencing contractor; his family of six had all been born in different States! Dan knew where his two sisters had married and settled down. Now and then he got letters, but, except through them, he wouldn't have been able to communicate with his three brothers. Two of the brothers had enlisted.

"You stay right where you are. In this war bullocks are more important than bullets."

That had been the beginning of a long session with the sergeant, who was a knowledgeable as well as a practical fellow. Dan liked him a lot. "After this war," the sergeant had said, "Australia ought to come out for once with a bit of credit in the Bank of England, not just a huge war debt and 80,000 dead. It's easy enough to kill and devastate, but to feed and clothe, that's slower and more difficult. How long do you reckon it took the first man to get a herd of cattle together?"

"Nine months to make a man and a second to kill him," said Dan.

"Nine months be ——," said the sergeant, who had a couple of small sons. "It's easy seen you're not married. Twelve years at the very least to make a man."

The argument went on most of the evening. For fifteen months afterwards it had held Dan confident that he was doing a good job for his country.

"Cattlemen don't grow on bushes," the sergeant had said. "With the best training in the world it takes nearly a year to make a pilot. How long do you reckon it takes to make a boss cattleman? Or a good farmer for that matter?"

"Production isn't something that happens in factories only," said the sergeant. "What's Wyndham meatworks without the cattle in the country behind it?"

*   *   *   *

Now, fifteen months later, Dan was sitting within hearing distance of the meatworks hooter, knowing that the Japs had carefully not bombed it, and wondering what he ought to do and what was going to happen to the cattle in his care.

The bill of sale was made, but if the meatworks wouldn't take delivery—? If they decided to evacuate and threw the onus of paying for the cattle on the government—?

Wishing he had got in three days earlier, wouldn't make any difference now.

He rolled a cigarette. Along the main track a horseman came galloping—an aborigine, by the way he galloped. It was a middle-aged aborigine with a few green teeth sticking out of a cheerful smile and greying hair showing under his wide-brimmed cattleman's hat. He pulled up with a flourish.

"Good-day, Boss."

"Good-day, Jacky."

"Old Gutsache want you over to the meatworks, Boss."

"O.K. Jacky."

It was the message Dan had been waiting for. He got to his feet. It was like a jack-knife unfolding. "Mr. Malone, I think you mean," he said, with deliberate clearness.

"All same Gutsache," said Jacky, with a perfectly uncheeky cheerfulness.

Malone, manager of the meatworks, was nicknamed Guts-ache by all the underdogs because of his habit of bellyaching about everything. There was an apocryphal story that once he had been doing a perish of thirst and his rescuer had handed him a drink of water and Malone said: "No germs, I hope?" And the rescuer said, "No, my wife filled the bottle up with bathwater specially to kill the germs." The only thing wrong about the story was that Malone wasn't the sort of chap ever to be in the situation of doing a perish.

Dan didn't bother to lecture Jacky. It would have been waste of time. He asked, instead, about the bomb damage in Wyndham, which he hadn't seen. He'd been out with the cattle the night before. The two men rode along the track towards the works, Dan gradually getting ahead. He was anxious to know how things stood.

CHAPTER VIII

No killers had been yarded for two days.

The processing, canning, storage and delivery departments of the big meatworks were still functioning, but the killing had stopped and the carcase butchers had worked their last shift. The blood-spotted overalls, head-covers, and dungarees had gone to the boiler room for the last time and the cleaning down had been more thorough than usual. The last run of tins was on the conveyor belts now. The steam would be let out of the boilers gradually.

In his big office upstairs the manager, Bert Malone ("Guts-ache"), had called a meeting of executives. The engineers and foremen of the different departments were there, and representatives of the cattle industry, and the union officials from the town, and several of the boss drovers who had come down with recent mobs. Dan had been summoned because his mob was waiting for the count-in and pay-off.

It was not a meeting to discuss—it was a meeting to take the news. Bert Malone was a worried man. The final news, when he gave it to these men, would be a big shock. Rumours had gone round and certain actions had been tipped as likely, but now the thing was actually here it was worse than any of them had anticipated. An earthquake is still an earthquake, even if it has been anticipated. He had put on plenty of beer to soften the blow. It would be the last beer the town would know for a long time. The Japs had got the last consignment. There would be no ice in the town anyway when the works closed down. This beer was beautifully iced, golden and sparkling, in the firm's best glasses. They were out of his private cupboard, the glasses the directors and personal visitors always used. The secretary of the slaughtermen's union, an old chap who used to be an I.W.W. and whose affectionate nickname was "Whiskers," because of the gorilla-like fringe of hair round his face, had an appreciative sparkle in his eyes from the beer. He had been making all sorts of cracks at the company, and the big shots present had to take them. For once they were more worried than the slaughtermen. If the company had to close down it was like the earth opening under their feet. How would they carry on? What would they do?

"Listen boys," said Bert Malone, at last. "Here's the news you're all waiting to hear. Here's what we've been frightened of, and now it's happened quicker than we thought it would happen. As far as I can make out it's part of a government plan and it's no use kicking against it. The directors were called to a government conference, I understand, and what we're under orders to do is no part of any private cowardice on the part of the company. If the army say they can't, in certain circumstances, hold the town, then the civilians have to do what the army want, what the army think safest. The army might not care to risk certain assets falling into the hands of the enemy . . ."

"The Brisbane Line!" sneered Whiskers.

"S'sh!" said a dozen voices. "Carry on, Bert," said another.

"The company might not care to risk its assets," said the irrepressible Whiskers.

"Far be it from me," said Bert Malone, with a frown at Whiskers, an old enemy of his, "to go against what the army and the government, as well as the company, think best . . ."

"Hear, hear!" said a foreman who was a close stooge to Malone.

"Oh, let's have the news," said the president of the local Pastoralists' Association, this delay was more than he could bear. At this moment Dan McAlpine edged quietly round the door. "Come in, Dan," said Malone, glad of the interruption. "Get yourself a beer." Dan took off his hat and squatted down in the cattleman's habitual pose. Someone put a glass of beer in his hand.

"As I was saying," went on Malone, "the wire I received informs us that the works have to shut down for the duration."

There was a buzz of talk. Malone mopped his face with a handkerchief. It was over. "Like to hear the wire?" he asked.

"Yes!"

"Go ahead."

"Read her out."

Malone read: "Close works stop. Load vital machine parts on s.s. "Toowoomba" immediately stop. Evacuate personnel destroy freezing plant stop. Regards Barton."

The men were all on the inside now. There was none of the antipathy Malone had feared. Dan blew a smoke ring from his stance on the floor. "Nice of him to send his regards," said Dan.

There was a babble of voices.

"This is it."

"Must really expect the Japs."

"We're through here. They were close enough last night."

"Too blooming close."

"Space, that's it," said Whiskers. "The scorched earth. They had to do it in Russia. We have to do it here." A belligerent intelligence lighted his seamed face.

"Have a cigar," said Malone suddenly to him, shoving the box under his nose. For the first time what he thought the old boy's habitual nonsense made sense to him. "There won't be any big shots up here for a long time," said Malone. It was the first time he had ever recognised to the union secretary that he was an employee, too.

"I don't mind if I do," said Whiskers. He bit off the end. "Going to burn the lot down?" he enquired. "There's nothing I like better than a good company fire."

Malone saw that it was dangerous being too friendly with Whiskers. He offered the box to the president of the pastoralists. Whiskers winked at Dan.

"You old firebrand," muttered Dan. In his cups Whiskers used often to boast of the sheds he had fired in the great shearing strike in Queensland.

Another round of beer was being poured out.

"Go easy on it boys, make the most of it. That's the last there'll be for a long time," said Malone.

"Here's to the skin on your nose," said the foreman. He had a particularly prominent nose. It was always sunburnt and always peeling. The toast was his favourite toast, but the joke was stale.

"Cheers!"

"Here's to the next canning down!"

"Here's to you, Bert!"

"Good old Gutsache!"

"Here's to the end of the war!"

"What about the cattle?" It was Dan, the boss drover, whose beasts were out at the Three Mile, speaking.

"The cattle?" said Bert Malone, as if the cattle were nothing to do with him. "What about them? We can't do anything about them. That's your job."

"The cattle are under a bill of sale," said Dan. "The owners didn't expect the factory to go out of action like this, without notice. Even if you don't formally take them I'm here ready to hand them over."

"That's so," suddenly put in the president of the pastoralists.

"Well, the Japs didn't give us notice, did they?" blustered Malone. "They didn't come over last night and the other nights with a by-your-leave and who's taking you to the dance, Danny Boy."

"Forget it, Dan," the foreman said. "They're not your cattle."

"They're my responsibility," said Dan. He was standing now, and he put his glass down on the table with a thump. "It's taken us more than a month to get those cattle down."

"And it'll take you more than a month to get them back, no doubt." Bert Malone was sick of this persistent drover. Who did he think he was, anyway! He had too much on his mind then to argue it out with a drover. He'd be working night and day till the "Toowoomba" sailed. The captain didn't want to put off sailing for the manager of the meat-works and his machinery and personnel. He didn't want to be caught by that jetty to-night. He'd go to sea anyway and he'd put back—well—maybe. But they'd better try to get their stuff on board to-day. He couldn't afford the time to worry about this drover. He didn't know how he stood, anyway, with these cattle. No doubt there'd have to be compensation, but from whom? The government? The company? Dan couldn't force the responsibility on to him.

But Dan was.

"It isn't as easy as that," said Dan. "Some of the runs are overstocked as it is, and with the war on and no market, the owners won't be able to stand it."

"The owners!" said Whiskers; "Always the owners."

"If the Japs land the owners won't stand much chance any-way," said Bert grimly.

"Say, you can't leave them here for the Japs to walk in and nab!" It was the tally clerk, who hadn't spoken before.

"You can't let them go bush?"

"The owners couldn't stand that either. Too much damage to property." The sardonic old Whiskers again. Malone was sick of him.

"Not enough grass anyway."

"They're wild enough as it is. In no time they'd be nothing better than scrubbers."

"Much worse for the industry than if the Japs did get them."

"Rangey stuff. Ought to be shot."

"That's what the sergeant of police suggested," said Malone.

"What!" So they'd talked it over, had they!

"Shoot the lot?" It was the president of the pastoralists again.

"You couldn't expect the knacker to knock them all on the head, humane like, could you? What do you think we're running here? The R.S.P.C.A.?" Malone didn't mind sounding brutal. He was not manager of a meatworks for nothing. "I've got plenty of ammunition for you, Dan." He turned to the other drovers. "You blokes coming south with us? The captain will give you a free passage. The company pays this trip." Evacuate personnel the wire said. That covered the drovers, Bert Malone reckoned. It would make it easier to deal with Dan, getting his drovers away from him.

"Sure," said the drovers, "we want to join up."

"Shooting the cattle. More than a thousand head. I don't like it," said Dan.

"Better the crows and dingoes get them than the Japs," said old Whiskers.

"How about sending up a few ships to get them down?"

"No hope. Too slow, too dangerous; just giving the Japs pot shots. Anyway, there aren't any ships." Bert Malone spoke.

"We could take them overland."

"That mob?"

"This time of year?"

"You've got another think coming, Dan!"

"I know it's hard, Dan, but that's war."

"Forget it, Dan."

The factory hooter boomed out.

"Smoko."

"That's the last smoko for a long time."

"There's plenty to do," said Malone. "Excuse me a minute, Dan." He got the staff of the various departments out of the door, giving them directions as they went. Dan walked to the large-scale map hanging on the wall. He blew a perfect smoke ring. It was like a bomb breaking against the map. Those most interested in cattle followed him, looking at the map too. The noise of the factory, that had accompanied the conference, was gone. The last conveyor belt had stopped rumbling, the last machine stopped its rhythmical thumping, the hiss of leather over steel was still. The silence of the machinery was welcome to Dan. He felt he could think better, make up his mind better, at once.

"I'm not going to leave them for the Japs," said Dan. "I'm going to overland them." To Malone, walking briskly from the door, he said: "I won't want that ammo, Bert, I'm not going to shoot those cattle. I'm overlanding them."

"You'll never get through, Dan. Look—just to prevent you committing suicide—look at the map. You either go to Adelaide or Queensland. Adelaide's two thousand miles away, Queensland's sixteen hundred."

"I'll go Queensland."

"All right. Taking everything into consideration, by the time you get to the Orde you'll be out of feed and water. Do you know how long the Duracks took getting the cattle in here? Three years! The war would be over, Dan, by the time you get there."

"There's been plenty of overlanding cattle since the Duracks," Dan answered. "There's been bores put down. The Duracks and D'arcy and Orr had to explore as well as drove. They had to conserve every head. They had cows and calves, weaners, bulls, every damn thing. I'm travelling bullocks. Just walking cans of meat. I know it's late in the season, I know there'll be shortages of feed and water, but if we lose forty per cent, even more, it'll still be worth while. There's armies coming to this country to feed, Bert. When it comes to the big push it's quicker to make bullets than it is to make beef, and the country needs both. Overseas need both. They really need our bullocks more than they do our bullets. Factories can be run up in a couple of months, but a bullock, wartime or peacetime, takes more than three years to grow. Even if the war is over by the time I get there, Bert, the people will still need to eat. More than ever they'll need to eat. Our people overseas will need to eat, our allies will need to eat. There's not so much food in this world that you can order me to shoot a thousand cattle and think it's not a crime and all the other blokes who'll have to shoot their cattle when the word gets around. Let me get my cattle through and other men will follow. Don't get it into your head that I'm running away either. It'd be a darn sight easier for me to go aboard your little steamer and have a soft time training in the army, spine-bashing it in a depot some place, because I'm thirty-three and my feet are crook for marching, than to belt a thousand head sixteen hundred dusty miles. I know better than you what I'll be up against."

"Well," said Malone, impressed in spite of himself, "Maybe there is something in what you say. I hadn't thought it out like that."

"Too right I'm right. If I can get a plant together will you let me have a go?" The hard word direct.

"I can't stop you, Dan."

"Don't give me that line of bull. You know I can't take those cattle away from here unless you give me the O.K."

"I've no authority."

Dan growled in his throat, a purely instinctive noise that conveyed contempt, anger, warning.

"All right then," said the manager. "I'll give you a personal contract and try to have it okayed either by the firm or the government down south. On the arguments you've given me the government ought to underwrite any sort of agreement like this because it's a national emergency and this move would definitely be in the national interest."

"Attaboy," said Dan, "talk like that to the politicians and they'll let you write your own cheque."

"Will they? You don't know them. That's their own line of talk. All nice to listen to, but when it comes to the dotted line— Oh, well, I'll get a contract form ready." Malone was sighing windily already. He went over and took a lugubrious look at the map. "You know what you're trying to do, Dan? You're trying to drive a mob of half-wild cattle the distance from London to Moscow in a bad season at the wrong time of the year. Now get out. I've work to do."

Dan grinned back at him from the door; "No wonder they call you Gutsache. See you in Moscow."

*   *   *   *

In the corridor outside the office he threw his hat up to the roof. Then he turned and sent it spinning sideways in an arc from one outstretched hand to the other. He had a stretch as long as his height. It was an impressive trick.

Chapter IX

The sailor had exhausted the sights of Wyndham, walked along its long main street several times, until he felt he knew it by heart. He was back now at the Post Office. Tethered to a ring on a verandah post was a drooping chestnut horse, who stood so that the line of shadow from the pole stretched straight along his backbone. The rider of the horse was Jacky, who had taken the message out to Dan. He sat sunning himself like a comfortable black lizard on the edge of the Post Office verandah. Leaning up against the verandah post was Nipper, the young aborigine who had been down at the wharf when the sailor left the ship. He smiled at the sailor.

The sailor would have liked to have sat down beside them and gossiped too. He would have liked to have learnt more about these friendly, strange, dark people. Before he had come to Australia he had imagined all the blackfellows were stone age, chipping weapons out with little stone axes and practising magic and throwing boomerangs and wearing no clothes. It was disconcerting to find this thin and rather elegant blackfellow, lounging up against the verandah post. He had on a pink shirt that was attractive against his browny-black face, and tight, long trousers of some heavy stuff, that had been washed so many times that it was a light pale blue. He had on short boots into which his trousers were tucked. His white teeth were magnificent and his hair had been recently combed. It was a handsome head of hair cut European style. Altogether he looked clean and exceedingly comely.

If the sailor had known more about the country he would have realised from their boots and their get-up that these aborigines were stockmen. Jacky had a humpy and a wife on the main road out of town. He worked for the meatworks on the cattle. Now the meatworks were shutting down he would be out of a job. It didn't seem to worry him much. He was a plump, well-fed, middle-aged native—his job, which he had stuck for a few years now, had fed him very well. Among Jacky's wife's relatives he was a king. There were always guests at the humpy. He was hoping to stick to the horse, which was meatworks property, when the meatworks did close down. The best way to do this, he reckoned, was not to let the horse out of his sight, then the bosses might forget all about it. The difficulty was that he was expected to help get the stuff loaded out of the factory and go messages. That brought him directly under the eyes of a great many bosses. It was a problem.

Nipper, the young stockman, who was some sort of a connection of his wife, might help him in this: form, as it were, another bodyguard to the horse. But confiding in Nipper raised a delicate situation. The uncle by marriage had prestige to maintain. He had always told everybody the horse was really his. In the meantime he was waiting for telegrams for Gutsache, the big boss. The telephone lines which could have carried the message were down and hadn't been mended yet. Everybody had so much to do. Except Nipper, Jacky and the sailor.

The sailor went to the other end of the verandah and sat on a wooden bench. He was self-conscious sitting there, but he would have been more self-conscious sitting on the verandah of the pub. He wished he had someone in Australia to whom he could send a telegram.

A tall man in a wide-brimmed felt hat with a plaited band round it and a whip over his arm and a thick shirt with breast pockets and long tight trousers, like something off the stage, walked briskly round the corner. He gave the sailor a nod and went inside the Post Office. It was Dan. The sailor felt more lonely than ever. He couldn't hear what the natives were saying and he couldn't hear what the tall stranger was saying to make the girl inside the Post Office laugh so loud. A little native boy, about nine years of age, came down the street, scuffling the dust between his toes that were spread out, individual, a little prehensile, never having worn boots. He had a long step with something disarticulated about it, like one of those single-line caricatures, animated and walking down the street. His shanks were long and skinny and his foot, by comparison, enormously big. He reminded the sailor of a long-legged bird at the zoo, all head and legs. His eye was bright, birdlike and intelligent too. He was quite different from any other little boy the sailor had ever known or seen. Quite suddenly the sailor thought of himself at that age—a pink pudding in a striped sweater and long golf socks, with a muffler round his neck. No doubt, if the little dark boy had lived on the Clyde they would have called him Nigger, the way a black cat is called Nigger, and had he thrown stones, his mother would have told him not to be unkind, in the same voice in which she told him not to tease the cat.

He got up and, hands stuck in his pockets and head bent down, walked off the verandah and into the street. Ever since the bombing he hadn't been able to get his mother, his boyhood and his home out of his mind. Everything reminded him of it, even a little darkie boy walking down a foreign street.

"Hullo," said the tall stranger with the whip, walking up behind him. "You can send a wire now if you want to. They've got the line working again."

"No one to send it to," said the boy; "Nothing to say." He felt that some explanation of his hanging around was called for. "Thought I might get a letter," he said, and at the same time knew that there was no one in the world who would know that he would be calling in at this little port with the jetty like a black foreign insect with its hundred legs sticking up out of the water.

"The mails are pretty irregular since the war," said Dan, to console him. "You're off the 'Toowoomba' aren't you?"

"Yes. Shore leave till midnight. Thought I'd look around and see something."

"Nothing much to see here. That's the most interesting sight in town." Dan indicated the biggest hole left by the bombing.

"I've seen worse ones than that."

"Like to have a look at some cattle?" asked Dan. He felt a curious attraction for this lonely, down-in-the-mouth, rather dour Scots boy with nothing to do.

The quick shine of interest in the boy's eyes was instant thanks. "Rather."

"I'll give you a ride out. You can easily get a lift in."

"Oh, thanks!" said the sailor.

"You don't mind a bit of a pack on the horse?"

"A horse?" asked the sailor. "I've never ridden a horse. Only a donkey once on the sands."

Dan had to smile. "Oh, well," he said, "We're quits. I've never been to England in a ship."

When he got the boy mounted he said: "I'll lead her till you get used to it. You won't mind that?"

The sailor smiled, his red lips were full and happy. It was a treat day after all, just the sort of day for a picnic. "Quite a good-looker," thought Dan, "when he's happy." He led the way out to the cattle camp, a natural arrogance couched in his own six foot six on a horse, nonchalant, easy-going, putting on a bit of swagger for the admiring boy walloping up and down on the trotting mare behind him. "Rise in your stirrups, son, take the weight in your feet," he called out.

"Aye, aye, sir," called the boy gaily. "What a wonderful bit of luck," he thought.

*　　*　　*　　*

Dan turned in at the meat works. There were a couple of big lorries being loaded with factory gear and other men nailing up crates filled with machinery. There was a lot of argument going on outside the freezing plant. Gutsache Malone was in the middle of it. Dan wanted none of these men. They were engineers, labourers, motor drivers and mechanics. He was interested in the drovers, gambling in the big two-up school in the sunny yard, out beyond the engine shed. Ever since the eleven o'clock hooter went for the last smoko the game had been in progress. Dan had to get a plant together or all his big talk would go for nothing. He couldn't drove a thousand head of cattle on his own to Queensland. Two of his own stockmen had come in for the game. The others out holding the cattle would be wanting to go south he knew. They had made the trip down on that understanding. It was these fellows or nothing. Dan tried to butt into the game once or twice but had no hope. The ring was tight and excited. Sitting on the stockrails at the back were half-a-dozen coloured boys. They didn't gamble directly. They passed their money down to one of the side bettors.

A fat individual, with a fringe of grey hair sticking out from under a deplorable hat and his belly held up by a tight belt, was calling the bets in a loud voice. He had the butt of a cigarette stuck on to his lower lip with spittle and magic.

There was something of the magician's parleyvoo about everything he said. He waved his hands about like a second-rate conjuror and licked his fingers every time he handled a pound note. "A quid to cover," he called, "a quid in the guts."

The bets and the two bobs came in. "Any more on heads?" called the fat ringkeeper. He caught sight of Dan sitting on the stockrails. "Coming in, Dan?"

Dan shook his head. "I want to talk to the boys for a couple of ticks," he said.

"Break it up, Dan. You'll never get through the Centre," yelled someone.

"It's the wrong time of the year," said someone else.

"You ought to go to Moscow with Whiskers," said another.

So they knew all about it already, thought Dan. Even Corky, the ringkeeper was primed.

"Come on, come on, gentlemen," called Corky, "business before propaganda." There was a laugh at that. "Everyone set? All right, come in spinner."

The spinner stepped forward with the kip, a flat little board with a place for the pennies. The ringkeeper inspected the pennies. A sudden silence fell as the spinner tossed the pennies, in a clean even spin. The heads of those watching went up as the pennies went up, the backsides straightened out, there was a momentary pause, breathing suspended, while the pennies slowed up, came to rest, turned downwards, the heads of the watching men bobbing down again and the buttocks jutting out again in the familiar up and down movement of the two-up ring.

"Tails!"

"Tails it is," shouted Corky.

The bets were settled on the side, a few poking borak at the spinner who had had bad luck. Corky was just going to call for a fresh spinner when Dan yelled out in a voice that would have turned a breaking steer fifty yards off, "Fair go for me, Corky!"

"He won't be happy till he gets it," said Corky to the crowd. "All right Dan, but keep it short. We're all in the money to-day. Even me. I've got a couple of quid out of it." He gave a wink as broad as a barn door. He was a good showman. The crowd liked him. It made a difference to the ringkeeper if he was popular. The tips from the winners were bigger.

"I want six men," said Dan, "to help me drove the mob to Queensland. Standard conditions plus a bonus."

"Wartime loading," jeered a wag from the ring.

"Exactly," said Dan. "It's a wartime job as much as fighting. Armies have got to be fed. It's no help to winning the war to leave all that tucker to the dingoes or the Japs."

"We'd rather fight," came the answer from about three places.

"Tell him about scorched earth, Whiskers," yelled the intellectual wag.

"Quiet, quiet," roared Corky, the ringkeeper, to still the baiting that began at once. "Fair go." To Dan he said, in the smarmy voice of a president at a meeting, "Time's nearly up, Mr. McAlpine. Anything more you'd like to say to the boys?"

"Yes," said Dan, "Get this straight. There's no medals or uniforms or pretty girls in it, but the recruiting sergeant down at Hall's Creek said to me, when he turned me down, 'Bullocks are more important than bullets, Dan.' I believe that. I don't want to stop you being bloody heroes, but this is the job that needs doing first. That's why I'm trying to do what I am. It won't be easy and I can't do it on my own. Who's coming with me?"

There was the kind of silence that makes the skin creep on the back of your hand. Nobody said anything, nobody made a move forward.

"Sorry, my boy," said Corky. "It was a fine oratorical effort, but the boys have their plans made."

"We're going to stick together," one of the drovers mumbled. "Enlist down south."

"Chuck it in, Dan. Come south with us."

"Well," said Dan, "I see I'm not much of a speech-maker, but if any of you think it over and change your minds I'll be over at the cattle camp."

He strode off, a melancholy and thin Don Quixote, to charge his own windmills.

The two-up ring tightened, again Corky's voice, blarneying and blandishing: "Any more spinners? Who wants to head 'em? Here you are. Five bob in the guts. Here you are mate, a tails over there. Put your bets on, gentlemen. Thirty bob she tails? You're on. She's going for a double. Fair go."

The confused and regular babble of the two-up game was on again.

The sailor followed Dan to the main gates.

"Two-up!" said Dan. "They'll bet on the bombs yet. They'll be betting on who gets the first Jap. I daresay the blokes in Singapore are already betting on when they'll get out. A nation of bloody gamblers, that's what we are." His voice was bitter and he kicked a stone out of his way with a burst of unexpected ferocity.

"This trip you're so keen on making," said the boy, "I suppose it's a bit of a gamble, isn't it?"

Dan looked sideways and downward at the sailor's inquiring face. The boy wasn't getting at him. He was just innocent. A grin spread on Dan's morose countenance. "You've got me there, sailor," he said.

"Pardon me, Boss," said a voice behind them.

It was Jacky, sombrero, boots, and the chestnut dragging along as if asleep walking. "You going south of the border, Boss? Take'em cattle? You want stockboy?"

"You a good stockman, Jacky?"

"All same Tom Mix. Draft, brand, cut-out, horsetail, break in wildfella brumby, muster big mob, sing 'em sleepy bye bye. Work cattle little fella so size." He indicated somewhere down near his knee.

"It's the latest craze," said Dan to the sailor. "Since the song, they think South of the Border's a wonderful new country. No, Jacky," he said to the aborigine, "Not south. If we go, we go east, towards sun-up."

"Plenty dry that way."

"Cross three borders that way; big mob travel that way. Westralian border, Territory border, Queensland border."

"How long it take, Boss?"

"A year, maybe more."

"All right, Boss, I come. Just tell the missus. Back in five minutes." He jumped on the chestnut, dug his heels in, and galloped off.

"That's one," said Dan.

"Will he really come back in five minutes with his luggage packed ready to go away for a year?"

"There won't be much luggage," said Dan, "not as you know it. He'll probably turn up to-morrow morning."

The sailor stopped and looked earnestly at Dan. "I'll come with you, if you'll have me."

"You! You're a sailor, aren't you?"

"I was called up after my mother was killed in the blitz. I've no home and no people. I hate the sea. I've been torpedoed twice. I spent nineteen days in a ship's boat off Greenland. I was in hospital for a bit after that, and I thought I'd got over it, but I haven't. The bombing last night brought it on again. I suppose I'm a coward, but I can't help it." He passed a hand over his eyes. Dan saw the hand was trembling.

"Any man's a coward if he's had too much of it," said Dan. "D'you think you could stand the life with the cattle? It's hard you know. No romance. No cowboy stuff. Just hard yacker and hard tucker."

"Yacker?"

"Work."

"I don't care how hard I work."

"What could you do, anyway?"

"I could cook. I was cook's mate on the second trip up north when we were torpedoed. I could learn to do anything you'd care to teach me."

"Um," said Dan. "How about getting a discharge from your ship?"

"I think the skipper would let me go. Medical grounds."

"Hell!" said Dan, "What a crew. Me, Jacky and you. I'll have to toss it in sailor, I'm afraid." They were getting on their horses when they saw the chestnut and Jacky coming up at a half gallop. "Looks like he's changed his mind, too," said Dan. Bitterness could go no further. It was the first time in his life that he couldn't get mates to go with him. "What is it?" he asked Jacky.

"That fella, Nipper," began Jacky hesitantly, "belong my missus's fambly; he a very good stockboy, Boss. Him come too?"

"Whacko!" said Dan, "You're on, boy. Let 'em all come. O.K. Jacky. Nipper's the one in the flash pants, isn't he?"

"Yes Boss."

"Tell him all right. Mind you both show up at the cattle camp to-morrow."

"Thank you, Boss." Jacky showed his three green teeth in a smile as reassuring as sunrise. "Jap bombs give all us fellas itchy feet," he said. He mounted his horse the way all black-fellows do when there is a gallery, with a flourish and the boot in for a gallop.

"Whose horse is that?" called Dan.

"Meatworks horse. I bring 'im." Jacky was all grin. The horse settled rapidly into a long walk.

"Jacky's all right," said Dan.

"Will you take me?" asked the sailor.

"It's taking a risk, but I'll take you if the drove's on. Wait till about six o'clock, or eight o'clock. If none of the other fellows offer by then the drove's definitely off. If they do offer you'll have time to fix up your discharge after that." Dan opened a gate without getting off his horse. "See those bullocks over there? They're some of them."

The sailor saw some animals in the long grass, only their backs and heads visible. At that distance they looked like brown slugs with suspicious antennae out, their horns were so long. Their heads travelled round to watch the two horse-men. The sailor could feel the big eyes still watching him through his back long after they passed by. He didn't know a thing about bullocks. Perhaps it was just as well.

CHAPTER X

THE police sergeant from Wyndham looked at the bundle of dust easing round the bend at the top of the hill. He screwed up his eyes and then he took the field glasses he wore out of their case and focussed. The dust turned, a moving cloud, and began the long, slow, sloping descent to the creek at the bottom, where the sergeant and his police boy were halted. "The Parsons," he thought, but he asked the police boy, just to make sure. "What you think, Peter?"

"Waggon. Six—eight horses; two horses, one behind one alongside. Little fella girl ride last one."

"Crikey, that's not bad at this distance. Must be able to see her plaits," thought the sergeant. "We'll wait here," he said aloud. "This is as good as any place to stop them."

The wind was blowing up hill gently, clearing the waggon of dust that floated now like red smoke at the level of the wheel-tops. Above it were two straight-backed figures with hats on, a man and a woman. The woman was only discern-ible because she wore a boldly-patterned dress. The waggon carried a big load under a roped tarpaulin. The horses were running smoothly—the three leaders, the three in the traces, the two polers. The dust struck up from their hooves, the sun gleamed on their sweat-stained flanks, the wind and the trotting downhill lifted their ragged manes. The girl riding beside the waggon, just behind the high seat on which her father and mother sat, cantered with an effortless poetry of motion; her horsemanship was as flawless as that of a crack outrider in a royal procession. The little girl on her white and tan pony came at the end of the outfit. Her hat, secured by an elastic, was blown to the back of her head. She rode with the carelessness of long habit, with the evident enjoy-ment of the whole expedition. In any show ring she would have taken a prize. There was about the whole cavalcade, seen in action at this distance, an indescribable exhilaration, an exact rightness, an almost miraculous feeling of proportion and placing, of utter harmony of the human, moving element with the dark, sombre green bush foliage, the heavy naked tree trunks, the dun and dappled earth.

The police sergeant dropped his glasses and watched with bare eyes. Not a poetical fellow by nature, the travelling waggon touched him with a sense of sharpened vision, an ex-traordinary freshness, a realisation that he hadn't really seen anything worth while for months.

Once he had seen a sailing ship come in, full-rigged, through the Heads; once he had stood guard outside Bucking-ham Palace while the carriages and the scarlet-clad riders and the white plumes and the black horses had swept past; once he had seen his wife under a canopy of orange blossom in a vast, dark church, and it had been like this. He sighed. "It's

a pity," he thought, "to lose such people from this country."
He had a personal sense of loss, of seeing the last of an epoch
that had known the stage coach, the bushranger, the pioneer.
He was reminded vaguely of the sporting prints that still
hang in little out-of-the-way bush pubs along with the calen-
dars, the Christmas supplements and the whisky advertise-
ments.

Then the whole thing passed, the waggon covered by the
timber at the bottom of the hill and a slight rise in the ground.
The next thing was the pounding of the horses' hooves in the
muffling dust, the noise of the iron-shod waggon wheels turning, the cracking of Pa's whip, and the girls' cheerful hulloo-
ing.

"Ho, there," said the sergeant.

The waggon pulled up.

The horses were just horses, breathing hard and none of
them much to look at; the waggon was just a waggon, old as
the hills nearly and not a lick of paint on it; there was dust
on Ma's tired face; the trace chains that had glinted silver in
the well-worn shackles on the swift descent were just rusty
old chains one sees lying about a stable loft; the wheels had
been mended so often it was a wonder they stuck together;
the leather of the harness, though recently oiled, might have
come out of a junk shop; Bill Parsons was a very ordinary sort
of fellow; the little girl had a dirty face.

Yet all his life he would remember how they travelled down
that long hill.

"How are you, Bill? How are you, Missus?"

"How are you, Sergeant?"

"Saved me a long trip out, Bill. I was coming out to get
you."

"Anything fresh?"

"Orders to evacuate civilians. Everybody's going South.
The 'Toowoomba' is lying in port till midnight. That's official.
Unofficially, I guess it will get out to-morrow's afternoon tide.
Unless the Japs get it to-night. They tried to last night."

"We heard them," said Mary. "It seemed awfully close."

"Close enough. A few near misses, a few more buildings
gone."

"The meatworks?"

"No."

"Any casualties?"

"A few, Missus. Not as many as there might have been."

"Well, I've done my bit," said Pa.

"The station's gone, Sergeant, most of the cattle too," said Ma.

"The Japs?"

"No. Pa."

"I'm sorry, Missus."

"What has to be has to be." Her lips tightened. The knuckles showed white on Pa's big freckled hands holding the reins.

"You'll be able to make it, I guess," said the sergeant.

"What?" asked Bill.

"The 'Toowoomba'."

"I'm not going on any b—— boat!"

"Orders are orders, Bill."

"We'll see about that."

"Now, don't go missing that boat on purpose, Bill. Think of the girls."

"I am thinking of them."

"Oh, well, I'll see you later," said the sergeant. "Where do you reckon to camp to-night?"

"On the flat out beyond the Nine Mile."

"That's safe enough. Keep well away from the aerodrome area. It got plastered last night."

"O.K." Bill gathered up the reins.

"I'm going on to the Taylors now."

"You'll find them hard to shift," said Bill. The waggon moved off, creaking.

"By the way," said the sergeant to the elder girl, "there's a parcel for you and your sister at the Post Office. The Misses Parsons. I would have brought it up but it was a bit bulky. Not much in my line, either—looked like a hat-box to me. Got a bit bashed on the way up."

"From Aunty Marge," said Mary. "Whoopee!"

"A new hat," said Helen. "That will be a change." She spoke sarcastically and screwed up her face into what she thought was a fashionable grimace. The sergeant smiled. Ma's eyes looked briefly amused. There was such a difference between the two girls, and the little one could be so oddly grown-up at times.

CHAPTER XI

DAN and the sailor had finished the evening meal. Tea, salt beef and pickles. There had been bread instead of damper. "I would have brought out something better if I'd known I was going to have visitors," said Dan. At the other end of the big paddock he could see a fat figure on foot moving towards the camp. "Why couldn't he ride?" he wondered. He could see the cattle getting up and moving away from the man on foot. "Frighten them a bit more and they'll go rushing into the holding fences breaking their legs." Corky moved cautiously, however, well away from them; there was no rush.

Dan relaxed. "I had a big feed of fish and oysters in town this morning. That's something when you come in from the track you always tell yourself you'll do. But you get used to corned beef. Fresh beef's good too, but you never get sick of corned beef—it sticks to a man somehow."

For an hour he had been regaling the sailor with stories of the bush and the track, not pulling his leg, though he could have done that easily enough and the sailor been never the wiser.

"And you just," asked the sailor, "sleep wherever your swag falls when you take it off the chuck waggon? You don't move it out of a puddle or on to a bit of softer ground or anything?"

"There's not often puddles," said Dan. "Cattle don't travel in the wet, and the ground's never any softer. A foot this way or a yard that. Sometimes we turn the spinifex upside down and that makes a good bed, quite the spring mattress."

"Spinifex," said the boy.

Dan liked the way he took to the new words: chuck waggon, swag, spinifex. It was queer to hear his Scots voice
saying richly, plaintively, familiar Australian words: yacker,
tucker, Bedourie oven, spinifex. It was like seeing another
man wearing your clothes.

"Here's where we get another volunteer, I think," he said
to the boy.

"It's that fat man from the two-up school, isn't it?"

"Corky. J. Claverhouse something Corkingdale, alias
Jimmy the Snoot."

"A crook?"

"No, a cattleman—and a good many other things besides."

Corky came up, made his salutations elaborately, sat on a
box, accepted a quart pot of tea, said it was a pity the pub
was wrecked and all the beer gone west, and, after beating
round the bush, offered his services to Dan.

Dan was astonished.

"I thought you couldn't get to the bright lights quick
enough?"

"Oh, well—you know—it's just a case of mistaken identity.
Some woman thinks I owe her money. I don't want to get
south too soon—not before the whole matter sorts itself out.
We get paid for this trip, I take it?"

"The usual. Six quid a week and tucker and a bonus at the
end if we get through."

"That's fair enough. I'll take it."

"It means work you know, Corky."

"I've worked in my time."

"All right, but remember, should you get discouraged, that
I told you it wasn't going to be a picnic."

"I quite understand, my boy. You don't have to explain
all that to me."

"And here," said Dan, "come the rest of the outfit. You've
brought me luck, Corky."

Les and Charley came on horseback in the gathering dusk.
Les was a big-built, handsome chap, with a face as empty of
meaning as a blank hoarding. It took him ten minutes to
think out a sentence, but he always looked wise enough,

clenching a pipe in his even white teeth. The dust of many droving trips had played up with his vocal chords and he spoke in a big braying voice like Bottom with the asses' head on.

Charley was slighter and darker, a shadow to the big blond Les. There might have been a little of the Chinese in him; he walked like a cat in the dark and could throw a steer American fashion. No cruelty of bush life ever revolted him. He could knock a motherless calf on the head and think nothing of it—it seemed to satisfy some potential of revenge or pessimism in him. When he polled or gelded or spayed it was with a latent ferocity instead of an impersonal calm. His particular quirk was to draw large obscene chalk drawings on all the water tanks along his travels. A wag had once called the pair of them, Les and Charley, "Night and Day."

They had changed their minds about going south in the "Toowoomba," because it meant leaving their horses behind. The captain wouldn't give the horses a passage, and they couldn't get a fair price for their outfit in Wyndham, now everyone was clearing out down south. Most of the money they'd got together in the last few years lay in their horses.

"If we can stick them in with your plant," said Les, "we'll come along with you."

Dan was glad to get the horses; they were good ones. He did the generous thing and offered a fair bit extra for the use of the horses. "It looks as if we're getting set at last," he said. He brought out half a bottle of rum and they sealed the bargain.

There were all kinds of arrangements to be made and Dan had his contract to draw up with Malone, and his waybill of stock and horses to get signed by the sergeant of police. The hurricane lamps were lit. "Might have to douse these later on," said Dan, "if the Japs come over again. Better buzz off while the going's good. See you all in town in the morning."

He lent Corky a horse. "Look after Sailor for me will you, Les," he called.

To the sailor he said softly, helping him on, "Get yourself fixed up right away kid—but don't talk about it on the way in."

"Thanks a lot for the grand day, Mr. McAlpine," said the sailor in a loud voice, "Good-night."

"He cottons on quick enough," thought Dan. "I hope he gets his discharge all right." He got writing materials and sat down, his long legs spread awkwardly round the box he was using as a table. "I wish I had a few more fellas," he thought. "A more dependable cook and two more good stock-men."

He began to work out stores, make lists of necessaries, think of all the gear that must be checked or obtained, worry about horses, formalities that he mustn't forget at the last minute. A sober, hardworking, methodical man, taking a big risk and working to minimise it. On what he remembered and checked to-night, the lives of all the outfit might depend six months later. The wrinkle marks of worry in his face were like gutters down eroded land.

CHAPTER XII

MA was sitting up in the waggon, holding the horses in the shade of a building, by Wyndham wharf. The heat struck back from the limestone hill sticking straight up behind the town and drenched even the shadow with warmth. There wasn't a breath of wind—the ridge kept it off. She could feel the starch in her crisp white collar wilting under the humidity. She could feel the heat draining the moisture from the flesh under her skirt, drawing off the fullness of her womanhood, withering her, as she sat, into a middle-aged husk, the body substance shrunken a little round the big bones. So it seemed to her. She was very tired.

The heads of the horses drooped, their uneven tails cease-lessly whisked the flies off, the loose-fitting harness lolloped from side to side as they stamped their hooves. There was no glamorous highway kingship about them to-day: they were just waiting.

*   *   *   *

It was thirty-six hours since the sergeant had stopped them on the road. The escape ship, the "Toowoomba," had to steam out and return again. There wasn't another ton of freight could go aboard. Bert Malone, the manager of the meatworks, had terrible trouble with the dismantling of the plant. The heaviest stuff had to be brought in by bullock teams. He had tried to get army transport to move it but there was none available. The days of ten-ton diesel engines in the north were far off then, and the through road to Katherine hadn't been opened up. Pa was talking to Malone now, in the saloon bar of the pub. Ma could hear their angry voices.

To her amazement they weren't arguing about any of the present trouble. It was about the cost of killing and loading bullocks for the south.

"The return I get for three years growing a bullock," Pa was saying, "is less than half what it costs to kill, chill and send to Fremantle. On top of that I have to pay agents' fees and take the risk of the market. There ought to be good large holding· paddocks, well grassed, for fattening before they're killed. We could afford to pay for agistment and the improved quality would pay you and us. How can we hope to compete with the Argentine for the European markets when the quality's not there?"

It was an old argument with Pa. He wanted smaller holdings and better beef. He wanted trucking facilities through to the Queensland pasturelands for relief in bad seasons, and in areas of uncertain rainfall. He reckoned the North was held back by the South and the Dead Centre. He wanted survey before stocking so that natural grass shouldn't be eaten out, and he hated the grip the canning factories had on the industry. Every time he met Bert Malone they had words.

Ma knew it didn't do any good. She knew that often some of Pa's best beasts got knocked back because of his rows with Bert Malone. The check-weighman knew very well what he could get away with when it came to the Parsons's cattle.

Not that it mattered now.

Ma sensed that Pa thought he had been too precipitate in destroying the homestead and a good part of the herd.

The Taylors had got ready to leave, but they hadn't fallen for this scorched earth policy. Of course, if the Japs came, it was the right thing. But still—. Now Pa was worrying lest

he had acted too soon. The bomb holes, the splintered buildings, the twisted galvanised iron sheets that lay everywhere,
convinced Ma that it was time to leave. In any case, the
danger to Helen had decided her.

A man passed by and raised his hat. Ma didn't know who
he was. She didn't know if they would be travelling on the
"Toowoomba" or not. It was very crowded. The risk of
being bombed was very great. A real apathy had come over
her. For the first time in twenty-odd years of her married life
she didn't want to face the future. Pa thought there might
be some scheme to dodge going south. He'd said he wouldn't
go. He said Ma and the girls could go if they wanted to. Or,
if they wanted to stay he'd camp some place in the area and
wait for the next boat south that wouldn't be so crowded, or
for something—he hardly knew what.

Bert Malone said Pa had to go on the boat with his family.
Telling Pa he *had* to do anything was fatal. Then Bert tried
to soft soap Pa into it and Pa got angrier than ever. "Don't
smoodge to me, you old take-me-down," he cried angrily.

Helen and Mary came out of the Post Office. Helen had
a wide leghorn hat with ruching and little forget-me-not
clusters in it and blue tie-up strings under her chin. It was a
very pretty hat for a small girl, but it looked odd with her
checked shirt and her long tight riding pants. Mary had a
flat-crowned hat of toast-coloured straw with a double edge
on the brim and a large organdie rose posed like a dancer
over one eye. It would have been all right to wear to a garden
party or some picnic races.

"Aunty Marge thinks we're civilised up here," she said,
"That's the trouble with everything she sends."

"I could have done with a silver-handled whip," said Helen.
"Something flash."

"They're very nice hats," said Ma, "but you can't take
them with you if we stick to the waggon and camp, and I
think somehow that's what we'll be doing."

"Why couldn't we?" asked Mary. "We could look at our-
selves in the glass sometimes."

"We haven't got a glass big enough to see that hat in,"
said Ma. "Besides, a horse or a bullock would be sure to
gobble it up."

"Yours ought to go well with golden syrup on it," said Helen, giggling, "I could nearly eat it myself." She looked as if she might start at any moment, just for devilment.

"Here's an apple each," said Ma. "I got them at Quong Kway's." An apple was a great luxury; these had cost Ma a shilling each. The hat did suit Mary. Ma could understand her not wanting to part with it.

"Bart Wells said he was going to organise picnic races if it hadn't been for the Japs."

"Him," said Ma scornfully.

"He's not as bad as he's painted," said Mary warmly.

"He doesn't need to be painted," said Ma. "He's a cross between a red fox and a weevily old wolf."

"He's only twenty-nine," said Mary.

"There's enough in his past to make him a lot older," said Ma, "if he ever thought about himself at all."

Mary thought to herself, "He's about the most exciting man I ever met, anyway."

Ma thought, "She's at a restless age." She asked, "Have you written to the boys this mail?" The boys were Mary's cousins at the war.

*   *   *   *

A woman passed with a sunshade up and a little girl about nine carrying a big celluloid doll. "We lost all our luggage last night," the woman said. "There's not as much left out of our clothes as would made respectable pocket handker-chiefs. We've only got what we stand up in and a few old things I was able to buy at the Chinaman's this morning. Nothing smart. Nothing warm if it's cold down south. They're nice hats the girls have on!"

"Yes," said Ma, "It's the first time they've put them on their heads." There was a little pause. "If we don't go down south," said Ma, "you can have them."

"You can have mine anyway," said Helen. She tied the big hat on the little girl; it looked very fetching. "I knew when I first saw it," said Helen, "it was a white pinafore hat." She put on her brown felt riding hat and Ma sighed with the pleasure of seeing her in it.

"The right thing is always smart," said the woman, also approving of Helen.

Mary dragged off the toast-coloured confection. "Do take mine," she said, smiling, a whole battery of unsuspected dimples coming into play, "before I make an ass of myself in it." She didn't want to give up the hat, but only her mother knew that.

"Oh, if you can spare it—"

It ended up in a bush swap, Mrs. Parsons accepting a couple of pairs of ducks, to be picked up in a very complicated way, and a roll of bedding that the Wyndham woman declared was "too good to give away and no use to us on the boat."

"I hope Aunty Marge doesn't go down to the 'Toowoomba' expecting us," said Helen, "and sees our hats walking off."

"We really will eat those hats," said Mary. "You didn't do so badly, Ma. Four ducks!" She laughed, showing all her teeth. "You must have had an intuition."

It was a tonic to Ma hearing her laugh.

"The bedding won't be much use," said Helen, "nobody to sleep on it."

"You wait," said Ma. "There's always somebody turns up in the bush." She didn't know how close the somebody was.

Pa and Bert Malone came walking over from the pub. "Nice looking girls," said Bert, thinking, "The elder one's a corker; belle of the North if it was a cattle judging."

"Not bad," said Pa, "with the cattle. Equal to a man or a boy any day."

Bert made his greetings to the ladies. "You ought to be going on board now, Mrs. Parsons. The captain gave a warning a while ago."

"I heard it," said Ma tersely. The silence that fell said: "It's up to Pa."

"I'm not going on any flaming boat," said Pa. "That's final, Bert. He balanced first on the balls of his feet, then on the heels, rocking forward to the toes, unconsciously imitating a boxer who says "Come on" to the world. His eyes, under their bushy eyebrows, scanned the comings and goings of the main street in a pre-occupied frown.

Bert Malone began a speech. "It's this way, Mrs. Parsons,

. . ." He was tired of old Parsons and his damned obstinacy. If it hadn't been for Mrs. Parsons and the beautiful daughter he would have said something pretty strong.

Pa interrupted. "What goes on over there?" He indicated a knot of horsemen well down the main street, surrounding a pile of equipment beside the road.

"It's Dan McAlpine," said Bert sourly. "Another of your 'won't be pushed around' sort. He's got a crazy scheme to overland his mob of cattle to Queensland."

"Why didn't you tell me before?"

Without waiting a moment Pa clambered up, took the reins from Ma, flicked his whip and giddapped the team into action. "That's where we're going," he said to the astonished Bert.

"Come along girls," Ma called to Mary and Helen. "We're going to Queensland." She had no doubt in her mind that Pa would be able to talk his way into it. "Worth speaks for itself" had been one of the old preacher grandfather's maxims. Ma still believed it. "I'm glad," she thought, "I got those hats off their heads. They wouldn't have been a good advertisement for stock-girls." She shrewdly went over in her mind points of the bargain that Pa ought to make with Dan. She knew Dan slightly and liked what she knew of him.

"I'll cook," she thought, "Mary is worth a man's wage. If he hasn't got a waggon of his own ours will do very nicely. Helen is worth her keep and he ought to be jolly glad to get Bill."

All her apathy, her life-is-over-at-forty feeling of earlier in the morning had gone. She watched carefully the men already gathered round Dan, estimating the capabilities of each. They all recognised her gravely and went on with their work of sorting and roping bundles. She sent Helen and Mary galloping back to collect the ducks, pressing money into Mary's hand. "Get a couple more if you can buy them," she said. Ma's roast duck was something a bushman remembered for a long time.

*   *   *   *

Bill wasn't finding Dan so easy to be talked over. He had a shy man's horror of women on a long trip.

"The language," he said, "the language. I couldn't make the boys cut that out."

"You'd be surprised," said Pa, "how Ma's being there just naturally makes them forget to swear. The girls," he said, "they know a lot more than Ma thinks they know. They're a cattleman's daughters and they know how to take it. They're not ordinary girls."

"The big one's not a bad looker." Dan said this as if it were an insuperable obstacle.

"In shop clothes," admitted Pa, "but when she's with the cattle you can't tell her from a man. All over dust and dirt she's nothing to look at. Besides, she's hardly grown up."

Dan was still unwilling, but he wanted to buy Pa's waggon. "Nothing doing," said Pa, "unless we come with it."

In the end Dan gave in, against, as he said, one part of his better judgment. He needed the Parsons's help too badly to say no to the girls.

"There's one thing we'll have to settle before we set off," he said. "I'm boss. You've had a lot of experience, Bill, and you're older than me, but on this trip what I say goes."

"Too right," said Pa. "What did you think I wanted to do? Grab your outfit from you?"

"You're such an argumentative old cow," said Dan cheerfully.

Bill Parsons laughed. "Look here, Dan," he said, "You're doing me and Ma and the girls a good turn and we're doing you a good turn and we'll all do our best for you all the way."

They shook hands. "I hope we'll be doing Australia a good turn," said Dan, very simply.

"Cut out the flap," said Corky, coming up at this moment.

Dan took Bill Parsons over to the rest of the outfit.

*   *   *   *

Helen, back from her message, had insinuated herself between Corky and the sailor, who were counting hobbles. "We're coming with you," she said.

"H'm. Won't that be grand," said Corky, in an "I don't think" voice. Little girls meant nothing to him. He liked large, fair women about thirty-five, barmaids preferred.

"Ma's going to cook," said Helen in a matter-of-fact way.

The sailor dropped the hobbles he was handling and lost count.

"What's the matter?" asked Helen.

"Nothing," said the sailor.

"Your Ma's done him out of a job," said Corky blandly.

"Oh, there's plenty for a man to do on a cattle drive," said Helen, composedly. "Even as it is, Dan will be a bit short-handed. I heard Pa say so."

The sailor went on counting.

Helen looked him over. His stockman's clothes still had the shop creases in them; he wore spurs, but they were upside down. "You thought you wouldn't be able to come?" she said, with the horrible way of little girls who see everything so clearly. The sailor said nothing.

"You're a sailor?" she asked.

"I was," said the sailor. He had got his discharge that morning. It was in his pocket, the ink hardly dry on it.

"You can teach me a few more knots," she said, "and I'll teach you how to ride."

He looked more gratefully at her. "Nineteen," he said aloud, keeping count of the hobbles.

"I'll call you Sinbad," she said. "He's the only other sailor I know. He was aged about fifty."

The sailor didn't mind.

She looked at Corky as if about to drag out his soul and history.

"Your mother's calling you," said that individual quickly.

"See you later," said Helen.

"I can't stand any of that third degree stuff from a kid," said Corky. "Sinbad. Not bad. Better than your own." The sailor had a cissy name he was glad to hide. "When a kid gives you a nickname," said Corky, "it means you're all right."

*   *   *   *

Up on the waggon Ma was talking to Mary. "Dan didn't want to take you girls," she said, "so I want you to wear this ring." It was a little turquoise heart with a surround of small pearls. Ma had had it since she was a girl. Mary had often **wanted to own it**.

"Oh, Ma," she said, beaming, and put it on her little finger.
It was too big.

"On your engagement finger," said Ma.

"But—" said Mary.

"That's why I gave it to you," said Ma.

"Nobody's ever asked me," said Mary.

"They will," said Ma.

Mary put it reluctantly on her finger. She had an instinct
that anticipating events might bring her bad luck.

"It's only a sham," her mother said quickly. "Just a sort
of protection. Play up to it, dear, and it will be better for
everyone."

Mary looked straight into her mother's eyes. They were
wise, bossy, and oddly tender. It wasn't often that her mother
treated her as a real equal or let her see that she really loved
her. The mother smiled. The daughter smiled back. It was
one of those odd little moments of communication.

Mary accepted all the implications of the ring. It must be
something really serious or Ma would never resort to subter-
fuge. She was as straight as a die and she hated women who
shammed anything at all. "Better tell Helen," said Mary, "or
she'll give the show away at once."

Ma gave a great cooee for Helen.

*   *   *   *

The "Toowoomba" was at last leaving, the captain on the
bridge, the deckhands getting ready to slip the hawsers, the
women and children crowding amidships and leaning over
the side waving. There was a lot of hand luggage still litter-
ing the deck. Most of the escapees would have to bunk down
on deck—the cabin accommodation was hopelessly inadequate.
There were black babies, brown babies, yellow babies, small
boys in pith helmets, women in sun hats, dogs yapping and
men swearing. The Parsons girls saw their two hats prominently on parade. "Got the ducks!" called up Helen.

The gangway was up, but the ropes not cast off, when Mary
rode up with some letters she wanted posting down south.
Some of the drovers and crew on the after-deck cheered.
"Love and kisses from Mary," they chiacked. They dropped
down a bucket on a rope for the letters and quite unashamedly

read the addresses. "Just my cousins," she said to someone next her. Succulent kissing sounds descended; with her blush working overtime Mary retreated to the end of the jetty.

Corky was on the wharf too. The crowd gave him a loud hoy. "We'll tell her you've gone to the Never-Never where the law will never find you," shouted a wag.

Another sang, mocking, "Wrap me up in my stock-whip and blanket," till Corky made a few dangerous flicks with his fifteen-foot long stock-whip that decided the joker to wait till distance made it a bit safer.

"Hang on to your gold teeth," yelled a third, "or he'll gamble them off you." Whiskers was one of the crowd.

"See you in Moscow," called Corky, with a histrionic bow. Dan's joke had gone round. Everybody laughed.

Bert Malone was there, in white linen, very important.

"Good-bye Dan. Good luck!"

"All the best, Mrs. Parsons."

Sinbad, the sailor, rode up on a little old mare, to see his shipmates off.

"Attaboy, Tom Mix."

"Where'd you feel it most, Scotty?"

"Don't say we didn't tell you."

"You'll be sorry!"

"You'll be sorry!"

"Good-bye-e-e."

The ship's siren let off a sudden startled toot. Sinbad's mare, already confused by the tumult round her, the clumsy weight on her back, the nervous handling of the reins, played up. She reared, and Sinbad fell off backwards. He scrambled up unhurt, but everybody on board laughed as if it was a pantomime.

"Quick, quick," said Helen, "Get on again. Might happen to anybody with that whistle. Quick!" She held the bridle and the mare let Sinbad mount again. He was in the saddle before he had time to worry about falling off. He gave a wave of the hand that told everybody: "I'm all right."

"Don't let the Japs get you, Sarge," bellowed Bert Malone, suddenly.

The gap between the ship and the wharf widened. The slate grey of water swirled, the churning propellors passed, the "Toowoomba" headed down the waterway between Wyndham proper, with its backyards melting into the shore, and the great salt pan opposite that lay like a yellow barrier between the town and open water.

CHAPTER XIII

THE first camp was only about four miles beyond the last boundary of the furthest holding paddock, but, as Dan told the sergeant, it was a start.

The sergeant had come to bring the licenses for Jacky and Nipper, the two aborigine boys, and to inspect Dan's way-bills. They put their right thumbs on the ink pad he had brought with him and then down on the documents. "This means," said the sergeant, "that you've promised to make this trip with Dan and he's promised to get you back here—that is supposing the Japs aren't here. Is that O.K.?"

"O.K., Sergeant," said the boys. They went back to their camp, near where the horses were grazing. All told, there were eighty-two horses and over a thousand head of cattle. Bill Malone had given Dan the meatworks horse Jacky used to ride, so he still had it.

Bill Parsons, Dan, Ma, and Corky, were still sorting out the gear. It had been got in a hurry and they weren't sure if it was all there. There were saddles, condamine bells, flour, hobbles, rawhide rope, soap, candles, billies, quart pots, water cans, canvas buckets, tin dishes, pannikins, fine and coarse salt, the blacksmithing gear, sugar, whips, spare harness, a rifle, lamps, axle grease, cocoa, jam, sauce, sugar, curry powder, tea, tarpaulins, medicines for man and beast, the camp ovens, blankets, matches, tobacco.

Each man would be responsible for his own swag, his own saddle and horse gear, his quart-pot, and his eating utensils.

There was a sense of uneasiness and expectation about everybody. Even the cattle felt it. They were restless. Les and Charley were riding round them singing discordantly. At any moment, thought Dan, the cattle might start something, might get the urge to break and travel to their rough home country two hundred odd miles away.

Les and Charley were grumbling to each other about the Parsons. They hadn't liked the girls coming. "Bet your boots," said Les, "they'll bring us trouble." "A priest on a ship and a woman on a drove," said Charley, "they just don't belong."

"I've heard of women droving," admitted Les, "I've met one or two. But the ones I met you couldn't call them women. More like men they were. Not like this bunch." He spat. His voice had the broken-down timbre of a lay preacher in an empty galvanised iron church with the thermometer at 105 degrees in the shade. He scratched at his head, then tapped the bowl of his pipe on it. The big skull vibrated like a half-empty water tank, hollow. "You'll have to wash behind your ears this trip, Charley," he wheezed.

Charley had the reputation of wearing his clothes till he got new ones.

"Like stink I will," grumbled Charley.

Helen and her father rode out to relieve them. They were early.

"Supper's on," said Pa.

Ma had done her best with the ducks. They were worth waiting for, crisp and brown, stuffed with a flavoursome seasoning, with real applesauce and roasted potatoes, floury and golden, to go with them; the gravy rich with pounded liver. There were dried green peas that you couldn't tell from real ones.

"You can have tinned peaches with them," said Ma, "or with custard afterwards."

Les and Charley were hungry. They said nothing until they had wiped their plates quite clean with a piece of bread. "That was good Missus," said Les. He picked at his strong, handsome teeth. It would have been no trouble to him to grind up a drumstick the way a dog does.

"Have some more," invited Ma.

They didn't need a second invitation to come again.

Ten minutes later Les said to Ma: "I'll see those abos get you plenty of wood in, Ma." With her back to him, Ma smiled in the darkness.

"Thank you, Les."

The Sergeant sighed. His wife and kiddie had gone off on the "Toowoomba" that morning. The lock-up was the only part of the police station that had survived the bombing. He would have to spend the rest of the night in one of his own cells. "I wish I was coming with you, Dan," he said—and half meant it.

"Best dinner I've had for a long time," he said to Ma.

"Just as well your wife can't hear you," said Ma.

"Wonder if they're sea-sick," said the Sergeant. The road home seemed emptier than ever. He was on his horse, ready to go, when old Jacky came up.

"You keep them plurry blackfellow away from my missus?" he asked.

"I'll do my best, Jacky," said the Sergeant.

Those round the fire laughed.

The Sergeant felt more cheerful with the laughter. He had a big job to do back in Wyndham. "So long, everybody," he called.

*   *   *   *

The sailor was rolled up in his swag alongside Corky. "That girl," he asked, "She wears a ring. Is she engaged?"

"Which girl?" asked Corky. He was thinking of a plump widow he knew once. Lying out under the stars you have to think of something like that.

"Mary," said the sailor.

"Her? Oh, I don't know. I wouldn't look that way if I were you. Her mother watches her like a hawk." He pulled his hat further down on his head and made his neck more comfortable. On the track he always slept with his hat on. He racked his brains for some good advice to give Sinbad, but he was much too sleepy. He had finished the last bottle of whisky in Wyndham and now roast duck sat on top of it, paddling with little strips of grilled bacon towards a nest of green peas. He was asleep in five minutes, snoring like the prima donna of snorers. In every snore his membranes blew three notes, an up and down ground-swell of sound.

"I'll have to put cotton wool in my ears," thought the sailor, but the next thing he knew it was pitch-dark and Dan was kneeling beside him waking him up.

"Our watch," said Dan. The Boss Drover takes the 1 a.m. to 3 a.m. watch.

The sailor was in all his senses at once. Seamen have that faculty. Change of wind, change of direction, change of the rattle and whine of the engine and the sailor is awake at once, though he may only be awake long enough to recognise the change, satisfy himself with knowing what it is, and fall asleep again. He was on his feet in a moment, startled, anxious.

"That's all right, son," said Dan.

The night horses were saddled ready.

"Take it quietly," said Dan. "Leave it to her. She's very steady. She could almost do it on her own." He walked his horse alongside the sailor's for awhile. "We ride round them steadily. No noise, nothing to startle them. They were b—— restless earlier on, —— the beggars."

In a few minutes he left Sinbad, going in the opposite direction himself, striking up a slow, deep baritone, a confident mutter of song that went on and on, a tune with variations Sinbad didn't recognise for a long time. When he did, the thing humming itself in and out of his mind like a constant wind blowing past a steersman, he realised it was the hymn, "Rock of Ages." Only a cattleman or a sailor would have inflicted it, at two o'clock in the morning, on a herd of drowsy bullocks. Presently it changed to "On Richmond Hill There Lived a Lass." The sailor had enough confidence now to whistle the refrain. He whistled and Dan whistled back. The cattle didn't move; their bodies warmed up the ground under them. The steps of the night horse lengthened, her ears stopped pricking back—she felt more at ease too.

"You're doing all right," said Dan when they passed next, "but don't fall asleep."

Sleep was far from the sailor. He had begun to enjoy the solitude, the sense of space, the outlines of darkness that were becoming familiar to him with every slow circle he took, the murmuring nearness of the cattle, the brightness of the stars that soon would pale into dawn, the quiet slow movement of the animal beneath him, the sense of quietly breathing in and out that the whole sleeping world seemed to have. He began a song of his own, "The minstrel boy to the wars has gone, with his . . . harp strapped before him. . . ."

"That's all the riding gear he's got on making him sing that," thought Dan with his special sense of amusement that often made his own company pleasant to him. "He's not bad. For a new chum a sailor wasn't a bad pick. He's not one of these sleepy bastards; he'll probably be all right once he gets confidence on a horse and can head off and cut out."

Back in camp Ma was already awake. "Daylight," she said, bending over Helen. "Daylight," she said, firmly, to Corky. It was his turn to take over.

Corky opened only one eye. He saw a faint star that was still there when he opened it a second time. "Must have been a dark night," he said. But he began to stretch, groaning, out of his blankets, put on his boots and wavered off into the bush, clearing his throat as he went like a very old motor car with its carburettor choked.

Nipper and Jacky went for the horses. Soon the cattle were up, moving gently forward, stringing out, eating with relish the grass still moist from the night, tender with dew. The condamine bells on the horses clinked and jingled. Pa stood with a mug of hot tea in his hand, listening with satisfaction. "The first night out's like a bridal," he said. "Get over that and you're set for the rest of your life."

"Speak for yourself," said Les, with a warm titter.

"I hope you're right," said Dan to Bill.

"Too right I'm right," said Pa. "It's a good beginning."

Chapter XIV

For the first month the track was pretty good. Surface water was still available and the feed held well. Ten miles a day is very fair going for a mob of bullocks—under difficult conditions the daily rate drops to five or six miles—but on this stretch Dan, with Bill's help, pushed the bullocks along, often fifteen miles a day.

Time was the enemy.

The plant knew this and they worked as one man to get as far as they could before they encountered the long stretch of six hundred miles of plains with the grass withered and the bores at twenty or twenty-five mile intervals. The sooner they got over the plains country the sooner would they come to the semi-desert, the sandstone and spinifex country, and the quicker they got there the less impoverished the bullocks and horses would be and the more chance of getting through safely.

The time margins were so narrow.

Bill Parsons had the confidence of the old-timer, the battler-through; a sort of unsinkable optimism. Action always made him cheerful, and now he slept better, ate better, and worried less than he had for years. He felt his family would get through. Of course, the cattle were not his direct responsibility.

That load of responsibility Dan carried. It made him terse at times.

It seemed to Dan, at first, that even the cattle were a bit on edge. With a first-class, experienced plant he had had trouble getting them to Wyndham, and for the next three weeks out it almost seemed as if they were conscious of the change in their destinies and resented it. It was ridiculous to imagine that, but the cattle acted as if they knew that the plant was a new one, full of diffidence, edgy themselves, and nervous of the distance and difficulties ahead. For one thing, the cattle didn't like travelling east. The slightest slackness on the ringer's part and they'd turn their heavy heads to the west and try to lumber off to the hills of their calf days.

The ringers were busy night and day. Les and Charley grumbled that it was hard on their horses. So it was. It was hard on the men too.

Although there were no bad stampedes there were plenty of jump-ups. A little thing would startle the cattle, either in the midday rest when the ruminants lay couched, chewing the cud but not sleeping, the sunshine hot on their ruddy coats, or, more dangerously, at night, when a momentary panic could run, like a shiver, through the whole mob. Mostly these jump-ups were nothing more serious than the sudden starting of the entire mob to its feet and a short, concerted rush that the ringers quickly controlled. Often Dan, Bill, Charley and

Les would jump, bootless, on to their horses, riding hard and determinedly to head them. Then the galloping bullocks would steady, tire out, the wings turned in on the leaders, the cattle ringing, confused, and then held. The impulse to rush madly from the suspected danger diminished when the original cause of the panic—the sudden sound, the sudden scent, the sudden strange vision—was no longer present to their scary sensibilities. Gradually calmness would return to the mob, as peace comes to a baby that has been howling, nobody knows why. The drovers suffered from these broken nights the way a mother suffers from a fretful baby.

Pa hazarded an explanation. "Where these cattle come from," he said, "the timber's thick enough to hide a man at thirty or forty yards. No animal likes that. So these fellas are just naturally suspicious. They don't trust their eyes. They listen. They don't wait to see the enemy; they're off if they only think they hear something strange or catch sight of some movement in the bush that they can't explain. Light on a white tree-trunk will do it, or a calico horse, or a flash of lightning—anything they think's sneaking up on them. A man on a horse riding round and singing they get used to —he never does them much harm—but a man on foot, that's different. They're really frightened then."

"When I took this mob on," said Dan, who was listening while Pa talked to Sinbad, "some of them had only been mustered twice. They'd run a mile without looking back."

"And they're not much better now," said Charley.

"They're much better," said Dan, smoothly, rolling a cigarette with automatic skill. Charley's grumble was the sort that Dan didn't like to go unchecked. "I can't let him get away with that," he thought, "he's making it out worse than it is, and that's bad for the kids and everybody." But he was not bad tempered. Bad temper does nothing for anybody on a long trip. "They'll be circus animals before we're through," he said, cheerfully.

Sinbad stared up at Dan, admiring his calmness, his competence, his six foot six of reserved assurance.

Les felt the admiration and resented it. He was a vain man, vain of his personal appearance and his skill. He never could stand too much limelight on the other fellow. If any-one in his company had ever done anything brave or com-mendable and a third party mentioned it, Les had always done something braver, riskier, in far more formidable circum-stances, and he was never long in telling everybody present all about it He now told the story of the piccaninny who was saved by being buried up to its head under Emily's Bush—the only shade for twenty miles—while the tribe tramped and died and the mother of the piccaninny perished, but the baby was saved by the stockmen who were camped at the next water. Les told the story as if he had been one of the original stockmen. "It was so hot," he said, "the abos had the soles of their feet burnt off, and no horse would walk in it. We had to take the camels to it. Fortunately we had camels . . ." Dan and Bill left him to it. In the slow way Les had of tell-ing it the well-known story of Emily's Bush lasted half an hour. Les chewed at his pipe-stem and got into a long dis-cussion with Corky about how far it was between two water-holes near Alroy Downs. He started off by making it 85 miles and ended up by conceding that it must have been more than twenty, anyway.

Corky treated Les with the skill of a veteran. He never contradicted. He just drew Les on and on until Les looked foolish. "Wait," said Les, puffing on his pipe held upside down, "Wait, Sinbad, till you've bunked under a log and had a thousand head of cattle jump clean over you. That's danger. That's nerve that is. Either you've got it or you haven't got it. That's what happened to me on the Diamen-tina, three seasons ago. It was . . ." Followed a long, circum-stantial account of how this had happened to Les when there was, unaccountably, not a white man with him, only one stockboy who was later reported missing on the track. Les's stories always were like that. No chance of checking them.

Helen had drifted up. She had heard the story of the piccaninny and the log story many times. Everybody had. But not Sinbad. He was drinking it in.

Corky now took a hand. "There's some terrible stories," said Corky, "about the old treks. There was a man named Clark once, out from New Well on his way to Maree with 700 head, and a sand storm came up. That's dune country, where there's no grass to hold the sand and it shifts and changes under the wind like water boiling, but. instead of falling back like water it banks and swirls. Stays put like glue or treacle. Before you know where you are you're caught in it like a fly on fly paper. It creeps up over your back while you're standing still, it can bury your horse to the rump. The only thing to do is to keep on the move or it buries you. That was all right for the drover and his horse, they kept moving, but the cattle bunched, the sand banked up. If you go there now there's only a pyramid of bones and bones lying scattered around as if all the animals had had a battle. He only had seventy left out of seven hundred."

"That's so," said Helen. "I've often heard Pa speak about that."

"Sheep'll do the same," said Corky. "What a bullick'll do because it's thirsty a sheep'll do because it's hot. This country's too hot for sheep, but the people who came here first they didn't know that. They'd try anything once. There was a mob of over 5,000, and a few little trees all the shade. The sheep piled in the shade, you know how they do, just like humans, first come first served, and lay down to rest in the only little bit of relief in all that landscape, and then others came and tumbled on them and pushed and others on top of them, and the drovers couldn't get them off in time, and finally there was only 200 left alive. Just suffocated the others were."

"Like cattle," said Helen. "Cattle can do that. Especially with water. That's why, Sinbad, we're always so careful at the bores or the small holes, watering them. You'll see. Only fifty, sixty at a time. Depends on how much room there is and how much mud. They can't hold themselves back. Trample each other down. Mad with thirst they get."

"I've seen men in pubs nearly as bad in the South," said Corky, meditatively.

"I saw a football crowd at home once," said Sinbad. "There were only a couple seriously hurt, but a lot more would have been if the police hadn't formed a line and charged. It was cruel for a bit, the police bashing one way and the crowd the other, but it would have been a real horror

if they hadn't. Like two waves in the opposite direction meeting, 'bang'. 'Bombora' you call it out here. We've no word
that I know of for it at home.

"What puzzles me about you Australians is that you don't
use dogs. You've got cattle and sheep dogs and sheep dog
trials and all that, but I never see any of you with dogs."

"Pa's all against dogs with travelling stock," said Helen.
"Dogs make the cattle nervy. Nip, nip, nip, nip. After them
all the time. Never give them any rest. Besides, there's
nothing a dog can do with them that a horseman can't, only
better."

"You'll see dogs," said Corky, "at the dipping. Dipping for
tick. Has to be done three times. I wonder if Dan thought
of that?"

"Bet he didn't," growled Les, his braying voice thick and
ass-like.

"Those dogs," said Corky, "aren't the real cattle dogs,
either. Just snappy, vicious brutes to bark and snap through
the race to get them down and swimming."

"Once," said Les, "there were two men, mechanics, going
out with a barrel of water on a two-ton truck to do a mending
job on one of the bores, and their engine broke down out
on the flat, with not a blade of grass around—nothing, just
hot and very thirsty—and travelling in the opposite direction
along came a mob of cattle that hasn't had a drink for two
days. Suddenly they gets a whiff of the water in the barrel
on the truck, and before anyone could do anything about it
they're milling all over the truck; one of the blokes under the
truck and the other up behind the cabin. They would have
been dead meat if one of the boys with the cattle hadn't shot
down the leaders. Terrible losses in the cattle. They trample
each other to pieces if they're thirsty enough or frightened
enough."

"You don't say?" said Sinbad.

"They're frightened of people on foot, Sinbad," said Helen.
"Never forget that. If you're in a jam, stand up and face
them. Of course, it would be better if you were standing
behind a tree if they were coming your way and you could
get there in time."

"A good thick tree," said Corky.

"Wait till you're lying down," said Les, "like I was, with a thousand of the brutes kicking their heels over you. And all you're hoping is that they jump high enough and don't tumble. If one of those bullicks had tumbled and dropped on top of me I'd have been for it. All the others would have piled up on top of him, and I'd have been right on the bottom of the sacks on the mill, flat as a pancake."

"Yet," said Corky, consolingly, "it's strange but true what an ignoramus can do and get away with—if that's any comfort to you, sailor. Mrs. Daisy Bates—a grand old person that one —told me once—you'll appreciate I'm not telling you this as if it happened to me—" he said, pointedly. "It was Mrs. Daisy Bates who once saw a whole mob of travelling cattle divide up like as if the Israelites were crossing the Red Sea, some to the right and some to the left—a real circus trick that no cattle-man would have attempted—just when down the lane walks a little Jewish pedlar, a couple of hundred miles off his beat, dead scared, but pushing a barrow and the Lord taking care of him and his haberdashery. It might be some consolation to you if you're ever really frightened. Just think of that little pedlar."

These tales weren't meant to reassure Sinbad. Les and Corky were enjoying themselves.

"There was once a man," said Corky, "the fastest rider on a night horse I ever saw. Any bloody risk at all, he'd take. He could see pretty well in the dark or else he let his horse see for him or else he didn't care. But no ground was ever too rough for him and no mob of bullicks too wild."

"You don't man the Man from Snowy River, do you, Corky?" asked Helen.

"I do not!" said Corky. "This man—his name eludes me for the moment—had a mob stampede in ironstone country, and their hooves simply struck up so many sparks from the ground it was like a fireworks display. He planned his strategy by the light from their fleeing hooves."

Helen whistled, but Sinbad was still drinking it in.

"Cattle," went on Corky, impressively, "have an uncanny sixth sense. Tell me. You must have noticed it yourself now.

A beast can be lying in the middle of a mob, sound asleep to all intents and purposes, and another on the edge, absolutely without any contact with him, jumps up, startled. In two seconds the whole mob is on its feet. How?"

"I don't know," said Sinbad.

"The chemistry of fear," said Corky. "Mass vibration, a sort of electric emanation, the whole basis of the herd psychology. What a student should do, a student of mass psychology, is to travel with the cattle, plot their reactions to fear and so on. When do they rush? what effect has thirst on fear? what effect has fatigue on fear? and so on."

"A cattleman could tell you all that," said Les.

"Horses have got a fear of ghosts all right. Cattle too," said Charley.

"You believe in ghosts?" asked Helen.

"Horse ghosts," said Les.

"I rode a horse once," said Charley, "every week round a bend we used to call the Devil's Elbow. Plenty of big accidents there. A good many horses killed or had to be shot afterwards. This horse used to shy every time. Never could pass it without shying. He knew damn right there were ghosts there."

"You think fear is just chemistry, Corky?" Sinbad asked. It meant so much to him.

"You know yourself," said Corky, "fear makes a man sweat and fear makes a man thirsty. You get thirsty for other reasons too, but even if it's to your harm to get thirsty, if you're lost and doing a perish, then fear makes you much thirstier. The only thing to do is to sit still and count your heartbeats till you're not frightened any more. It stops your sweating and it lessens your thirst."

"Maybe," said Sinbad.

"You have to sit down and wait till someone cuts your tracks," explained Helen. "When you're lost you follow your tracks back till you realise where you went wrong. You never keep just going and going. If you don't know where you went wrong, then someone is sure to come after you if you wait long enough."

Mary came riding up on her big chestnut. "Ready, Mary?" asked Corky. He firmed his belt under his generous paunch. He wore his trousers at the lowest elevation compatible with safety. Once on his horse he had a good seat, but it was years since he'd sprung into the saddle with anything like grace. He said of his own mounting that it was a middle-aged scramble. Corky and Mary usually rode behind the cattle. "Those horse ghosts," Corky called to Charley, "I always keep a pinch of salt in my pocket for them."

Charley didn't like being got at about ghosts. Perhaps it was the Chinese in him that respected them.

Sinbad couldn't tell what was true and what false out of all the tales he heard, but out of them all he was building up a bank of bush knowledge, learning to respect even the crudest of the drovers, even Les.

*   *   *   *

Dan watched Mary riding along, picking up a straggler here and urging a tired bunch on with loud and frightening cracks of her stockwhip. "She's worth her money," he thought. He was paying her a man's wage. It was nearly sundown, and they were coming up to the night camp. Ma and the chuckwaggon and horse-trailer had got there long since. The fire was going and supper being prepared. Dan was going to shoot a killer that night.

Les was edging in from the wing nearer Mary. Dan had often noticed that trick, just as he'd noticed the sheep's eyes the big fellow was always casting in Mary's direction. Any horseman could tell that Les often put on a show for Mary's benefit. Dan also had a pretty good idea that Les had boasted to Charley that he was going to make Mary. It didn't ever occur to Les that any girl could resist him. Dan wasn't the sort who talked about what he noticed. He noticed now that Les had on his best ten gallon hat with the band studded with nickel clover leaves, horseshoes, hearts, and round studs, and that round his neck he wore a gay silk neckerchief. "Quite the dandy," thought Dan.

He had been going to ask Les to cut out a killer, but now he changed his plan. Mary could do it. He had the feeling that

Mary knew very well what Les was aiming at, and he admired the girl because never once had she encouraged Les or risen to any of the opportunities there might have been to try to play up to him or impress him in her turn.

He rode up to her now. "Like to pick out your dinner?"

She smiled up at him. It was dull jogging along flogging the stragglers. "That one over there?" She pointed. "That slit ear?"

"He'll do."

She manoeuvred her way into the mob, picked up the bullock she had indicated to Dan, and, by a piece of clever, quick horsmanship, soon had him out of the mob and on the way to the night camp without any undue excitement. Cattle-men don't like a killer to be hustled in the last ten minutes of his life. They reckon it makes the meat tough.

"Nice work," said Dan to Les, who had come galloping up, very much the knight errant, to help his selected lady-love. "Leave her to it."

"You mean to say you're going to let her throw him?" asked Les.

"Watch," said Dan.

Not far from the camp there was a carefully arranged pile of green boughs. Mary had her chestnut close to the killer now. With a supple movement she was off, hanging on to the bullock's head, twisting it down, round and over. Now she had the bullock down, the tail twisted, the legs hog-tied so quickly that Sinbad, who was watching, astounded, didn't quite see how she did it. She caught her horse, sprang on, and rode away as the beast tried clumsily to rise to its feet. A rifle shot rang out and the killer stumbled, falling almost without a convulsion, stayed down and never moved again.

"Nice work," shouted Dan to Mary, riding off.

She waved her hand. "Nice work, yourself," she called.

It had been a neat shot, dead between the eyes. "She needn't have tied it," said Dan. "I could have got it without tying."

"I'll supervise the cutting, Dan," called Bill Parsons, riding up.

"I thought she'd be killed," said Sinbad to Les.

"She could have been," said Les, sourly. "A girl's got no right to do that sort of job." She had done it as well as he would have done it himself.

"She wouldn't have been killed," said Dan. "She's done it often for her Pa."

"She must be very strong," said Sinbad.

"It's not the weight, it's the way you use it," Dan explained, "and the knack and, most of all, the timing. You have to be a very good rider before you try that sort of thing on, son."

"She wouldn't have the strength to hang on to a bullock if it tried tricks or she was a bit slow," said Les.

"That's the point," said Dan. "She's not slow and she times her jump perfectly."

"It's the bullock that gets the surprise," said Pa. He had slit the hide down the back and sides, baring the ribs. With his sharp butchering knife he cut out the chuck steak and sent Nipper along with the meat to Ma, who had a good glowing bed of red wood embers ready to grill it over. Then he cut off the roasts—the aborigines would get the rib-bones —and removed the rump steaks. The rest of the meat he expertly cut off in big chunks, gashing it with the knife and salting it with coarse salt. This meat he left to drain over-night on the clean green bushes. By the time he had finished Ma was calling "Come and get it" from the camp.

The sun was going down, the sky packed with red and woolly cloudlets like a flock of bloodstained sheep. Behind lay low, rolling, timbered country, beyond was a grassy plain, dotted with, here and there, rosewoods and other light timber. The rosewood was a beautiful tree, Sinbad thought, and the bottle tree, many of which he had seen as they passed along, just as odd as the rosewood was beautiful. The shape of the bottle tree, with its quaint and thirsty trunk and its clutching, umbrella-like branches fifteen feet or so off the ground, he felt as something particularly antagonistic and alien. There was a bottle tree near the breakwind behind the camp fire. Now the grass caught a reflected redness from the sky, as if

the whole wide earth was a gigantic cooking hearth. Nipper
had dug a hole near the breakwind and now Ma filled it with
red-hot embers and put in her first batch of bread in the
biggest Bedourie camp oven and heaped more embers on top.
The Bedourie oven was just two big round baking dishes,
fitting perfectly together, secured firmly by a movable twist
of wire. There were a whole set of these ovens. On the
track they fitted tightly one inside the other, like a set of
cylindrically lidded basins. Sinbad had seen the slaughtering
place and he felt vaguely upset. These Australians, he
thought, were just a lot of savages, eating beef that twenty
minutes before had been walking along on four legs with a
white, squared-off face and big eyes and a pair of horns. The
bottle tree symbolised the savagery of the whole people,
natives as well. Nipper and Jacky had a fire going a little
bit behind the camp and the smell of roasting rib bones came
wafting over. He felt he could never fit in with these people
who took such things as a matter of course, or be at home in
a country where a girl could toss a bullock and a mother grill
meat still wet and warm from the beast.

Dan came behind him with a big plate of cooked meat and
bread. He sprinkled pepper liberally. "Get some into you,
Sinbad," he said. "You won't feel so lonely." He squatted
down, buttocks touching the raised heels, his weight resting
evenly between his feet. He saw Sinbad was a bit down in
the mouth and guessed at the underlying reason. "In six
months," he said, "you'll be able to throw a bullock like that.
Maybe." His strong jaws took hold of a large piece of steak.
"M'm, tender," he said, and called to Ma, "Done to a turn,
Ma."

She turned round from the fire, her face flushed. "Is it?"
She was pleased.

"It's funny how the chuck toughens once it's cold," she
said. "Have yours now, Sinbad?"

"He's turned vegetarian," said Charley, who had been
watching.

Mary and Helen came to the fire. They had washed and
brushed up. Mary had changed her shirt. Ma served them.
They sat down quietly by the row of saddles.

Sinbad held out his plate too. "I've got some 'bango' for you afterwards," said Ma. "It's a very simple thing, just flour and sugar. The old-timers made it a lot. I made it specially for you to taste." Sometimes she had this trick of mothering Sinbad as if he was a very dear guest, a stranger whom they would soon lose, a visitor for whom nothing was too much trouble.

"Thank you," said Sinbad. He sat down in his place. The sunset was still smouldering in the sky but the clouds were no longer bloodstained; they were purple barred with the last glimmering of gold. The earth was dark and wide and grow-ing cold. Never had he seen so wide a land. It went up like a broad and turned-down saucer to meet the sky. The red fire behind him was warm and comfortable, the big billy with the flat side that they used for tea hissed as it came to the boil; there was the smell of baking and roasting, the smell of lanawood burning, the smell of leather, of the packs and the camp, and the dung of the bullocks. There was all the friendliness of men sitting together round the camp fire, the family of human relationship in its most primitive form, the family of hunters and herders and killers eating together while their beasts rested.

Behind him the white blouses of the girls showed beneath their dark coats. He ran his hand through his blonde, longish hair and began to eat. As Dan had said, the meat was really tender. There was nothing to be ashamed of.

"Pass the sauce, Sinbad," said Corky, briskly. Corky liked tender steak, he had trouble with his teeth.

CHAPTER XV

DAN was riding out with Jacky to find a native soak or well for the next watering.

"There should be one about five miles off that sugar-loaf knoll," he said. "Only the last time I was out this way, the grass was six feet high. I know, because, standing up, I could just see over the tops of the grass heads."

"Different now, boss," said Jacky.

The plain all round them was covered with coarse kangaroo grass. "We're lucky, anyway," said Dan, "this stuff is good feed." He looked round the plain, trying to work out the exact location of the soak which he had heard about but not had occasion to use before. The aboriginals never direct attention to their soaks and wells; there was nothing conspicuous to catch Dan's eye. Moving across the plain, however, he discerned a small group of figures. His eyes narrowed, creasing at the corners as he scanned the far distance. "What you think, Jacky?"

Jacky stood up in his stirrups. "Kangaroo hunt," he said.

The horsemen galloped over. There were two natives in the prime of life, an old man, three lubras, one with a picca-ninny in a coolamon slung under her arm, a couple of young boys, and a girl about nine. One of the men was carrying on his head a dead kangaroo rolled into a tight ball like a sleeping kitten. The kangaroo, still wearing his reddish fur coat, smelled high. All the men had spears and throwing sticks. The boys had short spears too. The small girl had a digging stick. The lubras carried some half-charred small game, rodents and birds, that they had apparently got by burning out. They spoke almost no English, but Jacky was able to explain what Dan wanted and they gave copious directions, squatting down and drawing directions in the blackened soil. The well was more to the south than Dan had assumed.

Dan handed round some native tobacco that he took out of his pack-saddle. It was the black, coarse, loose-fibred sort that is imported duty free. One of the lubras had an old wax vesta tin, polished with long handling. When Jacky had assured Dan that he knew where the well was and Dan had assured himself that even, Jacky failing, he could pick it up himself, the lubra handed up three honey ants out of the tin —one for Jacky and two for Dan. Dan took a small insect with the three yellow bands on its distended abdomen. It looked like those "cherries" that children make out of burst toy balloons by sucking the rubber into their mouths. The light shone clear through the golden globule which Dan put in his mouth, nipping off the forepart as if it were no different from the shell of a prawn or the beard of an oyster. The

taste was only of honey—from acacia blossom if Dan was
any judge. He put the other ant carefully into his cartridge
belt, with a plug of earth on top of it and a pebble below.

"Might get it home to Sinbad," he thought. "Bit of a
curiosity." He doubted if the swollen membranes would carry
so far, but chanced it—though thin as a film of soap bubble
they were resistant enough.

Dan was taking a chance planning to cut the Orde lower
down than usual. It would save time.

He found the well, a roughly-timbered six feet square pit,
with plenty of water in it and running over into a boggy soak
alongside. "We'll water here early to-morrow morning," he
told Jacky. "We'll have to take care and not get any of them
bogged. Fifty at a time. They'll soon make a mess of this."

"Too right," said Jacky.

"A couple more days and we'll be on the river, eh?"

Jacky said that was so.

*   *   *   *

That night Les brought twenty-four crested pigeons he had
shot into camp.

"Aren't these birds protected?" asked Bill.

"They're dead now, anyway," murmured Ma. She didn't
want anybody upset. Nipper prepared them and Ma spitted
them on the long grilling-skewers. There was no more than
a couple of mouthfuls in each one, but the flesh was rich and
oily, a deep purple in colour after basting. It was a change
from beef.

Corky licked his lips, lay on his back, put his hat over his
nose, and said, "The fat of the land, Missus, the fat of the
land," in imitation of a well-known Wyndham identity.
Helen tickled him with the butt of her stockwhip. He didn't
mind. He sat up. He had got used to Helen and rather enjoyed her. She was so easy to take in.

"Come here," he said, "I'll show you something." Out of
the little washleather bag in his swag where he kept his gold-
prospecting specimens, he took three half walnut shells and

borrowed a couple of dried peas from Ma. "Watch," he said, "nature's masterpiece of prestidigitation. The quickness of the hand deceives the eye . . ." He had Helen every time. Her laughter bubbled out like a cool fountain after a hot day.

"I don't believe there's a pea at all, Corky," she said.

Nipper and Jacky had come up, smiling, to watch. Jacky did a card trick.

Bill began to play "Drink to Me Only" on his mouth organ.

"Food," thought Ma. "Fill their stomachs and they're all happy." She was busy making brownie for the next day. It would be a long day, Dan had told her, they would water the cattle till after midday and push on in the late afternoon. It was the last drink before the river, another thirty-four miles to go. Whenever there was anything hard to be done Ma always tried to bump the menu up. The men would take the brownie with the bread and salt meat for their midday meal. She looked round and saw Mary and the sailor lying side by side in the firelight.

". . . with thine eyes . . ." the mouthorgan wavered sentimentally and the sailor's eyes were fixed on Mary's. In the same moment she noticed how full and red his lips were, redder than Australian lips, and saw how his hand lay alongside Mary's hand, the little fingers touching, oh, so casually. Dan, she saw, noticed too.

"Mary," she called, sharply.

"What, Ma?"

"Your watch."

"O.K." the girl said easily, smiling, unworried. She went over to the waggon. Behind it Helen was getting ready for bed.

"I meant to ask you before," Helen asked, "what are you always wearing Ma's ring for?"

"Protection. It was Ma's idea."

"Protection? Against snake-bite? Sid-the-Chopper's Lily had a copper one against snake-bite, but I didn't think you believed that rubbish."

"Against men," said Mary.

"Men?"

Mary swaggered off. Sometimes there were things you couldn't explain to a younger sister.

Helen lay thinking it over. "It must be that Les," she decided. "I don't like him, either."

*   *   *   *

The next day there was quite a scene down at the soak watering the cattle. Sinbad, who didn't understand the danger, went in on horseback after a steer that had got bogged. He only made things worse. Dan swore pretty hard and Sinbad answered back. He was sorry afterwards and apologised. Dan was sorry it had occurred but didn't apologise for what he had said. That incident marked a difference in his treatment of Sinbad. "You're a member of the plant now," he said to him, "your initiation's over."

He left off thinking of Sinbad as a pretty boy, a poor kid who'd been through hell and whose nerves were bad. He didn't call him so affectionately "son" any more. "Looks like he's feeling his oats a bit," he said to Pa, with a grin. Pa quirked back his eyebrows at Dan. The two senior men understood each other. Sometimes it amused Dan seeing the mannerisms of the Parsons family. Mary moved her eyebrows just like her father, Helen was just as matter of fact as her mother. Actually it did Sinbad a lot of good not being nursed any more on the trek. He learnt quicker. Now that he was more or less safe on a horse he was picking up the droving business. The time was coming, and Dan knew it, when he would be able to spare nobody, not the girl nor the boy either. There could be no favouritism in an outfit.

"We're shaking down," thought Dan. "The plant's getting used to each other." Even Les had stopped making sheep's eyes at Mary and had put away his best bandana. Charley hadn't changed his shirt for a fortnight. Corky said "Excuse me" when he belched after supper, but he still belched. Sinbad no longer frisked like a lounge lizard when one of the girls lifted a saddle or a log of wood. Ma scolded everybody indiscriminately for their own good if she felt like it. Nobody minded. Jacky and Nipper looked quite glossy with the good food they were getting and smiled perpetually. They liked the movement with the cattle, the change from the everyday bore-dom of Wyndham. They were good stockboys, too, patient with the cattle and skilful with the horses. Nipper, the horse-tailer, hadn't kept the drovers waiting one morning. He had got to know which horses liked each other and stuck around together feeding. It made his job easier. He knew which ones had to be hobbled and which were all right if they were only belled. Even the cattle were settling down. They would move now, grudgingly, before the stockwhip cracked any-where near them. They were still wild-eyed and a bit scary, but they hadn't lost as much weight as they might have and there had been no strays so far, which was a wonder because there were occasional scrub cattle about, whuffing and bellow-ing in the night. It was marvellous, Sinbad always thought, the way the night horses sensed the presence of these scrub-bers before they gave trouble, and quietly headed them off.

"If there are any mobs coming down after us," said Dan, "they'll be unlucky, we haven't lost one."

"They'll be unlucky, all right," said Pa. "They won't find much feed. There's plenty of grass, but soon enough there won't be much in it for the horses."

"The horses are getting a bit poor," agreed Dan. "They've had a lot of work to do with these beasts. Nines and eights" (the year of branding) "take turning once they get it into their heads to go." He gave orders to Nipper to take the horses out further that night, to a patch of good grass he'd noticed earlier in the day. They camped at a gilgi that night.

The next day Bill, Dan and Jacky rode on to the river.

*   *   *   *

"H'm," said Bill, looking at the wide stream fringed with its dense tropical foliage, "looks bad. I've never seen so much water at this time of the year. Fair cow. How far's Coota-bulla crossing, Jacky?"

"Fifty mile, seventy mile, Boss."

"We'll have to swim them, Bill," said Dan, decisively. He had been examining the banks up and downstream. Some-times the boss-drover has to be like the captain of a ship. The course and the orders are his.

"You're right," said Bill, but he didn't like it.

At the camp fire that night Dan broke the news. "It's pretty deep," he said, "and there's a bit of a current. We'll have to make everything we can watertight and float the waggon. The horses will get over all right, but the cattle— It's a bit of a risk. If we had a few coachers it might be easier, but none of these brutes have ever seen so much water. The thing to do will be to get the waggon and stores over first— you can look after that, sailor. The canteens you can lash on empty. They'll help to float her. Then the spare horses, then the cattle. Bring them up slow and easy and drive them straight in. No waiting. Don't rush them, but don't give them time to think things over and get temperamental. If the leaders go in easy then the rest won't panic. If they panic and start ringing in the water we'll lose half of them. We haven't the time to go on looking for a better crossing. There's no better crossing for fifty or sixty miles, Jacky says. It'll save us a fortnight crossing here. We've got to cross. What do you think, Jacky? Can we swim here?"

"Yes, boss. Maybe lose the cattle though."

"Cheerful, isn't he?" The crowd laughed, but Les looked a bit annoyed.

"Straight from the horse's mouth," he said.

*   *   *   *

Ma worked late that night and Sinbad helped her. "Getting things shipshape," he said. It was remarkable what confidence he showed now he was in his own element with a responsible job to do. Dan recalled the nervous, shaking boy of eight weeks earlier. Nobody thought of Japs now. Nobody had heard or seen anything of the war. There mightn't have been a war on. The blacks with the kangaroo were the only other travellers they had encountered. But there was a war on. Dan never forgot it. Often he scanned the sky, thinking of bombers. Ma did too. Every moonlit night she thought of the last night at Glenrichard. All that was behind them now. Never again Glenrichard. They still had Helen.

*   *   *   *

The next morning Helen was watching Sinbad. "There's 'gators in the river," she said. "Aren't you frightened?" He shook his head. "They're cowardly creatures," he said.

Pa was taking no risks, however. He had his rifle out. He had seen too many heifers and calves pulled under by the nose when they stood too long drinking.

Corky told the tale of the man who went down with a bucket late at night and who never came back. He began to enlarge on it, telling how a crocodile waits up in the mud on the bank, still as a log, and how fast he can skedaddle back into the water, the mud flying as if he wore skates on his claws, and the poor victim tightly held in that nauseous, musk-odorous mouth, powerless, while the amphibian holds him under, slowly drowning.

Helen enjoyed her shudders—she was used to Corky. Sinbad took it all in, but he kept on working. He knew by now that Corky was only trying to get a bite out of him. For Corky, crossing the river was quite an occasion, the most exciting event since he had been magsman at the two-up school. He got flowers and a saucebottle, for champagne, for Ma and pretended she was launching a liner—the "Saucy Sue." He made a flowery speech. Helen was delighted, even Ma had to smile, but Bill took it badly. "Cut out the gab," he called. "There's work to be done. Dan's waiting."

Ma hastily threw the sauce bottle and the flowers into a pandanus by the water's edge. "Don't play the fool now, Corky," she said, softly. "It's too serious."

"Nothing is ever too serious, Madam," said Corky, with his mountebank's wistfulness. But all the same he put his shoulder behind the wheel and helped Sinbad launch the waggon gently. It just floated and it had a bit of a list. Ma was seated up in front and Helen was in the back, holding her horse, Rusty, by the reins. The sailor had rigged the canteens to poles like catamarans alongside. The waggon looked like a heavy water-beetle with wide outstretched legs. Dan had taken the team to the far bank and a long, strong rope was stretched from the harnessed eight round a tree and down into the water round the centre pole of the waggon.

"Take the strain gently," said Dan.

The horses strained and the waggon floated quietly into the water.

"O.K." said Dan, "bring it over. Not too fast, now."

Pa, seeing it was all right, went to see how Mary and the others were with the cattle. He didn't want them hurried either.

Sinbad stood watching. He was quite proud. The gallant little "Saucy Sue" was doing all right. "I never thought I'd turn a waggon into a boat," he said to Pa, whom he thought was at his side. But Pa had gone. He had left his rifle leaning against a tree next to Sinbad.

Helen gave him a wave from the back of the waggon. Ma was watching ahead. The horse Rusty was swimming well, but pulling. Sinbad could see its ears back, its rolling white eye, its head plunging up and down in terror.

"It's really terrified," thought Sinbad. At the same moment he saw the moving track, the snout and eyes of the crocodile, and heard the scream of Helen sharp as a knife. The pony was pulling her out of the waggon.

"Let go, you fool," called Ma, "let go." She couldn't move from her place quick enough. The waggon tilted desperately.

Crack! Sinbad had fired Pa's rifle. Whether the bullet hit the crocodile or only frightened it he never knew, but it disappeared.

"Keep her going! Keep her going!" yelled Dan from the other bank. Nipper and the team kept her going. The waggon moved in a distorted arc to the other side. Ma was beside Helen now, holding her by the shoulders. Helen still had hold of the bridle. The waggon creaked out of the river, streams of water running out of the tarpaulin.

"A bit waterlogged," thought Sinbad, mechanically.

Rusty galloped riderless off.

"Scared a year's growth out of me," said Corky.

"A good shot," said Pa, who had returned on the crack of the rifle. "Thanks, Sinbad." He rested his hand affectionately on Sinbad's shoulder.

Dan galloped to Ma. "Good on you, Ma."

She couldn't speak. She just pushed Helen ahead of her and mechanically wrung the water out of the skirt of the floral dress she was wearing.

*   *   *   *

Everybody was nervous till they got the cattle over.

The drovers swam cautiously beside their horses, but in all the excitement they had too much to do without worrying about 'gators.

The cattle paused on the downward dip of the bank, uneasy and lowing. The drovers behind yelled and urged them on. The cracking of whips was frightful, like a battlefield. Unwillingly, pushed from behind, the leaders got in. It was deep water at once. They tried to swim round, back to the bank from which they had come. "Don't let them ring," yelled Dan. "We're done if they ring."

Les, Charley and the girl held the right flank. Jacky plunged in on the left, urging his horse forward, giving the uncertain cattle a lead. They took it, they swam faster than the man on the horse, their horns began to bob regularly as they struck out for midstream. The current carried them down a little; the drovers on the bank kept the pressure up. More and more cattle took to the water. "One in all in," muttered Dan. Now the leaders were past midstream and swimming strongly, their eyes immense in their heads, startled, frightened, but not mad with panic. The wide river was coated with backs, with tossing horns like a debris of branches floating on a flood; there was a kind of long moan, a dull, continuous bellow of fear as the moving stream of cattle plunged each one into the dark, mirror-green water of the tropical river. By the right flank of the descending cattle a furious mill started. Animals got trodden under, began to fight, to swim away from the crossing, taking the easy way downstream.

"Hold them," yelled Dan, "get in with them." Nobody
heard him, but Corky plunged in. He slipped from the saddle,
grasping the reins and the pommel firmly. He was a heavy
man and a very poor swimmer. The cattle swam beside him.
Corky guided his horse to the opposite bank. "It was a 'save
who could'," he explained later, "and the bullocks saw my
point of view. They like company. They came too. But were
they close! Practically hugging me they were. I could have
hung my hat on any of their horns, but it didn't occur to me
at the moment. Bosom friends, that's how we all were in the
river." None of the plant minded how much Corky drama-
tised it. His presence of mind had saved many cattle. Sinbad
swam behind him and Les and the others too. Everyone did
his share. It was an experience.

When the last beast struggled up the bank, now torn into
a muddy chocolate bog by the thousands of hooves, the
drovers quietly got them on the road again as if nothing had
happened, as if swimming a wide, strong river was the least
sensational event in any animal's life. The water dripped out
of the drovers' clothes, out of their hats. Their boots and
their saddles sogged and sagged, Corky could hardly stagger
up the bank, but everyone was safely over. The stores were
safely over. Three or four bullocks had been lost, trampled
under in the furious rush on the flank. In a few days the
carcases would rise and stink, feeding the 'gators.

Dan took the next two long stages quietly. Everyone had
felt the strain.

CHAPTER XVI

THE flies were bad. They were small, black and sticky. They
stuck like beads of dirty perspiration on the backs, hands and
faces of the drovers. They exasperated the horses to the limit
and they made the cattle irritable and sulky by turns. The
men were the same as the cattle.

All the drovers wore fly veils. Ma was never without a
little bushy switch of green leaves and cooking was a nightmare for her. She kept covering everything with double-
mesh mosquito net throw-overs. "Fussy, aren't you?" was
Charley's comment. The flies troubled him less than anybody.

"Yes," said Ma, savagely, "I like to know it's currants I'm putting in the doughboy."

That shut him up.

Sinbad suffered more than anybody. Sandflies and mosquitoes bit him wherever flesh showed. He wore his shirt tightly buttoned to the wrists, but if he wasn't careful the sandflies got under the wrist band. His whole body itched. His face and hands swelled red and unutterably tender. "You'll have to watch those," said Ma, "or you'll be laid up with poisoning."

It was Nipper who helped Sinbad. He boiled up some aromatic leaves in an old milk tin and mixed some yellow clay to a paste with the liquid.

Helen came by, sniffing. "Citronella," she said.

"More like that graveyard geranium," said Ma.

Nipper wanted Sinbad to smear the paste over his face and hands.

Sinbad didn't want to. "Not hygienic, over these sores," he said.

"I don't know," said Ma. "The natives have some pretty good ideas on hygiene, sometimes." She was thinking of the way aboriginal women are brought to birth. "I'd try it if I were you." She dabbed on Friar's Balsam first. Sinbad danced with anguish. After that the cool, airtight clay brought immediate relief.

"You look," said Helen, "as if you're just done up for a corroboree." Whenever any of the plant saw Sinbad they laughed.

"At least," said Sinbad, not so philosophically, "I'm the court jester." But the clay was better than the bites. He kept it on and renewed it from time to time when it caked and fell off.

The country was getting worse. They met groves of lance-wood. It was easy to see how it got its name. The wood was extraordinarily brittle, and broke off into black, lance-like spikes that could penetrate a motor tyre or a hoof like sharpened steel. The clothes of the drovers suffered, tough drill as they were. Ma had to dress a few nasty knocks and scratches. Bill was quite a bush doctor himself. When Corky got an attack of what he called "the collywobbles" Bill administered the Painkiller. The girls were standing up to the drove well. Ma could see Helen getting taller week by week. Mary was almost her own self; "Pa's pal," as Corky ironically called her. Her restlessness was satisfied by the hard daily demands on her energy.

The deep green of the tropical rain belt had gone. The tall timber, ironwoods, giant ti-tree, turpentines, lofty eucalyptus, had gone. With them the birds, most of the small whistling warbling birds, the pigeons and ducks, the heavy-flying brush turkeys, had gone. The flowering creepers and white cockatoos and small gay parrots had been left behind. The murrangi scrub closed in. There was no escaping it.

"The drover's curse," explained Pa to Sinbad. "This stock route's named after it; tears the beasts to pieces. It's hard enough anyway on the feed available, but pushing through this slows them up to five miles a day. We've got a hundred miles of it, pretty well, to get through. The government ought to cut it down—bash a way through it for the cattle. A five hundred yard wide swathe. That would do nicely. Save weeks here on the track and weeks later in the fattening paddocks.

"Where we were before," said Corky, that know-all, "there were patches of volcanic soil with basalt and limestone hills. Here you're getting into the desert sandstone."

"The soil's good enough for agriculture even here," said Pa stoutly. "It's only that the tropical rain belt ends. The rains you can't depend on. Sometimes they come, sometimes they don't."

The small-leafed murrangi scrub varied in height from low stuff to eighteen or twenty feet high. It grew in distinct belts, with open, fine white sandy patches between. The wood was a hard dead fibre. In the scrub Sinbad couldn't see more than fifty yards. It was terribly gloomy. Somehow he thought of petrified forests and lost worlds. Now, added to the flies was the fine yellowy-red dust and the torment of the scrub. None of the men shaved. The dust caked on their faces, circling their eyes and mouths—"like concert coons" thought Sinbad.

He thought of the Blackpool pierrots. They were so far away. His morbid loneliness, outcome of the sandfly bites and the dreary landscape, lifted a little.

"Bet you," said Helen, riding up, "when you get all that clay off your face, you'll be sunburnt in stripes." She giggled cheerfully.

"Knew a man once," said Les ("You always do," from Helen, under her breath), "who put his face too close to a kerosene tin with a bunger in it to see what was the matter, and when it went off it blew the freckles clean off that side of his face. Fact."

At the camp-fire that night Dan said, "If the government want to bring down any more mobs they'll have to open up the stock route properly. More bores and better travel for the cattle." Mention of the government brought the war and the world beyond the cattle into everyone's mind. "We've got a thousand miles still to go," said Dan. He spoke for all. Les and Charley looked thoughtful; even Ma looked tired. They had done less than five hundred. Pa alone was still cheerful. His life had looked down longer perspectives than that.

CHAPTER XVII

THE cattle were bedded down just off the No. 8 bore on a harsh, bare-looking plain that looked as if all the top soft surface had been washed off. It stuck into the feet, hard and gritty. There were some scrubby bushes and a few grass trees about. Nipper had to take the horses a long way the night before to get grass. Now Dan rolled and stretched, waiting to hear him come back. For the first time he was late. Dawn had broken.

Bill rolled and stretched too. He got up on one elbow, listening. Helen, under the waggon, head on the ground, heard it too. She sat up, listening. Galloping hooves. Nipper came tearing up, dodging the clumps of bush, the hoofbeats of his horse drumming fear into the awakening camp. Something was wrong.

"Boss, Boss," yelled Nipper. He was dead scared.

"What's up?" Dan felt the doom coming.

"Poison weed. Plenty dead. Two or three very sick."

Les came up. "Any of ours?" His face had darkened with anger and fear.

"He only cares for his own," thought Dan. A great weariness rose through him, but he pulled on his boots, grabbed his horse, and went with Nipper. Bill, Les, Mary and Sinbad galloped after him.

The poisoned horses had strayed from where Nipper had left them. Lucky the leader's hobble was broken. Fortunately, Les and Charley's team had stayed in their customary bunch and not followed. The night horses had been on duty and were safe. That was the best of a bad business. There were eleven dead. Three more were streaming with perspiration and staggering. Another had its jaws firmly locked, its mouth askew, its tongue swollen so that it could eat nothing.

"What do you think, Bill?" asked Dan.

"They'll do no good," said Bill.

Dan nodded. He left it to Bill, turning away from the sickening sight.

Bill sent back for his rifle and investigated more closely.

"Get the bells and hobbles," Dan ordered Nipper. He rode slowly back to camp, thinking things out.

Sinbad watched the aborigine going between the dead horses. It reminded him of a ship's officer he had once seen collecting the effects of the dead. These horses were now just as grotesque and horrifying in death as those men had been. The sky overhead was sullen with cloud. Sinbad felt the old oppression returning, the pain at the base of the skull, the terror in the dry throat.

Then he heard the girl crying softly by his side. Suddenly he realised that for her, for the plant, these horses were individuals, as important as persons, that on these horses depended their own lives and safety. He had not thought she would cry out of pity so easily.

"They're so beautiful alive," she said, as if to excuse her-self.

Pa looked up and saw them watching. "Go back to camp," he shouted harshly. Under his breath he added, "Blubbing there." If she had been a boy she wouldn't have cried. Then he thought of his own first horse and how it staked itself in the stomach one night. The tears he had shed then. "Maybe not," he softened. He was going to open up one of the horses. Best to make really certain there was no foul play. They had seen smoke signals the day before. There were wild blacks about. It was odd, too, that none of Les and Charley's horses had been poisoned.

"Come on," said Sinbad to Mary. He led her by the arm. For the first time a warm protection passed between them, from him to her.

As they rode away over the plain they heard four shots ring out.

A cloud of wedge-tailed eagles rose up.

She moved her head sharply, but said nothing.

Presently, on the edge of a rocky razorback that scoured the extreme verge of a low ridge to the north-west, he saw a couple of naked aboriginals with a bundle of spears each. They were silhouetted against the sky, looking to see what had caused the shooting. Like a boy passing in a train Sinbad waved. The aboriginals waved back.

The plant worked hard that day. They flogged the bullocks along to get beyond the poison weed country.

"I've never heard of a patch on this route so far west," said Pa.

"There's plenty of it round the Palmer and the Coen," said Dan. "I did a trip up there once I'll never forget. Lost nearly twenty horses. But not all at once. Some of them we nursed for weeks. They were so bad they couldn't carry even a light pack. We threw the gear away to save them, but they never picked up."

"Lucky the bullocks had a good feed yesterday," said Pa, "though often they won't touch it when the horses seem to seek it out."

"It's hard to tell from the other stuff," said Dan. "The leaf's a bit broader, that's all. Flourishes where the grass is poor. That's what tempts the horses. I had a mind to lay into Nipper, but he couldn't help it. This isn't his country round-abouts, and anyway the beasts strayed. Just bad luck."

"Could be worse than bad luck, Dan."

"Yes, I know what you mean." The river crossing and the flies and the scrub and the poor feed had played up with the horses a lot. "No wonder Les and Charley are chewing the rag," said Dan. "I have a mind to go north by Paddy's Creek. There's always good grass there. Even at this time. We can spell up for a couple of weeks, maybe three weeks. If we don't spell up they'll all crock up on us. We can't afford the time, I know, but we can't afford to lose them, either. It's just taking your pick of two bad things."

"That's the way I see it, too," said Bill.

Les and Charley didn't like turning north. They said nothing, but they looked as if they were thinking a lot. The rest of the plant didn't know if Dan didn't notice them or was only pretending not to notice them. Nobody encouraged Les and Charley to talk. When a thing is serious between men nobody likes to be the first to spring the trap. Actually, in this case, Dan didn't notice them, beyond knowing they were a bit fed up. He never thought they'd get to the stage of pulling out. That is something that doesn't often happen in the north. He was too worried about the cattle. He was out and about all day and half the night too. "You'll wear your-self out," said Ma. Jacky had found some plains-turkey eggs in the grass and she made pancakes with treacle on them for supper.

"You'll wear yourself out, Missus," said Dan. "I never see you taking a rest."

"I get a good night's sleep," said Ma, "and I rest on the waggon going along."

Dan grinned. She went to bed last and she was up first. "The waggon isn't exactly joy-riding," he said.

"I like it," said Ma. She did too. She liked the clean air, the view of country expanding and contracting before her, the passage of hills and gullies, the timeless jogging and lumbering along, the brief spanking trots that now and again she got up to, the creaking of the harness and the iron scrape of the tyres as the big wheels turned rattling over stones and rumbling dully through dust. She felt she saw and knew and remembered and loved the country better than everybody else. "I reckon I get the best view of anybody from our old shay."

When they outspanned at Paddy's Creek it was like turning into a picnic ground. There was plenty of water in the six mile stretch of the billabong and plenty of feed. The grass was dry, but it still had body and nourishment in it. It was coarse, broad-bladed and in seed reaching to mid-thigh and looking a cross between kunai and ripe wild wheat. Ma sent Nipper down by the water's edge to polish all the pots and tins and plates and dishes in the sand. She scoured all her equipment and washed and mended her own and Pa's clothes. The girls washed their own clothes and went swimming. So did Corky and Sinbad. Corky wore a pair of ragged underpants for modesty. He fancied himself as a swimmer, but he dived like a stone. He began to tell Sinbad about Bondi and the conquests he had made there.

"In those underpants?" asked Sinbad.

"In these underpants," said Corky. Then he began to laugh. He laughed as if the world had only just begun for him. "You know what she called me?" He could hardly tell it for laughing. "Cockalorum. And after that, every time I called, instead of ringing the doorbell I crowed like a rooster. Did she like it!"

Sinbad threw a clod of grass at him and it caught him off balance and in he went. He rose up spluttering.

"Did she?" asked Sinbad.

"Did she what?"

"Did she like it?"

"Till I was broke," said Corky. "You know women—or don't you?" He flashed a look at Sinbad. "They're not mercenary! Oh, no! But if you've got no spondulicks you may just as well cut the traces clean and tell them so and step out.

Life—" said Corky, meditatively, "it's a funny thing, but bathing always makes me randy. The salter the water the quicker it happens."

"Come off it," said Sinbad.

*   *   *   *

Helen splashed water over Mary, then she sat in the shallow, kicking her legs up and down. "I like Sinbad," she said, "I think he's the nicest person I ever met. He doesn't show off. He's really good-natured without being soft. Everybody picks on him when they want to show off, but he doesn't mind. He smiles and he takes it in good part. He says he's a learner and he acts like a learner. Some people never learn, but Sinbad will."

"You sound just like Ma," said Mary. "Do you really like him better than us?"

"Outside the family I meant. I wish he was our brother and belonged to us. Do you like him, Mary?"

"He's all right."

"I think he's tops. My ideal."

"Your ideal? You're only eleven."

"I can have an ideal. Sinbad's it."

"You're starting early."

"Don't you tell him!"

"I might."

"Don't you dare!"

"Very well then, but why don't you want him to know?"

"He might think me goofy."

"So you are."

"I'm not; but he's my ideal, all the same." Mary was going on with her washing, spreading out handkerchiefs, panties, blouses on little bushes beside the water. "Who's your ideal, Mary? What sort of man would you want to marry?"

"A commando," said Mary, "about six feet two but not skinny like Dan. Red hair, blue eyes, very good on a horse."

"You have got him picked out. We don't know anyone like that—" Mary was silent. Helen eyed her off. "—or do we? Do you?"

"I only met him once."

"What's his name?"

"I'm not telling. I was only joking, really." But she hadn't been joking.

"I know your secret now," crowed Helen. "Now you can't tell Sinbad about me or I'll tell him about you. It's wonderful being in love, isn't it?"

"Wonderful," said Mary. "Except that I don't know I'm in love—not like you." She had to smile at Helen. Love was so much more than having an ideal. It was dreaming about hands that burnt when they touched you, it was not knowing whether to write or not to write, it was the way men looked at you and the way Ma made you wear an engagement ring that you had no right to, it was what sent you galloping like mad on a moonlight night picking white flowers out of the scrub, it was . . . "Corky says love is just chemistry," she told Helen. "Being near people of the opposite sex. Male and female created He them."

"I don't believe it," said Helen. "That's just Corky, as usual, sneering at something he doesn't understand. If it were true it would mean I'd think just as much of Les or Charley as I do of Sinbad—and how could I?"

"You couldn't. Nobody could. But that's what Corky said."

"I'll tackle him on it," declared Helen, who never let anything rest on her mind.

"Don't do that. Ma wouldn't like it."

"No," said Helen, "she wouldn't." She got up and said, in the same tone of voice, as if it were of equal importance, "I suppose I'll have to wash out my jodhpurs. Damn."

"And I wouldn't let her catch you swearing, either," said Mary.

"Did I really swear? Gosh, I didn't notice it."

*   *   *   *

Camped in a bark hut at the other end of Paddy's Creek was an old prospector. Corky, who was always friendly, called on him and found him at that stage of senility and loneliness that talks to itself without knowing it is talking. Corky had taken up a piece of Ma's cold plum duff. It was sweet and rich with suet, quite a treat for an old bushman. He made tea and handed it to Corky and himself with elaborate cere-mony. "Will you have a cup of tea?" he asked himself, and replied, "I don't mind if I do." His eyes were a washed-out watery blue and he wore a big old-fashioned hat, hand-plaited out of dry pandanus palm, with a fringe of bobbing corks. His hair and beard were long and white. Corky said after-wards it was like having tea with the Mad Hatter, Robinson Crusoe and Father Christmas rolled into one. The corners of his hut were piled with boxes and rotting sugar bags of specimens, but Corky was sure the old man would never be able to find any locality where he had ever found anything of value, supposing it were of value. With a childish duplicity the old prospector showed Corky all that was of no value at all, hinting all the time of rich and secreted treasures that excited the cupidity of the get-rich-quick villain in Corky, even though he knew all the time there was probably no truth at all in the old man's delusions that he was on the track of new and immensely rich fields.

Corky knew, like everybody else, that the mineral resources of the Northern Territory had only been lightly scratched with a comb, many of whose teeth were missing. While every gambler is not a prospector, every prospector is always a gambler. Corky was a born gambler. He had never settled down and never would, although he had plenty of ability. Now the lure of avaricious dreams enticed him. He planned to come back here when the cattle trek was done and the war over. There were good signs. He even meditated how he could leave the plant now and settle down with the old prospector, making his living off the land. The old man showed him some topazes and sapphires. One of the sapphires was uncommonly fine. Corky offered to take it to the store at Anthony's Lagoon and get credit for the old prospector to take out in groceries, but he declined. With trembling fingers he put it back in its cottonwool bed in an old match-box. "There's plenty more where that came from," he said, and, "What's money? I don't need money. A little flour, yes. A little tea, yes." He was like a child. His crazed mind could not see the necessity for the link between money and bread.

Nailed on the wall beside the chimney was the picture of a woman with a rose in her hand, her hair puffed high up at the sides and a lacy, low-necked gown on her bosom. It was covered from the flies by a thin sheet of unprocessed mica. There was a faded inscription underneath it, but Corky could not read what it said. "We've got a couple of nice girls in our outfit," he mentioned.

"Girls!" the old man exclaimed. Had Corky said vipers or death adders or tarantulas he could not have been more horrified. "Don't bring them up here," he besought Corky, and looked around as if his little hut were a refuge no longer, as if he would have to pack his portmanteaus and leave at once.

Going back to camp Corky thought it over. A misanthrope, a woman-hater, a self-immolated Carthusian—and obviously a remittance man, one of the old sort, because he spoke with a faded gentility that somehow matched the tired transparency of his eyes. The old prospector still ate and drank not like a wolfish old solitary, but with the restraint and elegancy imposed so firmly by a childhood training long ago that it was still part of his nature.

"I'll try Sinbad on him," thought Corky.

He warned the girls not to disturb the old man and begged a little parcel of luxuries from Ma. Bread, sultanas, a billy of thick kangaroo-tail soup, some tea and sugar and fresh steak. Her medicinal bottle of brandy she wouldn't open for him.

"If he's run away from wine and women I'm not going to tempt him now," she said firmly.

When Sinbad arrived the door and window of the humpy were shut and barred. It wasn't much trouble to him to open the sheet of bark over the window-opening, and he did so. There was nobody inside, but he saw clearly the photograph that had excited Corky's fertile imagination. When he turned round it was to face an old double-barrelled shot gun.

"I beg your pardon," he stammered, wondering if he ought to hold up his hands like a covered gangster. "I apologise for breaking in, but I thought you might be ill, sir." The recluse lowered his gun. The "sir" disarmed him. "Mrs. Parsons thought you might like a little fresh bread. She baked this morning. The old man's nostrils twitched. "If I'd had a little cheese," Sinbad told Corky afterwards, "I could have caught him like a mouse in a trap." It ended up with Sinbad and Robinson Crusoe taking tea and talking oddly together like an old vicar and one of his young parishioners. They spoke of the Clyde and the Wash and King John and the Crown Jewels. Then Sinbad shook hands and went back to camp. "There was a lot of formal politeness," he reported to Corky, "but I don't think he'd welcome any more visitors. It might push him really off his rocker if any more of us went up."

The drovers decided not to trouble the old man any more.

"That photograph," Sinbad told Corky, "That was an old actress, Nellie Stewart."

"Of course, of course," said Corky. "The name I just happened to forget."

"How was he off for tucker?" asked Dan.

"He wasn't worrying," said Sinbad. "He never mentioned being short."

"That sort doesn't," said Dan. He made a note to leave a few stores on their last day at the Creek.

"I think he eats crows," said Corky. "I saw one of those old crow traps out beyond his hut." The talk about the Crown Jewels had him intrigued. "Straight from the subconscious," he told Sinbad. He began to work out plans for floating a big company down south with the object of investigating the mineral and precious stone possibilities of the locality. He sharpened a pencil and at odd moments began to write down the long, glib generalisations that company promoters of Corky's type go in for.

On the third morning Dan had a deputation from Les and Charley. "We think we should push on, Dan."

Bill put down his needle and palm. He was working on a saddle.

Dan went on plaiting at a rawhide thong. "We've got to rest the beasts, Charley, or we'll lose the lot," he said amiably. He didn't realise the seriousness of what had come to a head.

"Then we're going on," said Charley.

"And we're taking our horses," said Les.

Dan rose. His six foot six was like a stockwhip uncurling. "You realise that means standing the cattle and us up?" he asked, with terrible quiet.

"That's not our funeral," blustered Charley.

"It may be ours," said Dan.

"If we wait we're liable to lose the horses as well as the cattle," said Les. "The horses again!" thought Bill.

"The whole trip's crazy," said Les.

"You had your chance to think of that before you came in," said Dan.

"You're yellow," said Bill. Dan gave Les a push in the face with his open hand. Charley made a swipe at Bill and Les charged Dan and butted him in the stomach. "You long cow," he sneered as Dan reeled back, doubling over with pain. Les bashed him with the butt of his stockwhip as he went over. As Les stepped forward to let Dan have another butt Corky stuck his foot out and gave him the larrikin trip-up. As Les went down he cracked his head on a stump Nipper had brought in for firewood, and lay sprawling. Charley turned from Bill to Dan and made a furious swing as Dan tried to come again, but by this time Ma had armed herself with a heavy frying pan and stepped between them, shouting, "Stop it, both of you. In camp I'm boss and I won't have fighting. That goes for you, too, Dan McAlpine." She turned to Les, slowly picking himself up. "As for you, take your good-for-nothing mate and your precious horses and clear out while the going's there."

"But, Ma," said Bill, wondering, "we need their horses."

"We can get along without them," said Ma, vehemently. "We don't want any rat-bags with this outfit." She put down the frying pan and wiped her hands together as if dusting Charley and Les off them. "They've been asking for it for a long time," she said. "They've had it coming to them."

Charley and Les didn't wait for the noon-time meal in camp. They rolled up their swags and took the tucker Ma silently laid out for them and rode off, driving their twenty or so horses in front of them.

Dan accepted Ma's rebuke; he accepted the decision she had made for everybody. He rolled a few more cigarettes than usual, that was all. He thought about it all day. After supper he said, "On a trip like this, if the blokes aren't with you, they're no good."

"Worse than useless," said Pa.

"We said we could do without them, but how? That's the point," said Dan. He smoked for a bit. "With Jacky and Nipper," he said, "I could get to Brunette Downs, get horses, and be back in a month."

"You'd have to spell them for a fortnight after," said Bill.

Dan agreed.

"Could we leave the cattle here and pick them up after the wet?" said Corky.

"You wouldn't find fifty," said Bill, fiercely.

"*You* don't want to pack up, do you Corky?" asked Dan, slowly.

"Me?" said Corky, "Ah, no. I rock myself to sleep each night counting that bonus, old chap." He would never have admitted to honour, though the Crown Jewels of the old prospector were a temptation.

Sinbad came into the gathering. "You know, Dan," he said, full of excitement, "I saw dozens of horses. Just dozens! and not ours, all grazing out beyond that gully where Jacky killed the kangaroo. I was sneaking along thinking I might get a shot at one myself when I saw these horses. They saw me and they galloped off, but not far!"

"Horses! Whee-ee!" exclaimed Helen.

"Brumbies," said Dan. "Wild horses. No use to us."

"I'd best go out and shoot the stallion," said Bill, "or he'll cut out our mares."

"But horses!" said Sinbad. "Why shoot them, Bill? Isn't it horses we need? Why can't we catch a few?"

"Tell him," said Bill wearily.

"Tell him—hell," said Corky, suddenly. "The kid's got the right idea. Why not? It's worth a go."

"Brumbies," said Bill. "Brumbies. The only good a man ever got out of brumbies was the worth of their hides. That's all the good brumbies are. Ruin your best horses, break your own legs getting them, and then they're no good to you. Brumbies!"

"It's been done," admitted Dan. He was not enthusiastic.

"Been done! Too right it's been done."

"Not by you, surely, Corky?" asked Bill sceptically.

"Not by me." He laughed, remembering. "But it was done all the same," said Corky. "Not the word of a lie. It was in the Downs country south of the Gulf and an anthropoidal old professor came up to me wanting horses and I sold him as wild a bunch of brumbies as you ever got within five miles of. And what did he do? He made money on them, the stinker. Caught them, used them, and sold them afterwards. I took a hundred off him and he got a clean four hundred on the lot of them after all the exes were paid. Never gave me a penny of it, the old ——."

"Some of the old-timers weren't bad at it," admitted Bill, grudgingly.

"This was a bloody new chum, green as grass," said Corky. "That's what made it hard. A new chum and a couple of abos."

"I bet he was six months breaking them in," said Bill.

"Three months," said Corky.

"That's no good to us, then," said Bill.

"Wait a bit," said Dan. "How many did he break, Corky?"

"About a hundred."

"A dozen would do us."

They all thought it over.

"We'll give it a go," said Dan at last. "What's the routine, Corky?"

"Damn foolery," said Bill angrily. "Just something for nothing rubbish. It won't work."

"It might work," said Dan, "it might."

"A gamble," said Bill. "Go to all that trouble, miss them the first time and they're off for keeps."

"We'd be no worse off," said Dan.

"A week worse off," said Bill.

"And maybe five weeks and fresh horses better off," said Dan, "and in the meantime the cattle rest up. There's feed here for three weeks."

"O.K., O.K.," said Bill crabbily, "you're the boss. But it's a flaming wild goose chase to me. You'll lose out. You'll see."

"I'll take you," said Corky. "Five to three. And the first one we catch will be Wild Goose——."

"Out of Corky's Folly," said Dan.

"By Flaming Gamble," said Helen.

Ma took her by the ear. "You ought to be in bed," she said.

As Helen went off she called back, "We'll put it in the Melbourne Cup, Corky." They all laughed.

"Seriously," asked Dan, "what do you propose, Corky?"

Chapter XVIII

IT took three days' hard work getting ready to trap the brumbies. Everyone kept well out of the way of the wild horses and the camp went about its business very quietly. Jacky and Nipper took it in turns watching them, noticing which way they came down to the water and where they mostly fed. The presence of the cattle on the other side of the long waterhole that went by the name of creek didn't seem to trouble the brumbies. There must have been nearly fifty of them.

The plan of catching them was to run out long wings of rope to which were attached fluttering white rags. When the ropes were tugged the rags would jig and jiggle very fright-eningly. These wings would run like fences inwards towards the watering place, which, as luck would have it, was a deep quiet pool with sandy shores, between two high rocky bluffs. Beyond the wings, on the other side of the water, the drovers built a trap, a square stockade that took in most of the water-hole and a strip of sand and grass beyond. The fencing of this stockade was not very strong. They had no time for that. Branches and bushes camouflaged it. "Horses that have never seen fences," argued Corky, "can be held by the slightest fence if they're sufficiently frightened. They don't try to crash through, they just run round and round. Before they get educated to that extent they're hobbled and broken in."

"I hope you're right," said Ma. She was as sceptical as Pa.

The most difficult part of the scheme was the gate. It was stronger than the rest of the stockade and built at the narrow-est part of the canyon, where the rocky bluffs approached most nearly. Dan had utilised a couple of trees that grew opposite each other to conceal it, and had propped bushes round the uprights and in an arch overhead as naturally as possible. This gate was held up by two ropes and could be raised and lowered smoothly.

The trick was not to frighten the brumbies till after they came down to drink. When they were drinking the scaring was to begin—the ropes pulled, the calico rags fluttered, a grass fire started behind them, and a general din created so that the one quiet way open to them was through the gap, through the gate and into the trap. As soon as they were in, the rope that closed the gate was to be released.

That was the plan.

There were many points at which it could go wrong. The brumbies might go elsewhere to water—though that was un-likely. The signs were that they used this approach regularly. Instead of running forward, down the wings, they might run back and there was nothing to stop them, save the howling men. If the gate did not work or were not shut immediately the brumbies got past it, but was open a fraction of a minute too long, then they would come wheeling out and away, beyond the wings and the fire and the noise into the free wild spaces. Once frightened like this they would never come again. Not, at any rate, while Dan and his plant were still camped there. It might be months or years before they got over their fright. Another big obstacle in the way of success was the natural nervousness of the wild horses. The slightest scent or suspicion that anything unusual was up and they would be off like the wind. They had got used to the cattle feeding and not having been molested and to the sight of men on horseback in the distance.

Dan drew the plan of campaign in the dust and drilled everyone in his or her part. The whole plant was in it. Nipper was left with the cattle. Ma and Mary had to keep the plant horses quiet and then help drive the brumbies forward. Sinbad had to light the grass fire, Corky and Jacky were on one wing, Bill and Dan on the other. Helen was out of danger of a stampede of wild horses and the flying hooves of the other riders high up in a rock beside the trap, but she had a most responsible part, to cut the rope that released the gate of the trap.

Dan explained it all to her beforehand. By dusk he had his gang planted and the ropes lying slack, hidden in the grass. In the absence of sheets the women had torn up old dresses, old shirts, blouses and the new dresses they had been keeping for the townships ahead.

"We can get more in town," said Ma, sacrificing her best pink floral. "Out here," she said, "time's something you can't buy."

"Or anywhere," said Mary.

"It matters more out here," said Ma. "It's funny that. Sometimes life goes on, week after week, season after season. A day or a week doesn't seem to matter much up here. We have to keep date clocks so that we won't lose count of the days of the week and the days of the months. If we didn't we'd get like the abos and tell them by the rains and the grass, the coming of the pigeon and the going of the duck and the migration of the grey geese. Yet once we get on the track almost every hour counts. Certainly every day. There's the rations and the way the feed holds and the distance between drinks. It's a silent race against time all the while."

"Down south," said Mary, they're always racing against minutes. If you're ten minutes late that's a black mark against you. Here, if you're within a week of when you're expected everything's all right."

"It'll be a matter of seconds to-night," said Ma.

"I'll have my stop watch on you, Helen," joked Corky.

They were all tensed up.

It was a dark and moonless night. Even the stars seemed shrouded. Dan moved very quietly giving his last instructions. "Don't be in too much of a hurry," he warned the sailor. "When you hear the noise start, Ma, wag the ropes like mad. They're heavy, but keep it up till I tell you to stop." "When

you see me mount and drive, Corky, you get to it too."
"Helen," he said, "you can make out the gate?"

"Yes, Dan."

"You've got your knife?"

"Yes, Dan."

"It's sharp?" He had seen to that himself, but he still wanted to know.

"Yes, Dan."

"Then when you see them all in, all of them mind you, let her go."

"What if they don't go in, Dan?"

"Then we're sunk, Helen."

"Oh!"

"All right then. Clean as a whistle mark you. Wham! As soon as they're in. Don't hesitate for anybody to tell you."

"Yes, Dan."

"Are you set, Bill?"

"Yes, Dan."

They settled down to a long wait. Insects made little droning noises close to their ears, moths flew on crepuscular wings right into their faces. "What's to do?" "Deary me," "Mopoke," called the occasional night-crying birds. Gradually a dimness of light appeared in the sky from the late-rising moon, and with the rising moon the first brumbies came stepping silently to the watering-place. Dan saw them first in dark silhouette. He nudged Bill and moved, thin as a knife cutting the darkness, to warn Ma. The leading brumbies hesitated; the watchers hardly breathed. Then a small mob of brumbies drew down to the water's edge. Helen could hear the faint slivering and sucking of the water going in their mouths. The sudden croak of a frog set her almost in panic. "Not yet," she said, "not yet." She had to grind her teeth together. A pulse began to hammer in her throat. The sailor on his tree watched. He saw the rest of the brumbies coming, a dark, quiet jumble of moving shapes, well down into the centre of the wings. He could see no more beyond. This, then, was it. He should have to give the signal. He strained his eyes, fearing to make a mistake. Then he tugged the signal cord.

Dan and Bill felt the first jerk. "Let her go, Bill!" "Let
her go, Corky!" The ropes danced with their terrifying
devil-devil rags. The men rode in shouting. Under Sinbad's
tree the brumbies crashed, racing mad and frightened. They
struck the ropes and wheeled, rearing and plunging back.
The shouters caught them in the rear. "Ten to one the field.
Even money Wild Goose. Wild Goose, come on!" yelled
Corky. Jacky let out a corroboree cry that would have frightened any opposition ghosts. "After 'em! After 'em!" yelled
Dan. The canyon took up the echoes. The din was frightful.
The brumbies wheeled once more and made straight for the
gap in the darkness, splashing through the water, aiming at
the silence and peace of the valley beyond this fearful
hubbub.

As she watched them come Helen prayed, "Oh, go in, do
go in. We want you. Do go in, oh, go in—" till it was un-
bearable. The last ones were just in and the first ones hadn't
turned back when she began to hack the rope with the knife.
It took seconds that felt like minutes. Then, just as Dan
shouted, the gate came down, "Crash!" just as he had said.
A brumby screamed in fear. The mob milled back. Helen
started to slide down off her rock and lost her grip. With a
thump she fell on Sinbad, hurrying underneath. She knocked
the wind out of him. Dan came up, running hard, to see the
gap was closed. Mary's cool voice spoke through the darkness, "They're all in, Dan. Good work, Helen."

"Good work everybody," said Dan.

"If the fence holds them," said Pa, grudgingly. "And
then . . ."

"Then we've got to break them," said Dan.

CHAPTER XIX

THE wild horse on his native plain is wonderful to watch;
there seems no other freedom to match it. With the sun
shining on the dark bay backs, the manes and long black tails
tossed by the wind, they stream from cover to cover, wheeling
and turning, unassailable in their speed, moved by needs and
impulses that the observer can only guess at, creatures of light

and motion, seemingly as capricious as the wind, their un-
bridled gait apparently as effortless and smooth as water flowing down a long sluice, their untrammelled existence and
their playful running about wholly delightful, noble and somehow indescribably poetical.

Until they are caught.

Then the now timid mares tremble and are afraid of every
hostile motion. Thirst rather than fear conquers them, some
quicker than others. The old stallions are shot, the rubbish
got rid of. In this case, since there was plenty of feed and
water and no station stock to consider, Dan simply turned them
loose again. All but one, a newly-born foal whose mother
was kicked to death in the stockade on the night of the cap-
ture. Helen kept it to rear by hand, on the bottle, otherwise
it would have died or been knocked on the head. Everyone
in the plant said it was folly to keep it, that it would be a
terrible nuisance, that it would assuredly die; but no one took
it from the child, who sat under the shade of the waggon
with the foal's head in her knees and her hands fondling its
fawny, tousled coat. "Wild Goose, this one is," said Helen,
"our very own little Wild Goose, Corky."

"A promising colt," said Corky, looking over the spindle-
legged little thing. He made a hammock from a bag to sling
under the waggon so that the foal might travel with them.
Dan didn't say no. He didn't say yes, either.

"After all," said Helen, looking sideways up at him from
under her long fair lashes, "we were very lucky, Dan." So
the outfit spared the foal as a kind of thank-offering.

The brumbies that met with Dan's approval were kept
corralled and hobbled with the old-fashioned strap hobbles.
There are many different methods of breaking horses. Some
are crueller than others, some take longer. These were broken
in the Territory manner, which, some claim, is adopted from
the South American method. In any case the approach afterwards is the same, the would-be rider crouching low and
catching the horse by the front fetlock, working upwards till
the bridle can be easily slipped on. It is as effective a way as
any and remarkably quick. In about a week of handling a
four- or five-year-old horse, broken in this way, will allow

himself to be caught out of a big mob of plant horses. However, it takes patience and skill and, at the critical stage, when
the horse is mounted for the first time, great courage, horsemanship and endurance. Bill, Nipper, Jacky and Dan took
turns at it. Mary broke one in. They each handled the same
horses every day for a week till Dan said they were good
enough.

It was hard work. Jacky and Nipper did the work of four
men, lunging on the rawhide halter as the unbroken horses
plunged and reared till the horses were worn out. Often it
seemed that the men would be worn out first. The stockboys liked the breaking in, although it was hard work. It
appealed to them, the mastering of something as primitive and
savage as a wild horse. They were very good at it, but Dan
and Bill liked to break the horses they fancied themselves.
Dan picked the toughest and most difficult, three or four
regular buckjumpers.

Mary and Sinbad watched for hours. Sinbad would have
liked to have tried but Dan wouldn't let him. "You're not
up to it yet, son," he said, with some of the old affection returning. "I couldn't risk having you disabled—you're too
good a man to lose now, now I've broken you in." Praise
along with refusal. Sinbad's ears burnt proudly. "Too good
a man," Dan had said, and Mary had heard him.

"I'm not frightened," he assured Mary.

"Of course not," said Mary. "Who thought you were?"

Nobody except himself. That was an old secret anyway.
Even Dan, who knew, seemed to have forgotten all about it.
Sinbad tackled him about it afterwards privately. "I'd like
to show you I'm not frightened of trying," he persisted.

"No one thinks you're frightened," said Dan. "It's just
a special sort of skill that takes getting used to—like ice
skating. Can you skate?"

"Yes."

"Well I can't. But if I was learning I wouldn't go in for
the fancy figure championships till I'd done a lot of track
work. Get me?"

"Yes," said Sinbad.

"Then forget all this tommy rot about being frightened."

Dan knew what he was talking about. That morning he sat the biggest and the strongest of the brumbies. Jacky brought it out with a bag tied over its head. Blindfolded and with the ears pinned back a horse is a bewildered fool—hence the good Australian expression, "Go and put your head in a bag." Dan mounted and then Jacky whipped off the bag and for ten minutes it seemed as if hell were let loose. The brumby put out every trick, pig-rooting, propping, rearing, tossing sideways, seeking to roll, dashing madly into obstacles to try to brush the man from his back. Sinbad was sure the horse would kill itself if not Dan. Dan stuck on. He stuck it out, the sweat pouring down his face, the thick shirt he had on drenched. He stuck on till the brumby had worked itself to a standstill and stood trembling; then quietly Dan rode the horse round and round. "That'll do," he said at length. Jacky slipped the halter and the hobbles on again.

There was a buzz of admiration from the watchers beyond the fence. "Couldn't you do with a nice long beer?" Corky asked.

Dan ran a tongue round his parched lips. Helen ran to get a water bottle. He rinsed his mouth and gargled his dry and clotted throat. "You'll have to wait till Anthony's Lagoon for that beer," Corky said.

Dan interrupted his drinking. "Anthony's Lagoon? We're not going there."

"By-passing it! Man, you're mad. We've come a thousand miles without a drink!" shouted Corky. There was no good humour about him. He was savage with annoyance and frustration.

"And we can go a thousand miles more, for all I care," said Dan. His tone was: "What I say goes."

"You like a drop as well as anyone," said Corky, angrily.

"That's the trouble," said Dan. "So do you, so does Bill, Sinbad too, I've no doubt. We waste a week—maybe more—and who looks after the cattle? No, I'm sorry, Corky, but Anthony's Lagoon is definitely not on the schedule."

"So," said Corky, "So."

But he was an old campaigner.

Chapter XX

THEY turned south-east again. They had been seventeen days at Paddy's Creek, but they had got fourteen new horses to replace those that Les and Charley had taken out of the plant. The cattle and the remaining horses had had a spell and were in much better nick. The creases had smoothed out a bit from Dan's face, his mouth didn't look so tight or strained. He used to sing again riding round the cattle, getting a lot of pleasure from the quality of his untrained baritone voice. He had a special repertoire of Territory songs, droving songs, blackfellow songs, and dirty songs that were so dirty they were almost clean. Sometimes he didn't put the words to them, but just whistled them through. Helen picked up the airs and whistled them too. Ma hardly knew what to do. She tried to make the tunes taboo, but that was too difficult. "I only know the nice verses, Mummy," Helen protested.

"Yes," said Ma, "but everybody else knows the others."

Mary raised her comical eyebrows at that.

Ma had to laugh. She compromised. "Well, don't sing it when there are strangers about," she said.

"That's not hard," said Helen. "Except for those abos on the Sugar Loaf knoll I haven't seen anybody the whole trip."

"You will," said Corky, "if we drop in at Anthony's Lagoon. I suppose you need more milk for Wild Goose?"

"Indeed we do," said Helen. "He drinks quantities. Just quantities."

"H'm," said Corky, "he certainly needs it if he's to do any good in the Melbourne Cup. I suppose you've got plenty in stock though, Missus?" he said to Ma.

"Well, we haven't," said Ma. "We're getting short of all sorts of things it's hard to do without."

"Pity Dan's so set on not calling in," said Corky. He had the technique of dropping the seed.

Later he had a word with Bill.

"I suppose you're checking the contract when we get to Anthony's Lagoon, Bill. Bert Malone only made out a provisional bill, didn't he? Wasn't there some talk of getting the government to back the first payment to the owners and to arrange for a further interim payment?"

"Search me, Corky," said Bill. "I only came into it at the last moment. I missed out on all that. In any case, we won't be calling in at Anthony's Lagoon."

"H'm. You might find you and your family working for nothing, Bill."

Bill swallowed the bait. "I'll speak to Dan about it," he said.

Mary was easy meat. "Lovely to get a letter, wouldn't it?" sighed Corky, sentimentally, as the two of them rode round the cattle that were beginning to drop into their familiar attitudes of repose as the sun went down. Sometimes the cattle took longer to settle than other times. It made all the difference if there were flies and mosquitoes about or if they'd had as much grazing as they needed, or if it were the night before they were watered or if the camp was what Dan called "a natural." This night they took time before they dropped and even longer before they slid into the relaxed posture they would hold, if nothing untoward occurred, till morning.

"Letters would be lovely," agreed Mary.

The sunset was amethyst and purple. There was a heart-shaped cloud of polished gold floating above a bank of solid indigo. The atmosphere was pure and translucent.

"Like a locket on black velvet behind a jeweller's plate glass window," said Corky, who always thought in terms of display. "I should get some letters too. Pity Dan wouldn't give us the chance to collect them. Only take two days at the most."

"There was someone who was coming in to Wyndham to say good-bye," said Mary. "I don't know if he got my letter telling him not to come."

"It's the overseas letters that matter most," said Corky.

"Yes, it's nice to hear from the boys," said Mary. "It means so much to them, keeping in touch."

At this moment it didn't clearly mean so much for her.

Corky dropped an ostentatious glance at her ring-finger.

To avoid his probing further she wheeled to quiet a steer that was taking a long time to settle down. That night she asked here mother, "It's a bit of false pretence, keeping this on, isn't it?"

Ma looked at the ring and then the girl.

"It's working very well, isn't it?"

"A bit too well," said Mary, half under her breath.

"Keep it up," said Ma. "It's for the best, really."

Ma herself favoured calling in at Anthony's Lagoon. "Give us a chance to get stores and to break the monotony," she said to Bill. "Give Mary a chance to think about something else." She had almost said "someone else."

The result of all these hints and conferences was that Dan changed his mind. He felt the group pressure and knew he was being yarded into a visit to the township, so he yielded with a good grace, but not without having a dig at Corky first. "How about you, Corky?" he asked one night when the subject of Anthony's Lagoon came up.

"Me? Immaterial to me, old chap. You know the cattle come first with me, Dan."

"That sounds too good to be true," said Dan. "I'll think it over," he promised.

Corky knew he had won.

*   *   *   *

The country was rough and it was hard to get any real work out of the brumbies, but the spirits of the drovers were high. Dan scouted ahead for likely camps and Ma drove the waggon a zig-zag course between the last of the great ant-hills. They were coming out of the ant-hill country that stretches like a band of latitude almost across the continent. Sinbad never ceased to wonder at these insect palaces that the Australians took for granted. They rose over miles and miles of territory, like solidified sand castles, crenellated and turreted in weird gothic pinnacles, mute monuments to the frightening industry of the ants. They were six, seven, ten, even fifteen feet high. Sometimes there were the broken-off tips of ones that had been even higher. The earth, red, yellow, or black, of which they were made was saliva'ed into a sort of insect cement that resisted the downpours of the Wet. Sometimes Sinbad took the trouble to knock one over or shatter it into big lumps to see the curious twisting galleries of the inde-fatigable ant builders. "From the insect point of view, they're a cross between the pyramids and the skyscrapers," he told Helen, "and they're a bit like a graveyard, too." He surveyed the plain, pin-pricked by these monuments. "At dawn," he told her, "when there's ground mist rising, you know what they remind me of? Stonehenge. Stonehenge is just as lonely. It's the most savage part of England I ever saw. The big stones the Druids used to worship with, grow out of the ground like something natural, the way these stone-like ant-hills do. I got lost once, when I was a Boy Scout, out on a cy ling trip, and I saw Stonehenge when I wasn't expecting to, when there were no trippers and no people to tell me what it was. There was a big thunderstorm coming up and it was like nothing I ever saw before—or since either for that matter, till I came here."

"You know what they remind me of?" said Helen. "Those pictures in books of fairy castles, and real castles perched up in mountains where knights were put in dungeons and trouba-dours came singing."

"Well," said Corky, "if you're going spooky, I'll put up a notice, 'This way to fairyland'. Then the next bloke who comes along on his own will really think he's going ding-bats."

He chuckled, working out ways to make the mischief seem likely, and then, having thought out how it might be done, imagining it had been done and glossing up the story as some-thing that had really happened, something to tell when he got with a new lot of people.

The group, so ill-assorted at first, had got to the stage of comradeship when their own company didn't pall. They had pulled off the brumby-catching together. That was a big thing, almost like the first flush of unexpected happiness that unites a group of lottery-ticket buyers who have drawn a prize. With the drovers the unanimity and the happiness lasted longer. Bill laughed quite happily at Corky's jokes now. He thought him no end of a good fellow. At the beginning of the drove he hadn't been able to stand a bar of him. "Just a shyster," he had told Ma. Now, in the evenings, beside the line of pack and stock saddles, he played his mouth organ while Corky unmelodiously sang Pa's own songs, "Drink to Me Only" and "Thora," or Corky's two favourites, "Madamoiselle From Armentieres" and "Jackie and Frankie."

Little domestic preparations went on for the township ahead. Mary heated up the flat iron and ironed her best blouse. Jacky was working down the thong of the long stock-whip he was plaiting. It took time. Helen started on her boots and her saddle. She wanted to get them looking like mirrors. Ma stroked with her darning-needle. She had plenty to do. The weather had got colder. The flies had gone—at least almost gone. The days were still hot and the nights brilliant, but from dusk till the sun was well up again it was very chilly. Jumpers and leather jackets had come out of swags. The hair on the bellies of the bullocks had begun to curl, their coats to seem longer, rougher, warmer. Dan got closer to the fire at night, reading. He had exhausted every scrap of reading matter they had with them—Helen's few school books, and even such surviving pieces of yellowed newspaper that had been wrapped round garments or stores to protect them. At the prospector's camp Corky had picked up a coverless old book from some outback circulating library of forty years before. It was the first volume, in small print, of "The Tale of Two Cities." Everybody, except Dan, said they knew how it ended, but when it came down to taws nobody really remembered the story. Dan watched Ma with a ravelled plait of darning wool, the beginning firm, the end knotted securely, but the middle a jumble of possibilities. "That's how I'm left with this story," he said, "but I may pick up the second half at the Lagoon."

"We should cut the North-South day after to-morrow," he told the camp. The wheels of the waggon had rumbled over nearly half the way, the stiff-muscled bullocks legs carried their owners all the way from the lush tropics to the half desert. Now the going on was almost automatic. "I believe," Dan said once, "Socks" (his favourite horse) "could take the night watch on his own."

"I had a horse like that once," said Bill.

"Don't any of you," said Dan, "try it on." Corky had a sweet little mare. It was as well to warn him.

CHAPTER XXI

NEAR the North-South road they caught sight of air traffic overhead, mostly like giant eagles, the Kittyhawks. The war came into their minds again, but high and far away, like the planes. Always the cattle and the needs of the cattle were closer. Until they came to the fringe of brown and dusty grass that marked the straight, long, dusty highway they had not seen a glimpse of the war since they left Wyndham. Nowadays the North-South highway is a river of sunshine-faded bitumen with the dust and the rocks soft or inert on either side, but then it was hard or soft surface according to the country it crossed and corduroyed in the bad places against the Wet. After the Wet there were always wash-aways.

They were on the move to cross it about half-past-three in the afternoon. For Helen it was like crossing the equator for the first time, only more so because here the line was visible, drawn like a dirty yellow crayon mark from horizon to horizon. Beside the road grew marsh grass with rounded stems and beyond that the silver-yellow of the Mitchell grass growing in wind-bitten tussocks. It had been windy and dusty all day and the drovers were anything but clean, their tempers held hard on a short rein because of the crankiness of the beasts. It was low scrub country, mulga and gidgee and smoke bush. Along the road from the South came a cloud of dust, moving too fast for bullocks. Dan, riding in front, halted the mob to let whatever it was pass.

It was a convoy of 200 trucks with troops, going north.

They rumbled and rattled past at the uniform rate of fifteen miles an hour, all camouflaged but of different makes, weights and sizes. The Army had been glad to get whatever service-able new trucks were on the market. Later on in the war heavy diesels were used and standard truck types for different service requirements, but in those times the road through had only been opened a couple of months, by pioneering bull-dozer units. These troops who passed the overlanders were the cream of the Australian Army then available in the country. They carried full equipment with them, and were seventy miles off the next staging camp. They were dust-dirty and dog-tired, but they gave a great cheer to the drovers, hanging out of the trucks, shouting and barracking. When they caught sight of Helen and Mary and knew they were girls by the checked shirts and the plaits sticking out from under their hats, they gave a great whoop of joyful recognition and the long sibilant whistle, straight from the gutter, of the hunting male. Corky tossed his hat up in the air, and all of them waved and smiled. They were singing, but only one word was audible, "Hardships—." Ma, her team drawn up and waiting to cross, got a special cheer all to herself. A staff car, leading the convoy, drew out and passed round to Dan to have a word with him. "The Japs landed yet?" asked Dan.

"Not yet," said the C.O.

"What's the big news?"

"The boys have come back from the Middle East and are holding them up in New Guinea."

The officer began to explain, but at that moment, with only half the convoy past, the cattle could stand no more of the din. They turned tail and scattered from the noise. Bill, who had been expecting it, galloped off with Nipper and Jacky to hold them further off the road when their burst of energy failed. Mary and Corky followed. Dan satisfied himself that everything would be under control and got the rest of the news briefly. In camp that night, four miles over the crossing, he told the plant.

"The Americans are sending a big army to help hold Aus-tralia. The Jap navy's taken a big beating. The advance Yank organisation has already arrived in Melbourne. They'll need this beef more than ever. The C.O. said he saw some-thing in the paper in Adelaide about cattle herds from the north, but he doesn't remember now what it said, whether there were more coming down and the government were taking care of them, or if there ought to be more coming down and the government ought to look after them."

"That's the way with newspapers," grumbled Bill, "they're supposing and supposing for so long beforehand that when it comes you forget if it was the same thing or something different."

"It makes a hell of a difference to us," said Sinbad, laughing and showing his teeth. You could hardly tell he was from the Old Country any more, thought Ma.

"Just as well you decided to call in at Anthony's, Dan," said Corky. "There's sure to be something definite there."

"Yes," agreed Dan, but non-committal. It was wonderful, he thought, how Corky put that "you decided" over, and how things kept going Corky's way. "You know, Corky, I bet you were born lucky."

"Lucky at cards," said Corky, "unlucky in love. I've been married, well—er—three times. Like a game of poker, Dan?"

"Not to-night," said Dan. "I've got a couple of books to read. The C.O. handed them out." He always dodged cards with Corky. In a normal plant Corky would have won wages and bonus in advance from all hands and left at the first opportunity with the takings. But Bill and Dan didn't gamble; Sinbad wasn't interested; Nipper and Jacky, even if they had been worth Corky's time, wouldn't have been allowed.

"I scored too," said Ma. "The kitchen was already at the staging camp, but a cooks' helper from a store truck at the back ran over with these." These were tins of peaches, tins of jam, tins of cream, and tins of tomatoes. Not many, but enough to make a welcome break in the diet. Dan had got some tobacco.

"Didn't they look tired," said Mary. "Poor things. It's very uncomfortable in those trucks. They've got a long way to go."

Corky put his head on one side. "I suppose when they looked at us they said, 'Poor things, they've got a long way to go. I bet they'd like a ride in a nice motor lorry'."

Helen laughed. It had been an exciting day. The noise of the lorries lasted in their heads a long time after the convoy passed by, the sight of cheering, crowding faces lasted in their dreams well into the night.

"The poor boys," said Ma, "going maybe to their death." To her the night sky was like a blanket over the grieving earth, draping all mothers.

"Poor boys!" exclaimed Corky. "They looked like prime fats to me!" The joke was too grim for anyone to laugh. Ma sighed heavily.

"At any rate," said Dan, "they need the beef. They must have it." He felt a further justification for his decision to overland the cattle, come what might. It comforted him and steeled him for what lay beyond. He was the commander of a little army of cattle and the enemies, time, starvation and thirst, were strong and subtle. He would need all his skill. He went out to see that Jacky was not sleeping. The wind had dropped with sunset and the cattle were resting calm. It looked like being a good quiet night. "Hullo, Boss," said Jacky. He was not asleep.

"Everything all right, Jacky?"

"You bet, Boss."

CHAPTER XXII

IT was twenty days later. The country was poor and scrubby with patches of spinifex. The best feed lay along dry watercourses where the water had remained longest after the Wet. No cattle had been down this part of the route for some time, and the feed was adequate. Bores had been put down at regular intervals by a previous administration, and though some of the equipment at the bores needed renewing and checking over, Dan's plant was able to manage. Dan kept note of which bores were in need of repair and exactly what was needed at each one. He thought that if other mobs were to be brought down, it would save time and many losses if the inspectors were notified early. He wrote regular short reports to the Federal Department of Commerce. He intended to mail these from Anthony's Lagoon.

The bullocks, all told, were in pretty fair condition. They had lost about twenty, six or seven of them in a bad dust storm on the edge of the Tablelands. "Another mob might pick them up," Dan said.

"Any mobs after us would have a bad time," said Bill. He had expected their own mob to be leg-weary by this, but they weren't.

"We've been lucky so far," said Dan. It was as near as he went to thanking Providence.

They stood on a slight rise, looking down on the little township of Anthony's Lagoon: two or three tin roofs, with out-buildings.

"Thought there might have been a race meeting on," said Corky. He had been filling Helen with visions of grandstands, wonderful horses, colourful aboriginal jockeys, tall bets, crooked runs and straight owners. Her own colt, Wild Goose, was alive, but not doing as well as he might. She was anxious to compare him with others of his own age.

"Breeding tells," Corky said, shaking his head over the brumby colt. "Maybe we'll enter him for the Newmarket and not the Cup." Then he explained learnedly that the Newmarket was tougher than the Cup.

There wasn't a sign of life at Anthony's Lagoon. The cattle camped beyond the township, and the four men and Mary rode down, full of impatience.

"Wine, women and song," said Corky enthusiastically, holding out his arms, "here I come!"

Dan gave him an odd glance.

In the post office there was another man, a cattleman, leaning against the counter while the postmistress sent a long telegram on his behalf. There was a woman with a sick baby in the repeater station down the line, and the telegram took a long time to send. Corky made to reach over the counter and look in the initialed letter boxes himself for his mail, but the postmistress, with a haughty look, stopped him.

"I won't be a minute," she said. She was the thin spinster type, and Corky said afterwards that she curled her hair every night with government red tape.

"You could never fatten her out of being a store," he said. He liked his women plump.

"Couldn't you just see if there's a letter for me?" whispered Mary.

"First come, first served," said the postmistress, indicating the stranger. "Mr. Carter's just in from Camooweal."

The sailor said, rather proudly, "We've come from Wynd-ham."

"Cattle all right?" asked the stranger of Dan.

"Pretty fair."

"They need to be," said Mr. Carter. "The next bit's bad."

"How bad?"

"The heart's eaten out along the route and water's short. All the Gulf cattle have been coming down in big mobs."

"I thought it might be like that," said Dan.

"McAlpine?" called the postmistress, taking her ear from the telephone for a moment. Dan held out his large brown hand, and into it she put a long, thin, blue, official envelope.

"That all?"

"That's all."

The stranger and Dan went talking out of the door.

"Now," said the postmistress.

"Parsons."

"Corkingdale. J. Claverhouse Corkingdale." Mary and Sinbad looked at Corky, astonished. "It looks beautiful on a cheque," Corky assured them.

"Maxwell?" asked the postmistress.

"Yes," said Corky, reaching for it.

"Captain Hector Maxwell?" said the postmistress, in a tone of cold disbelief.

"Certainly," said Corky, "that's me too." He put on an ambassadorial and ingratiating smile. It looked odd under his old felt hat. She handed the letter over, but said, "I hope there's no mistake."

"None at all."

Mary had three letters and began to read them at once. Sinbad stood by, letterless and lonely.

Corky disapproved of his correspondence. He glanced at it and thrust it away, going outside. "Contract all right?" he asked Dan.

"Same as before," said Dan.

"No bonus?" asked Corky.

"No mention of it," said Dan.

"B—— Malone," said Corky. "All belly and no heart. We save his cattle from the Japs and he lets us rot. Forgotten men! That's what we are." He kicked at a stone.

"You'll get your bonus," said Dan easily. He was more uneasy than his words showed. He felt let down too. "Mary got what she wanted at any rate." He smiled at the girl eagerly reading.

She looked up at him, smiling back. "Nothing special, Dan."

"Go on," said Corky, "he's having a good time with the English girls."

"Shut up, Corky," said Sinbad.

"All right, all right," said Corky, as if he knew a thing or two, smiling because Sinbad had been so quick to scowl in defence of Mary's supposed boy friend. "Come and have a drink. Man may let you down, women are sure to let you down, but wine never lets you down. Likewise beer."

"See you later," Sinbad said to Mary.

She smiled, reading a letter from a school friend. There had been one from a cousin in the forces, and a large, scrawled, provocative word from Bart Wells. "Man-shy?" he queried —and gave his full regimental address. The letter had been forwarded from Wyndham by air. Someone had been kind. He could not have known, when he wrote it, that she had gone overland with the cattle. "I'll get another one," thought Mary, "as soon as he finds out. He wants me to answer back." The corners of her mouth turned up with pleasure. She hadn't really expected to get a letter. It was amusing to keep the notorious Bart dangling. How could she answer him in his own coin? Say so little and so much? She walked away from the post office about a hundred yards and then turned back. The sergeant of police rode by. He pulled up and saluted her. "Dan McAlpine and my Dad have gone for a drink," she told him.

"Pretty thirsty job you've got," he said, approving of her. He rode on. "I'll look them up," he called back.

"Lock them up?" she called in reply, not quite hearing.

He laughed. "Look them up," he shouted.

She turned into the post office that was also the bank, and wrote out a telegram. It was to a regimental number and name and it contained one word and no signature. The word was "Foolproof."

"You'll have to sign it on the back," said the postmistress. She stared at the telegram form again. "Is this code?" she asked crossly.

"No," said Mary, "it's English."

The postmistress frowned. She was over thirty. Nineteen seems very foolish to thirty. "There are military precautions now——" she began.

"Let them censor it, then," said Mary. Her eyes were bright and her dimples showing, though she pressed her lips together to stop them.

"It is the silliest telegram I ever sent," said the postmistress. "One and a penny, please." She stamped it angrily.

Mary got on her horse this time and rode away. The further she rode the more she agreed with the postmistress. It was silly to have sent it. Everyone who handled it would gossip about it. She galloped off, penalising herself and her horse in the hot afternoon. But by the time she got back to camp she had worked off her worry about it. It was only a joke. Bart would take it the right way. Old people were so clever and sensible they never had any fun.

"Where are the others?" asked Ma.

"Having a drink."

"Any news about the contract?"

"I think Dan got a letter," said Mary.

"So vague," thought Ma. "At her age I had much more sense."

"Corky's talking about forgotten men again," said Mary.

"Oh!" said Ma. "I'll give them till midnight," she thought.

Chapter XXIII

FOR the man doing the job the government always seems a lot of fatheads and slow, deplorably slow. It doesn't matter much which side is in power, they always catch the curses. Just now Corky was expending the full range and colour of his vocabulary on the so-and-so so-and-so's down south. By silence, Dan and Bill were agreeing with him. Sinbad was a willing audience.

Only those in charge of a government department can know why these delays occur. Politicians have their own methods. They feel the public pulse, take soundings, fly a kite, walk warily, talk it out with the experts, modify the scheme to suit the estimates, check it for precedent and for all the possible ramifications with other interests, mention it to the news-papers, accept praise or blame, and finally write the letters that give effect to decisions.

Then, when the men on the job have really given up hope, something happens.

In a modern office, with shiny wooden furniture, thick carpets and the filing systems, switch girls and secretaries out-side, a small, calm man man had just finished a long conference on droving cattle. The contracts were signed. Approximately 90,000 head of cattle were to be moved across the continent. What Dan had started other men would finish. Bert Malone, sweating, and with the disapproval of the general manager of his company, put in a word for the special bonus he had promised Dan. "Why not?" said the Minister. He saw him-self shaking hands with Dan at the end of the trip and a large photograph in some of the papers. "This man took great and special risks. It is largely on the basis of what he has been able to do that the Department is now prepared to go ahead. Give him any facilities he needs."

"In that case," said Gosport, one of the Departmental heads who was more closely in touch with the needs of the man doing the job than any one else present, "we should get a bleeder out to him as soon as possible. As far as I know the McAlpine mob weren't innoculated before they left, and there's been no opportunity since. He'll be getting into Queensland soon and we don't want any outcry from the cattle owners there. They've got enough pests of their own."

"Fly one out to him, Gosport," said the Minister, with the quick insight into the needs of a situation and the largeness of decision that had got him where he was. "You're in charge of all that side of it. Go yourself. It will give you a chance to survey the route from this end. Congratulate him from me, will you?" The perfect politician's touch, thought Gosport. The Minister left the conference room for lunch, satisfied with his morning's work and ready for a good, long, iced drink.

*   *   *   *

The beer at Anthony's Lagoon was not iced. It was kept in a drip safe. After the war, the storeman promised himself a kerosene refrigerator. The store had been shut for a long time and his predecessor had let stocks go right down and neglected making improvements. All equipment was still in the pioneering stage. But the previous owner had been a European, with a knowledge of and taste for wines. Liqueur bottles stood on his shelves that you would find hardly any-where else in Australia. The drovers did not like liqueurs, they stuck to beer. "I'll let them have another three bottles," thought the storeman. Beer was hard to get. He sold it at six bob a bottle.

Corky was still talking about forgotten men. "Two bob per head, per hundred miles. That's a hundred pounds for a hundred miles, for a thousand heads. Sounds good, doesn't it? Just like a little walk-over, just a Sunday school picnic from here to there. Some josser, in Sydney, measures the miles and he says, 'These b—— drovers are rolling in dough; forget 'em', and every time a bleeding bullock drops that's two bob a hundred miles that same poor bleeding drover won't get. I wouldn't walk a hundred miles for two bob paid into somebody else's pocket—"

"You've ridden a thousand," said Dan. "Have another drink, Corky."

The contract lay on the table-top, ring-stained from the overflowing beer glasses. "If a bullock puts his skeleton down to rest by the wayside," said Corky, "he's got sense. You see what I mean, sense. Where's the policeman?"

"He's gone to perform his duties," said Bill, with a wave of his arm that swept a glass off the table, "inspecting way-bills for poor b—— who take on droving for a living."

Sinbad sniggered. It suddenly seemed very funny to him that the only day for six months they'd been away from the cattle they kept on talking about bullocks.

"That for them," said Corky, picking up the contract and throwing it behind him with a dirty implication. "Forgotten men, that's what we are." He broke into the song the men on the trucks had been singing, "Hardships, you bastards, you don't know what hardships are."

Dan took up the song, so did Bill. They sang it line for line, banging down the glasses with every chorus.

The storeman brought out one more bottle than he'd meant them to have. They had a thirst a thousand miles long behind them. Dust, flies, thirst and bullocks. The army got beer, but these blokes didn't. He felt sorry for them and sleepy himself. "This is the last, boys."

"How come?" said Corky, "We're still thirsty."

"The policeman's gone home," said the storeman. "You can't drink after hours without a policeman in the pub."

That was the sort of reason that appealed to Corky. "Quite right, too," he said. "Mustn't break the law. Come, friends," he said in his special Shakespearian voice, "hides, hooves, tails and away—the beer's off."

"It's the war," said the storeman, shutting up behind them. "There's not enough for anyone to get stinking any more."

"No matter," said Corky, "how much they need to. 'Hard-ships, hardships. You don't know what hardships there—are—'."

They stood on the top of the wooden steps by the verandah, their arms linked, their voices trailing discordantly up to the stars. Bill and Dan were steady, but very solemn, Corky was magnificent, at the height of his enjoyment. He should have had buskins on. Sinbad retained his disposition to laugh; he felt completely free, a man among men in some quite spacious planetary existence that had been under his feet for a long time now and that he hadn't suspected before. The stars, swinging low to the horizon, seemed like good friends coming nearer. . . . He caught his spur in a bag laid for a doormat and fell down the steps, dragging the others with him.

They sat up in a heap, nobody hurt, but the silliness of the entire universe suddenly hitting them hard. They began to laugh as if the same cosmic comic cuts were spread out before them. From a box under the shadow of the verandah a muffled figure rose.

"Come on, you lot," said. Ma. "We're moving the cattle in a couple of hours."

"Ma!" said Dan, getting to his feet and looking about seven feet tall in the starlight. "Ma, you're wonderful."

He held out a hand to the others and they walked giggling to their horses, still singing "Hardships." It hadn't been a bad night.

"A boose-up," thought Ma. "It's like lancing a boil. Unfortunate, but sometimes necessary. Corky will be good for another five hundred miles now and Mary will see Sinbad's only like all the rest of them." She excused Bill. Bill was different. Bill had had a hard life. Bill could take his liquor. Bill walked with her back to the camp, his arm round her waist, the horse tailing behind them. Now and again he spoke of contracts, but sleepily.

She made strong, hot, sweet tea. Nipper had the horses in. The cattle rose, switching their tails, stamping their hooves, uttering plangent bellows, disapproving of Man, of the track, of the inevitability of going on, of their whole lives, which were nothing more than a continuous thirst, a continuous snatching after disappearing herbage. They strung out, plodding on; in an hour they would fan-out, feeding. The sun came up, winking a bloodshot eye over the rim of the world; the familiar dust rose, the drovers sat in their saddles like leather men, saying nothing. Their whips spoke in snarls. Ma set everything in order, tidied up, broke camp, got the waggon going. It looked like being a hot day. She tied a square of green mosquito net like a veil over her old felt hat. The men pulled their hat-brims down, made sure their water-bottles were full. It would be a thirsty day. Anthony's Lagoon lay behind. Ma had got them going again in spite of the disappointments.

Chapter XXIV

They were crossing a gibber plain. The small rocks lay like outsize red button mushrooms petrified after a flood of fire from a million years before. The bullocks winced crossing it They put their feet down with the tenderness of a mob of ballet dancers in stained stockings whose tendons had been half cut through. "They're getting muscle-bound," thought Dan.

"Meat on the hoof," thought Sinbad. "I'd as soon eat an old, tired grandmother as these. They'll be nothing but string and gristle when we get there." He said as much to Corky.

Corky thought it over, but he only said, "I'll get myself a new set of teeth in Sydney." He had no idea of being funny. He spent quite a lot of time laying out his cheque and bonus to the best advantage. New suit, new teeth, new shoes, new friends. No beer, at least not much beer, till he had bought everything. Then the prospectus. Ever since he had met the old prospector in the hut he had been planning how he could launch out into company promoting. That was where the money could be made. Slogging along after bullocks was a mug's game. There must have been a verbal attraction in it for Corky, who loved words. Prospectus, prospector, prospecting, prospectus. . . . He had got a letter-writing outfit at Anthony's Lagoon, and on most nights when he was not too tired, he got out the old writing pad and licked the stumpy pencil, crossing out and re-writing and thinking hard how to make everything go his way without it being noticeable, and how to make his knowledge and experience and bonafides seem like paying dividends and director's fees at the same time. When he had written "golden opportunity" for the seventh time he crossed it out. "Sound investment and solid bottom," he wrote instead.

"Any mine you're in," said Bill, "would have a solid bottom all right. Solid rock."

"What's salting a mine, Corky?" asked Helen.

"A very reprehensible practice, my dear," replied Corky, and then explained in great detail and most convincingly how it could best be done in three quite different ways.

*   *   *   *

They needed day-dreams to get over this stretch. It was as bad as the man from Camooweal had said. There was little feed, no surface water, and the earth was as dry as a bone. The dust rose from it finer than flour, finer than bone-dust, sometimes white as a precipitate of calcium left dried out at the bottom of a chemist's prescription, sometimes grey as the ashes of a turpentine-wood fire, sometimes black and soft as soot without the oiliness that makes soot cohere, sometimes red as the wind-ravaged earth, the individual particles so small they would shake through a hair sieve, but clinging and sticking to hair, face, hands, and clothes, till it seemed the drovers had been dipped in a dry, red, powdery dye. This was the real bull dust country. Under the hooves of the bullocks it rose like the most expensive sort of talcum powder, hanging, tickling in the air, a moving pillar of dust that showed the dreary progress of the mob shuffling along in a red twilight, the sunshine quite clouded out unless there was a wind blowing. If there was a wind blowing it was worse for the drovers.

What vegetation there was was of the prickly and inhospitable sort, except for the graceful mulga with its pine-like foliage that hungry travelling stock had eaten to the height of their lifted muzzles.

The water was slow coming in to some of the bores. There was a mob ahead and one two days behind. Shorthanded as they were it made the big drag worse. Tempers got a bit edgy. Whips were not the only things that snarled. "Don't play at being a cowboy," yelled Dan to Sinbad once as Sinbad rode to keep the main mob from milling to the troughs where about fifty were watering. "Get off your horse and scare them. You ought to know by now when to scare 'em stiff."

"Shut your trap," said the sailor. He knew perfectly well Dan was right, but he hadn't thought quick enough. The instinct is for a stockman to stay on his horse. Sinbad wasn't yet a trained stockman, but he was getting that way, he was picking up the habits. He never walked now when he could ride.

"Hardships, hardships . . ." hummed Corky. He could easily get indignant, but he rarely lost his temper. When it came to breaking point Bill had a more explosive temper than he.

Helen was grieving. It looked as if the colt, Wild Goose, would die. It had walked well on many of the stages, springing about with a funny knock-kneed gait, but now the absence of any sort of tender grass, and some sort of deficiency in the tinned milk they were able to spare, showed in its debilitated frame, its apparent weakness, and its staggering walk.

Mary though less of Bart Wells now than she had before she sent her "Foolproof" telegram. She sometimes wondered if he ever got it, and in what circumstances, but the laughing face with its bright blue eyes and shocking red hair no longer disturbed her imagination. There was Sinbad closer at hand, and Sinbad, Mary could tell, thought of no one but her.

Nobody seemed to notice it. They all had their own preoccupations, drifted, each one out of his close awareness of the others into his own hard integrity of carrying on. If the bullocks sometimes walked as if they were mesmerised, so, Mary thought, did the drovers. Now they were no longer bad friends or good friends. They just lived from one stretch to the next, for Dan from one watering to the next, for Ma from one meal to the next. The aborigines were far away from any place they had ever known before. At night they camped a trifle closer, by day they scouted round, noticing, learning the landscape as a politician remembers faces and names that may be useful to him some day, as a shopkeeper remembers prices, as a musician keeps phrases, brackets of notes, snatches of pure harmonies in a storehouse into which no one can go but himself. The name, nature and condition of every bore Nipper could reel off at a moment's notice. Once Helen came up to him in a dry gulch where there was one sod of marsh grass lying pulled freshly slantwise. "My people do that," said Nipper. He lifted the tussock. Under it, and under it alone, and under no other tussock, was a tiny soak or spring, holding about a cup of water. He drank and covered it again with the sod.

"I would never have found it," said Helen, marvelling.

*　　*　　*　　*

Corky was still singing away, "Hardships . . ." He had made up a couple of new verses and loved them. The words

comforted him above the dust, the wind, the strong smell
of the cattle from some pea-podded bush they had eaten.

"We had a drink at the Lagoon,
We got there late and left too soon,
Hardships, hardships,
You don't know what hardships are.

Now Camooweal's a very fine town I'm told,
Where the beer is hot and the women are cold,
Hardships, hardships,
You don't know what hardships are."

Mary had her silk handkedchief tied round the lower part
of her face, walking behind the cattle. She could hardly see
for the wind and the dust. Sinbad walked beside her. His
blonde hair was reddened by dust and there was a rim of
white round his eyes, but the rest of his skin looked as if a
painter had run a brick-red flat-wash all over him with a
kalsomine brush. "I don't know how Corky can sing in this,"
he remarked.

"What?" asked Mary. The wind made it hard to hear.
Sinbad's words were blown away before they reached her.

"I don't know how Corky can sing!"

"Why not? We're getting near the border hills. Look.
Over there. Won't be long now," she shouted back to en-
courage him.

"I'll be sorry when it's over."

"When this is over?" Her glance implied the wind, the
cold, the dust, the awfulness of everything. Her eyes smiled.

"When the trip is over."

"You'll be going back to England."

"I might try for a shore billet here. I like Australia."

"Well, you've swallowed enough of it."

"If I stayed here, Mary, how about you?"

"Me? I'll follow the cattle with Pa, I suppose."

"Can I come too?"

She stopped, suddenly angry. "Look here," she said, "this
is just fun for you, an adventure you'll talk about in a pub
some day, but with us the cattle are our living—we've got
to go with them. You don't really want to go on droving."

"Oh, yes I do, Mary."

"You only think you do."

"I mean it."

His eyes said what his tongue found difficult.

She gathered up the reins and said lightly, "You'll change your mind when we come to port, see if you don't." Then, suddenly, she leaned forward and added, pressing his hand, "But no drove will ever be like this one—for me," and galloped off.

They camped early that night, the horses and riders exhausted as much as the cattle. Wood was very scarce. Nipper came in with some brigalow that burns when green and Helen brought in some dry grey branches and a pocket full of kindling. She was singing.

> "I've just come down from Darwin town,
> Where the men are black and the girls are brown,
> Hardships, hardships . . ."

"Helen," snapped Ma, "I thought I told you—"

"Yes, Mother," said Helen. She stopped singing and only whistled the next verse. "Where's Wild Goose?" she asked.

"With the other horses, I think," said Ma. "He was running behind for a while and then I lost him in the dust."

But Wild Goose was not with the other horses. Helen, with Jacky, went back on their tracks. Two miles behind they found the foal behind a little clump of mulga, dying. Even Helen could tell it was the end. The foal could no longer stand on its feet, its eyes were filmed, and the rough coat was clotted with sweat and sand. Helen rested its head on her knee and tried to revive it with water from her water bottle. The foal swallowed a little and shivered. "Close up finish," said Jacky.

The tears were running down the little girl's face, but she did not cry aloud. It was getting late. They would have to go and they could not carry the foal with them, even if that would have helped. "I don't want to leave him to the crows, Jacky," she said.

"Leave him to me, missee," said Jacky. "I hit him, finish him dead. You give me matches, crow never get him."

She gave him several matches she had in her pocket, and patted the foal for the last time. She put a few grains of sugar on his tongue, but he did not even seem to taste them.

There was nothing else she had that would do any good
Sadly she walked through the trees, the tears coming faster
and faster. What everyone said about keeping the foal had
come true, but it did seem a shame. It did seem a shame.
Along the track a bit she sat down and waited for Jacky.
Sunset had gone and in the sky wind-clouds still raced, dark
clouds ragged as the manes of racing wild horses. The horizon
was misted with dust. It was impossible to tell where cloud
began and dust ended. The hills they hoped soon to cross
were obliterated, shut away by the ingathering night that
crept stealthily over the vast plain, the few stunted trees so
many lonely dwarfs in that wrinkled immensity of ancient
earth, earth the colour of bullocks' blood, a succourless bosom
of soil without covering of grass, an earth that denied nourishment to even one little foal, motherless and born free in that
land.

Then through the dusk a fire flared. Helen could see Jacky
moving to and fro, wrenching at scrub, hacking through it
with his knife, getting a blaze going. She saw the firelight
flickering along the black feathery branches, licking at logs
and shadows, turning the night into a cave, its illumination
spilling like blood on the thirsty earth. She turned away.
She did not want to smell the burning hide, or see the last
of her pet. As she walked in the tracks of the bullocks back
to camp she felt different, wise and unhappy, grown out of
the last of her childhood into the perplexing torment of girlhood.

She sat down in the suppertime circle without saying anything. Ma asked after Jacky, but nobody said anything about
the foal. She was glad they said nothing. Everybody was
tired and quiet. The brushwood fence against the wind was
stronger than usual. Pa thought the weather might break.
Helen looked up and saw Sinbad watching her. His eyes
were clear and understanding. They told her he was very
sorry about the foal. They said something else, which he did
not know he was saying, that he was happy about something,
unsure at the same time, tormented—as she was. His eyes
were the eyes of a friend, a comrade; they looked at her as if
she were only a little girl.

Chapter XXV

The aeroplane came in over the hills looking for Dan's mob It was the second half of the afternoon and the cattle expert, Mr. Gosport, had it worked out that the mob should be within the next twenty miles. The grass, dry and flattened, looked like the combed-down hair of a blonde, the hills in their hollows were already draped with shadows, purple over the green. From that height the spinifex looked soft as plush.

The navigator was getting nervous. He knew how deceptive that smooth golden sweep of plain could be. Under the blonde hair of the grass the rust-red earth was ravaged with gutters and channels. The smoothness of the plain was entirely fictitious; the grass grew in tussocks, bumping any one of which would slew around the large transport plane, tip it on its wings, rock it to a crash. "We can't land here," he said to the cattle expert. He went forward to the pilot, a sunny-haired, large-handed youth with a grin like a slit in a watermelon. He was hand steering.

The country flowed beneath them in striations of tone from biscuit to indigo. Outcrops of stone in the hills showed the colour of blood and iron. The plain ran up into the hills in a series of crumples like a loosely-held tablecloth. The plane dropped lower, searching. To Mr. Gosport it was like falling down a step in the dark. The bullock penned in the belly of the plane gave a sickening half bellow. It had been frightened at first, and then calmer, but now it was terrified again. The air crew made jokes passing over paper bags for it. One of them had a little housemaid's whisk broom which he flourished over the dung. "Never thought I'd be a cow hand," he said.

His mates chipped him on the "cow."

The plane passed over a construction of heavy logs that looked like blackened matches. "The old mustering camp. Good as ever," said the cattle expert. He had the nostalgia to be back at his old job again. It was all very well to have got on in the service, to have a couple of children and a nice home and superannuation when he retired, but the best years of his life would be those with the cattle, round the camp

fire at night, boiling the billy, and so on. He thought of it
with the sentimentality of a man who has got soft with office
routine.

"It'll be good work if we catch them within coo-ee of that,"
he shouted to the navigator. "Save a lot of time." The
navigator nodded. He had his heart in his mouth again. Fool
civilians who didn't know the risks they were taking.

There came a message back from the pilot. "Are these
they?"

Mr. Gosport squeezed for'ard.

The plane circled.

"About the size of the mob."

He looked through the glasses, trying to focus quickly.

"Seems like the look of the cattle." He had to make up his
mind; the decision was up to him. "We'll chance them. If
it's wrong blame me."

The pilot made a lower sweep, rose again over the hills,
came back hunting, rose and circled, swept in again, lower
this time.

"I'll try," he said, "for that hard stuff on the edge of the
grass near that cart."

"That'll be the chuck waggon," said Gosport.

Down below all hands were staring at the plane. "You'd
think," said Bill, " it wanted to give us a message."

They all waved in a friendly fashion upwards. Helen went
to her mother. The last night at Glenrichard came back.

"Wonder if it's a Jap?" quizzed Dan, his eyes following
the plane, intent.

"Struth," said Corky, "I never thought of that."

Ma patted Helen's hand.

"Might be a damn politician," said Corky, "come to congratulate us." His fierce sarcasm raised a laugh. "Pin a few
medals on your chest, Ma."

"Maybe they're in trouble," said Mary. The plane had
turned and was coming in again lower, against the wind.

"Going to land."

"Got its flaps down."

The undercarriage came down under the flat body like a
grasshopper's legs kneeling. The heavy pneumatic treads
touched, bounced, touched and the plane was down, dust

whirling behind it, the pilot stopping within ten yards of a rock that stuck tooth-like out of the wind-swept pebble-pitted plain.

"Done it again," whispered the navigator, his palms marked with the pressure of his nails. "Nice work, chief."

The young officer winked. "The thing about this sub-soil," he said, "at least it's hard."

The plant moved en masse towards the stationary plane.

"Nipper!" called Dan with stentorian lungs, "Catch the horses." The unsaddled horses had gone off, tails streaming, hard as they could make it away from the plane.

"Regular racehorses," said Corky, turning to look.

"Bloody brumbies," said Bill.

The big doors of the aeroplane opened. Mr. Gosport jumped down. Dan stepped forward. They shook hands and made themselves known. "Wasn't at all certain it was you," said Gosport.

"Why, were you looking for me?" said Dan, astonished.

"Well yes, we've brought you a bleeder."

"Kind of you, but why the attention?"

"With the Department of Agriculture's compliments. The Minister sent his personal congratulations. You've done very well. The Bill authorising the movement and compensation for all cattle from the north has gone through. You're to get a special bonus for the resource and initiative displayed." He smiled with the air of being on Dan's side against the world.

"You don't say?" But Dan took it with less astonishment than he might have a sudden fall of rain. The crew of the aircraft were setting down a gangway of planks. "Wait a moment, don't say anything to my boys. Just listen to what they say," said Dan.

The group out of hearing behind him had their attention fixed on the gangway. Corky ran a hand over his lips. For some reason he had the brain wave that an actress was going to get out. Mae West. Actresses, he knew, took turns visiting the troops. But instead of a pair of million dollar legs he saw a pair of horns, two ears, and the familiar outlines— a bullock.

He threw his hat to the ground, jumping up and down on it, waving his arms about and clamping them over his chest

as if he were in a land of snow and ice and would freeze to
death if he didn't exercise violently.

"A bleeder, Corky," said Dan.

"A bleeder be beggared," said Corky. "We've only been
bashing a thousand of the bleeders a thousand bleeding miles
and—there's no beer and all you can do is bring us a bleeder!
—a bleeder!"

"What's the matter with *him*?" asked Gosport, ravaged,
pointing to Corky.

"The climate," said Dan. "The dust's been like curry
powder the last three weeks. The only difference is it doesn't
taste so good."

Gosport laughed. The airmen climbed out. The family,
the drovers and the cattle expert began to chat and exchange
news. Helen climbed inside the aeroplane. The pilot let her
sit at the controls. "How long," she asked, "would it take
you to get to Wyndham in this?"

"About six hours."

"Six hours! Do you know how long we've taken? Six
months!"

"Ah," said the navigator, "but you get there."

"He's in love with terra firma," said the pilot. "He got
engaged last trip and he can't get home quick enough."

"You wouldn't get there quick if you rode," said Helen.

"Remember the tortoise," said the pilot. His face reminded
Helen of the Jack of Lanterns you cut out of pie-melon. He
was nearly as nice as Sinbad.

Gosport talked over plans with Dan. They would use the
old mustering camp for the innoculation. It would have to be
done in two days. There was not much water and a big mob
from the Gulf was three days behind them. "We'll have to
get a move on," said Dan. They drove the cattle another
couple of miles before sunset. Gosport said he would stay
and finish the innoculation. He looked forward to a couple
of days with the cattle.

*   *   *   *

"Makes it easier," doesn't it?" said Gosport as the first of
the cattle passed through the crush rails. As Nipper and
Jacky secured the head of each beast he made a quick injec-
tion at the base of the tail. He worked cleanly, with a deft

flick of the wrist like a man marking at billiards. They took
it in relays and kept the beasts going through. At night they
went back to the camp by the aeroplane. The air crew, with
the help of any of the drovers who could spare any time, had
been making preparations for the take-off. "Good practice
for a crash landing," said the pilot. He didn't seem to have
any concern about the success of his jump-off; he took it for
granted with such confidence that Ma had only the vaguest
idea at all that it was quite dangerous. She blamed the aeroplane for frightening the horses. It had taken Nipper hours
to collect them. He had been up all night.

*   *   *   *

All day, as the men worked, the galahs came around, sitting
on the fences like old grey wiseacres, then rising in clouds,
their red underneaths a sunset on wings, flying into the scrub,
and melting into the greyness of the foliage, their folded wings
making them almost invisible, nondescript prolongations of
branch and twig.

There was good feeding for them in a few acres of seeding
grass round a dried up watering hole beyond the mustering
camp. They flew down to feed and then, their crops full,
went back, a chattering horde of overseers, to see how the
innoculation was getting on. For some reason there were a
couple of strands of fencing wire strung between two poles
and on these lines the galahs did acrobatics, swinging, twirling
from their beaks, grasping and letting go, putting on a show
the whole time. They were like tumblers in a circus ring,
comical clowns, trained troupers of the air, jesters in a pretty
feathered uniform. "I've never seen so many parrots in my
life," said Sinbad. He wanted to catch one, to clip its wing
and keep it for a pet.

"Trust a sailor," said Mary, laughing, "to want a parrot in
a cage."

"He'll only die," said Helen. "You won't be able to get
the right seeds for him."

"In the markets in Sydney you can buy one for half-a-
crown," said Corky. "They're all over Australia."

So they talked him out of it.

But he was fascinated enough to try to. He tried to sneak
close to them and they let him come so far and then lifted,
jeering, their roseate umbrellas parachuting them to the
nearest timber. "Simply can't get near them," he confessed
at last.

"Haven't you ever heard of a cockatoo outside a two-up
school?" asked Corky. He explained the term by reference
to the galahs. "There're one or two always keeping watch
and giving warning of the policeman coming along."

"How like Australia," said Sinbad.

*   *   *   *

On the second night in camp one of those discussions rose
that are as sudden and devastating as a willy-willy. They were
all lounging round the campfire finishing their last cup of
tea. Sinbad and Jacky were out with the cattle and Helen was
fast asleep with her blankets tucked tight to her neck. Corky
had been doing a lot of figuring and talking with the navigator, who in civil life had been a stockbroker's clerk and
whom Corky had interested in his prospectus. He had also
flashed round a collection of semi-precious stones and some
specimens with the gold showing. He had actually dolly'd
off a little and panned it out in a dish borrowed from Ma.
"If it were false gold," he explained, "it wouldn't sink like
that. You'd have no hope of clearing it out from the sand."
The navigator had no objections to getting in on the ground
floor, as Corky suggested. A young man about to get married
thinks a great deal about money. He suggested debentures.

"What," asked Dan of Corky, "are you cooking up now?"

"Like to see our prospectus?" replied Corky, flourishing it.
Dan read it slowly. It was written across the long side of the
paper in bold blue pencil. The heading, in large letters, stated:

NORTHERN TERRITORY EXPLOITATION LTD.

J. Claverhouse Corkingdale, Managing Director.

CAPITAL   -   -   -   £100,000.

Objects of the Company.

1. To exploit the vast potential pastoral and mineral
   wealth of Australia's Northern Territory . . .

As Dan read his face grew grim. The lines wrinkled round his mouth, and he pursed his lips up as if to spit out something that tasted bad in his mouth. Corky, standing behind him, proud as Punch and rocking to and from with his hands behind his back as if he already stood on the directorial hearthrug, missed that grim countenance. Ma saw it. She could sense when things were serious, as she had the time of the fight with Les and when they were all in the grip of a crazy carelessness at Anthony's Lagoon. She got to her feet, prepared to intervene. This time it was Dan.

"Sounds good, doesn't it?" said Corky, cockily.

"Sounds damn bad to me," said Dan.

"Why?"

Dan read slowly: " 'Objects of the Company. To exploit the vast potential pastoral and mineral wealth of Australia's Northern Territory.' That's what's wrong with it." He tore the paper in two and flung it in the fire.

"Hey!" said Corky, "What's wrong?"

"Exploitation's wrong. That's the trouble with the whole caboodle down south. That's the trouble with the whole of this country from the coast to inland. We've torn the heart out of it. We've lost the timber and we're losing the soil. We're losing the rivers and we're losing the grass. All these getrichquick exploiters think of nothing but money, how to make money as quickly as possible, and not how Australians are going to live twenty, thirty years from now. Exploit men if you like, they can fight back, but the land can't fight back. Punish it too much and it gives up. The desert creeps in. I love the Territory too much to see it go the way of a lot of the rest of this country. And it won't take so long to ruin it. It's a peculiar country. It's got to be handled right by people who know it and can use it to the best advantage for the future as well as themselves."

"You mean leave it to the cattle kings?"

"I do not. I mean leave it to people like us, Bill and Ma, all the soldiers who'll be coming back once the war's over, all the ordinary Australians who don't want what you call the potentialities gobbled up by fatarsed exploiters."

"It needs capital," interrupted Corky. "You can't do anythink without capital."

"Capital only means facilities," said Dan. "If you give ordinary people facilities they'll make use of them. The tax-payer has the right to decide how this State ought to be developed. It's a national job, not a job for the racketeer. It's too big for a lot of mushroom £100,000 companies out to make quick dividends and leave a lot of heartbreak behind them."

"I like that," said Corky. "This isn't racketeering or senti-ment. This is business."

"A bad business for the country."

"Would you like it better if I put in 'scientific exploita-tion'?"

"I would not. That would be only inviting Dr. J. Claver-house Corkingdale inside." He put the accent on the "Dr."

Corky shaped up, but half-heartedly. "Oh, come off it, Dan. What did you throw the prospectus in the fire for? Now we'll have to write it out again."

"That's the way I felt about it," said Dan.

"You're an idealist."

"Better an idealist than a rogue."

"Dan!" said Ma, sharply.

"I'm not a rogue, I'm a realist," said Corky. The plausible oil of his good nature threw off insult like water. He had talked himself out of worse disagreements. "You ought to take a sporting chance on the future of this country, Dan."

"It's not a gambling matter. It's sober and conscientious enterprise."

"Hear! Hear!" said Gosport.

"That's what I'm all for," said Corky, "enterprise."

"Not your sort of enterprise, Corky. It's too big for you."

"Nothing's too big for me once I get going."

The row had fizzled out. Dan threw more wood on the fire and Mary got up to take her watch.

"Tell Sinbad to hurry or his supper will spoil," said Ma.

Mary zippered up her wind-breaker and combed back her hair. It fell loosely. For once it was out of plaits.

"A pretty girl," thought Gosport, "if she were dressed properly." "We're off early," he said, "I'm going to turn in now. Had a hard day and I find I'm not as used to it as I was."

"Good-night," called Mary, riding into the darkness. It was one of those nights when the air floats in layers, warm on the flats and colder where the currents of air have swept round and away from the hillsides. It was still except for the night-sounds of far places, the scurrying of little plains rodents and marsupials, the whinnying of a horse a long way off, the singing of Jacky, distant and indistinct, putting its thin, shrill stockwhip of sound round the drowsing cattle.

Then, closer than she had expected it, the sailor's voice rose, "Ye banks and braes of Bonnie Doon . . ." It was tender and sad and, like all love, foolish. As he sang the moon rose, large and red from the dust that still hung in the air, a lamp as golden as the 'one on the last night of Glenrichard. But for all it was there to remind her, Mary did not even think of that night at this moment. She rode towards the singing.

Chapter XXVI

SINBAD heard her coming and stopped. "Go on," she said, "I like it."

"I'm too shy to listen to myself," he said. He smiled at her. In the distance they heard Jacky still singing. He was singing one of those chants that go on and on in a minor key, a song about droving cattle and the moon carrying her firestick through the sky. "That fits in better," said Sinbad. They sat on their horses, listening to Jacky's song. The moon-light had given an incandescence to the night air, the sus-pended dust refracting and reflecting the beams so that the light was as though filtered through alabaster, what clouds there were moving in mottled and broken patterns without sharp highlights, so that the sky was like the dappled hide of a silver grey pony. "What do you suppose he's singing about?" asked Sinbad.

"About when his people were happy, I suppose, long ago when the land was theirs to roam on." She spoke as if some part of her mood was unhappy with the wistfulness of Jacky's song, as if her being was flooded with the sentiment of pity and unhappiness and forever aloneness that moonlight sometimes drags out of people ordinarily unemotional, as it tugs at the streams and underground artesian reservoirs of

waters that lie under the continent, on top parched and dry
and thousands of miles inland, but beneath responsive and
surging in unaccountable rises and falls towards the surface.

"Aren't you happy, Mary?"

"Sometimes I am and then I don't know. I get very dis-
contented. I'd like to be wild and adventurous like a man and
go on and on with the cattle, laughing and joking and doing
all the things that men do when women aren't about, and
then I realise that it's impossible, that a trip like this only
came my way because of the war and Dad and Mum joining
up with Dan, and Dan needing help so much that he took me.
Another few trips, perhaps—. But I'm not a man and I want
other things besides—."

"I'm glad you're not a man, Mary."

He said her name like a caress, bent his head so that his
cheek touched her hand resting on the saddle. He turned
his head so that his lips touched her flesh. As he was going
to kiss her hand, his other hand stealing up to hold her, his
lips touched the metal of her ring. The claws of the setting
scratched his cheek with the tiny menace of a barbed grass
seed. He lifted his head away from her hand.

"Don't mind me, it's the moon, I guess," he said, with a
roughness that pretended to be casual. "I really got off"—
now he tried to speak like a man in an office dictating com-
monplaces to an unattractive typist—"so you could have
Lassie. She is excellent on this sort of a night."

"Thank you," said Mary, "I like her the best of all we've
got—on any sort of night." Now her voice had lost its
unhappiness; it was the voice of the typist, the very attractive
typist, mocking her boss. Her face was in shadow under the
dapple of night, but her hair shone a little, tangled with
moon-shimmer. She slid from her horse at once, so close to
him that his hands ran up her sides and held her gripped,
under the armpits. Her head tilted backwards and her lips
were shadowed crescents. He bent to kiss her and her first
drawing-back was the sharpness of bush honey and then the
sweetness of it was all honey, the more delectable for being
wild and long-sought after. Her full hard breasts breathed
under his fierce pressure; then he loosed his embrace.

"Oh!"

"I've wanted to do that for a long time."

She put her head into the curve of his neck and he held her. "So have I," she whispered.

He kissed her again, but with gentleness, thanking her for the wonder of it.

"Maybe I should be sorry, but I'm not," he said. His fingers found the ring on her hand and twisted it so that the little turquoise heart went inwards to the palm. Then he pressed her hand shut tight.

"That—that's just Ma's idea of protection," she said, "nobody gave it to me."

"I thought—" he said. "You got letters—" he said.

"I have—a sort of cousin. He's very attractive. And there's a friend at the war. But nothing definite. They're really strangers—compared with the way I know you."

"Let me kiss you again."

She shook her head and moved back a few paces. He took her reins and, with his own, slipped them on a low branch, then he moved into the shadow of the tree. She sat with her back against the cobbly bark and clasped her hands round her bent knees. Her blouse was as white as magnolia and drew him cup-like. He lay beside her on the ground, his head touching the curve of her thigh. Her hand rumpled his crest of hair.

"Just a kiss can't hurt," he said, "when you're not anybody else's girl." He had the subtlety of surprise and kissed her below the ear in the curve of the neck and, as her body trembled, stirred in some secret place, his lips melted over her skin to her mouth. An electricity of desperate enjoyment flowed between them. Then she sat up, letting him hold her but determined to talk, to quench fire with talking. Every-thing was as before, the horses together, Jacky's singing further away drawing its slip-knot of sound round the couched cattle which are never altogether quiet, altogether still, but rest like light sleepers frightened of the dark and on the qui vive against burglars.

"It's silly," she said, "getting emotional like this."

"Oh, no," he said, "it's quite real—real as—" He looked around, but the night and the landscape and everything about him, except her, was quite unreal and full of the illusion, the make-believe of moonlight and the moth wings of a semi-luminous darkness. "Real as my boot." He tapped the leather against a stone and the horses moved, nervous at the sound.

She laughed with the deliciousness of the unexpected. "Oh, no, it's not real. It's just the sort of night it is. The stars, night after night travelling, and the moon, romantic as can be, and the journey. You know we've crossed half Australia together—such a long way. We can't help feeling like this. Corky says it's just chemistry."

"Corky couldn't feel like this—ever." He kissed her gently, softly as a leaf falling, with the tenderness of loving her and looking after her forever. "Why, I've loved you ever—ever since the first moment I saw you come riding up beside the waggon looking as if you didn't care a hoot for anybody, and as if it wasn't a road underneath you but the whole world— You can't imagine how you looked to me, just a sailor off a ship."

"I saw you," she said. She cuddled into him, her head on his shoulder, his arm cradling her waist, their breathing mingling. "I pretended not to, but I saw you counting those hobbles backwards and forwards all the time Dan was making up his mind."

"I got the numbers boxed," he said. "It was a wonder nobody else noticed . . ." They were at the first intimacy of lovers, uncovering their true minds. He kissed the vee of her chest, bare from the turned-back collar of her blouse, and had no thought yet of discovering further, the delicacy of innocence upon them both, the wonder of kissing for the first time sufficient.

They had forgotten the cattle completely.

To forget the cattle on a night watch is like taking one's hand from the tiller of a little ship in mid-ocean when the wind and the high waves tolerate no unpreparedness. It is the unexpected hazard that swamps and drowns. Mary's and Sinbad's horses, Hero and Lassie, had been harmlessly nicker-ing at each other, excited to a sort of instinctive love-play by their tethering together and the soft sounds of the lovers nearby. How could such sensitive animals, accustomed to respond to the slightest needs and temperamental requirements of their riders, but be disturbed by the unusual circumstances of the night and the breaking of their habitual routine? The mare cavorted coquettishly back and knocked the low branch with a distinct thump. Then out of that tree not one but hundreds of galahs rose, and out of every neighbouring tree hundreds rose, till the air was swirling with wings and the host of birds sailed like a grey magician's cloud over the scrub then settled down again, invisible as magic. They had squarked but little, moving with a collective eerieness, quite different from their daytime behaviour when they are all noise and nonsense; but before the first bird had time to settle the cattle were on their hooves, galloping madly.

"It's a rush," said Mary, on her feet and grasping for the reins and the saddle. "Look out, Sinbad. You keep out of this. I'm riding to head them."

She was gone and he stood for a moment nerveless, uncertain what to do. The cattle rushing on that hard ground sounded like thunder in a dark wood, like surf on a reef, like the falling of many great trees to the ground in a storm. He had Hero by the bridle and now he rode out and saw the cattle moving like a river over rocks, sharp and fierce and hissing with speed, their backs and their horns humping and flowing, pressing in the close hysteria of movement that marks a stampede which, like a flood, is folly to enter and death to be caught by. That insanity of animal fear is something that only time, distance and the science of the trained drover can check. Sinbad rode off wildly in the direction he believed Mary had taken, his impulse only to be near his beloved, to protect her, feeling and fearing with horror the trampling of the hooves, the tearing and rending of the horns, the crushing into nothingness of the softness he had held in his arms.

*   *   *   *

At the camp, silent after the argument, Dan sat by the low fire, turning over the embers with a stick and gathering his feelings together. He ought not to have got mad at Corky personally—it might have smashed up the entire attempt to get the cattle across if Corky had been another Les. On the other hand, he couldn't sit by and say nothing while parasites calmly plotted to nibble and gnaw, to white-ant with their flaccid rottenness and impoverish with their petty profit-mongering a territory that he saw as the home of a future nation, a nation of horsemen and bushmen, of cattlemen, miners and land developers, of natives who were happy and properly fed, not vestigial savages with sore eyes, rotting with pox and scratching with scabies and breeding out through malnutrition and heartbreak.

The stockbroking clerk he saw quite clearly as a parasite. As for Corky, he had always hated the city slicker in him. Corky was a man of two worlds, a bit too smart for the drovers and not quite crooked enough to do really well in the town. Yet it was quite possible that in an enterprise that required selling the outback to the town Corky would, for once, hit it off. It was that possibility that had made Dan tear up Corky's prospectus. Yet why he had acted so violently, without meditation, puzzled him now. "Getting my shirt off over a thing like that," he brooded. "I'd better take a dose of salts and run it out of my system. It's the dust and this hold-up with the innoculation that's got me down." He unrolled his swag and took off his boots, preparing for sleep. The navigator and Mr. Gosport were sleeping beyond the waggon, the pilot and the rest of the air-crew inside the plane. Dan listened for the cattle but could hear nothing. Because of the plane the camp was further off than usual. Dan settled his long frame, nudging a hollow in the ground to get his hip more comfortable. In a moment more he would have been asleep, but in the lulling of the senses before sleep he heard the noise that sounded at that distance as if a violent wind had sprung up, and was knocking over houses. He sprang to his feet, listening intently.

"North!" he shouted, "All hands, a stampede."

Bill, listening, shouted, "Straight for the scrub. They're going straight for the scrub."

Corky, struggling into his boots, demanded, "Who's on watch."

"Mary and Jacky," said Ma. She looked to the fire and saw Sinbad's tucker tin as she had left it, untouched.

Dan was back on horseback, shouting to Bill, "You take the right, I'll take the left. Ride for all you're worth. There's no time to let 'em tire." He was galloping even as he spoke; so were the others. The hooves of the horses drummed away, further and further, merging in the general roar that crashed like long rollers breaking on a distant beach.

"What's up?" asked the navigator, sleepily. He had been dreaming of twenty per cents.

"A night rush," said Gosport, the cattle man. He wondered if he should get up to help. But he had no horse caught and bridled.

"How do they stop them?"

"Ride round the leaders and flog them to a standstill."

"Pretty dark, isn't it?"

"They take a risk."

"Sounds dangerous to me."

"Damned dangerous."

Ma lay listening. She couldn't tell yet how it would go.

"If they get into that scrub," she said aloud, "it'll be weeks and weeks before we can round them up. If ever." But her worst fears weren't for the cattle. In a rush as fast and furious as this anything could happen. Bill and Mary were out there. She scuffled into her clothes and sat by the fire, waiting.

* * * *

The scrub was low stuff, myall and mulga. In front of it stretched clumpy, low Mitchell grass. There was a hillock reaching out in a goose-neck from the main ridge, with a huddle of big rocks where the goose-neck met the plain. Mary made straight for this point, cutting off ground in her race to overtake and pass the mob. She could see the bump of rocks sticking up like the door-knob on a door laid horizontal. The night that had seemed so bright before was grey and shrouded now, treacherous as thin, bright ice over dark water. Mary trusted to Lassie, the best night horse in the camp. She was creeping up on the cattle, riding hard, urging Lassie on, taking a chance on holes, rocks, crevices and logs. The mare could see or sense obstacles that Mary would never have seen in time or, if she had seen, could never have avoided.

Sinbad caught sight of her for an instant as she came up on the skyline beside the projection of rock. He galloped, less steadily and with increasing diffidence, his flamboyance of protecting changed to a lust to survive, to cut off the mob, to wheel the leaders in and turn the brutes; to ride, to ride, and to ride, not to fall off. This was like nothing he had ever known before. The horse seemed sailing on solid air, buffeting him against invisible obstacles, for Sinbad was not a good enough rider to feel with the horse, tensed and easy automatically, the mind free to think above the body's behaviour. Hero stumbled once and Sinbad was flung against its neck. He recovered his seat, but now his mind was divided between cattle and his own danger. Yet he galloped on, urging his horse clumsily. He passed cattle and more cattle. He was catching up with the lead, but he had no exhilaration. It was too dangerous. He had only apprehension. On the other wing Jacky was catching up, riding to point the cattle on the horn of speed. Speed was now something as tangible as distance and Jacky measured his distance against the speed of the cattle. His direction of speed was like an arrow feathering the dark night with the phosphorescence of haste. He would cut Mary's approach before the edge of the scrub, but just, but only just. The leaders of the cattle were still ahead, horns branching, hooves pounding, the panting breath of the following cattle a sound hoarse as air drawn through a mine shaft down into the ventilation tunnels, dark and invisible and noisy as water falling, a mirage of hearing, an emotion of insecurity and plunging fright.

Mary was into the scrub hard behind the leaders and Jacky beside her. For a moment the girl and the aborigine were neck and neck; then they drew apart, weaving, dodging the tripping bushes, the menacing boughs, their stockwhips angry above the hooves, threatening, cracking with curses, arguing with the familiar persuasion of pain and fear, calling on the leaders to halt with the established overlordship of armed warders among criminals; expertly reckless with their strength, their endurance, their mental dominion; demanding surrender; insisting with the voice and the horse and the lash, on obedience and pause. So the brutes yielded, falling into a slower trot, into the lesser panic of knowing what they were avoiding, into the turn back and gradual return, spent and slavering.

But Sinbad, caught in the scrub, not knowing how to dodge and duck, how to follow and how to stick on without thinking, how to ride light and sit tight, was as much at the mercy of the pitfalls and the branches, the trampling hooves and the entrail-spearing horns as the small craft in high seas whose helmsman has been washed overboard. The third time he ducked he was not quick enough. The bough struck him in the throat, knocked him off his horse, which continued riderless, galloping through the scrub, undirected, away from the commotion, well away, following its own instincts towards safety and peace. Later, when it had quietened and fed, it would trot back towards its mates and water.

Sinbad lay motionless, the whirlwind of sound drawing down on him in a cracking of branches and tornado of earth trampling. He lifted his head and saw cattle charging through the scrubby small timber and he had the thought that their eyes were on fire, red as coals slumbering, then he shielded his head with his arms and, heavy and earthbound as a man in a nightmare, he half crawled, half rolled into the narrow protection of a log a foot nearer the beasts.

*   *   *   *

Dan was beside Mary, the cattle turned, her stockwhip flaying the air and their hides indiscriminately. His big horse, Socks, was lathered with foam. Dan's whip cracked with the solitary belligerence of rifle fire, while his oaths streaked out with the regularity of bursts of machine gunning. "That'll teach them," he said. He noticed the girl's wrists below her short sleeves, fine and flexible and strong. She was slogging away at the still stupid followers-on who hadn't got moving back. "You did well, Mary," he said. "Good on you. We've got 'em now. I thought they'd got away from you when they touched the scrub. Another forty yards and nothing could have stopped them. It'll take time to pick them all up as it is, but we'll get them. You want to get back to camp?"

"Oh, no, Dan. I'm quite all right till daylight."

"We'll bunch them and drive them beyond the goose-neck and get them going down the route. They won't settle after

this, and we may as well have the advantage of an early start.
They'll tire quick enough once the excitement's over. Tell
Bill to check count. I'm going to comb through again."

He whistled shrilly to Nipper to give instructions about the
horses.

"O.K., Dan." She went after a group of cattle slipping like
thieves into the edge of the scrub. Dan hadn't enquired how
the rush started. No post-mortems. That was good old Dan
all over. It might, of course have been different if she hadn't
been lucky enough to help turn them.

CHAPTER XXVII

DAWN comes so often like commonsense into the world,
chilling it. Grey and cold on this morning the dawn broke.
The moon, like a spent witch who has outlived her hour of
power, dropped wraith-like to the horizon. The men and the
girl had the cattle going again along the stock route, a route
without fences for a thousand odd miles, a route which could
not be lost because the watering places, like the arrows on
marked trees, kept the direction safe and immutable. Where
the cattle went first, roads would go afterwards. War came
as the only interruption to that cycle of development in the
Territory. Under the stress of war, soldiers who were a little
more than men dug a route for themselves straight across
country, dodging the detours that cattle must take. They had
to dig a road because they rode in wheeled vehicles, and
wheels that can buzz through dust almost up to their hubs
get stuck during the Wet in a plasticene of soil more tenacious
than clay. The road from the Katherine to Wyndham went
straight, and soldiers pioneered it with the shovel, the axe, and
the bulldozer. They pioneered it in the Wet that came after
Dan and his cattle had slogged through following the stock
route that cattle and cattlemen had pioneered during the
eighty years before this war came.

Now back in camp, Mr. Gosport, the expert, was telling
Ma what would have to be done to make the stock routes
better, and the hazards for drover and beast less wearisome.
Scrub cut, gradings made and more bores sunk. He was saying

in cold words what Pa had been saying for twenty years passionately, but it had taken a war to make the office-sitters see it. "Why," he said, "on that very route you've just pushed through there are already men at work in the bad places. The orders went through a month back, and one of my assistants says the route's as clear as a tennis court in the thickest parts of the Murrangi."

The pilot said, "From the air they look just like outsize tennis courts, Mrs. Parsons, but I wouldn't like to land on them!"

"Really," said Ma. She was tired and had had a bad night. Sinbad's supper was still in the tucker tin, dried up to a frazzle. She was wondering how the men were with the cattle. Nipper had brought a message in about three o'clock that the rush was stopped, and all well, but Ma had a misgiving that she couldn't place. "I'm getting old," she thought. Now, when anything discouraging happened, she always felt tired. The untouched supper worried her. By rights Sinbad ought to have been in and eaten it long before the cattle rushed.

"Why wouldn't you like to land on them?" Helen asked the pilot. She was eating damper and plum jam and drinking black tea. The only stipulation Ma made about tea was that Helen only had one pannikin, and that it was watered down.

"Because I want to go home to mother," said the pilot, and winked. The air-crew was already at work on the plane.

"What do you think, Mrs. Parsons? Shall we wait to say good-bye? Perhaps there's something we could do for you? Dan might want something or other."

"You're taking his fresh batch of reports aren't you?"

"I've got those."

"After a rush," said Ma, "they're liable to be late for breakfast. If they come at all. As a matter of fact I think Nipper will soon be back with the horses and word for me to strike camp and follow on. They won't trouble to come so far back if they've got the cattle on the road again. I don't think you'd better wait. And don't do any stunts over them on your way home, please. It doesn't seem to worry the cattle much, but it does frighten the horses."

Mr. Gosport smiled. It was a long time since he'd met a woman as forthright as Ma. "Very well, then," he said, "If you think Dan will understand. These airmen chaps like to get going almost as early as drovers. Call you in the middle of the night, and you're lucky to be off by noon."

The pilot only grinned. The Air Force always had this complaint from civilians.

*   *   *   *

Out on the track Dan and Bill had finished counting the cattle. Dan made it that they'd lost about four, Bill that five were missing. "Mary and Jacky did well," said Dan.

"I said she was as good as a man," said Bill with satisfaction. The labours of the night had not tired him. He was the sort whom adversity strengthens. The day was quickly growing hotter—cold at dawn it didn't take long to warm up. Mary had discarded her windbreaker. She was tired now and looked it. All that had happened before the cattle rush seemed far away and, for the time being, unimportant. The really important thing was that the cattle were safe. As for Sinbad, what had happened between them seemed like a remote act of madness, a few kisses and the touching of souls drawn up like well-water in a bucket by the moon. Now, in full daylight she felt almost antagonistic to Sinbad.

If it hadn't been for him she wouldn't have let the cattle stampede. Nobody blamed her, but she blamed herself.

Sinbad? Since the ride to head the cattle and the round-up she had not had time to think of Sinbad. He had gone from her mind altogether, along with the consciousness of her guilt. Now, thinking of herself as guilty, she suddenly remembered the partner in her guilt. Where was he?

"Hey!" shouted Dan suddenly, "what's that horse doing there?" It was the bay, Hero, still saddled but feeding by a thicket on the edge of a box scrub. Jacky galloped over and caught Hero. There was nothing obviously wrong with him or the gear he carried.

"Sinbad was riding him," said Mary. "I changed horses at my watch."

"Follow the tracks up, Jacky," ordered Dan.

Nipper and Corky remained with the cattle while Dan, Bill and Mary followed on horseback. Jacky went on foot.

The track was fairly plain, but it took two or three hours to trace. Once while Jacky was casting round where Hero had evidently spent some time, Dan brewed a quart pot of tea over a little bushman's fire. It revived Mary. She blamed herself to Dan and Bill for changing horses, but they pooh-poohed the idea of that being in any way out of order. "The sensible thing to do," said Dan.

"When the cattle jumped up," said Mary, "he wanted to help head them, but I told him not to. He might have tried though—he's got some silly idea of proving his bravery all the time."

Dan looked at her, knowing what she meant about bravery and wondering if he put two and two together about something else would that make five. The implication that she had been talking to Sinbad when the jump-up occurred had quite escaped her father.

Dan said nothing. What really mattered now was if the boy were hurt or not.

They scraped through bushes and by stunted mulga hung with papery caterpillar nests. On the powdery soil there were all sorts of marks which normally on horseback they would see but never notice; the bird marks small and large, and the tail marks, furred a little, of sitting kangaroos; the monstrous wreaths of the ants who scaffold the rising domes of their underground nests with circles of twigs laid end to end so that the shifting dust will not blow in and keep them toiling endlessly at the same galleries. These same twigs crackle, too, under the movements of enemies. On the trails leading to the ant nests camped mountain devils, like horned pieces of grey bark, ancient as the acacias of that region. There were lizards too, of an appearance from before the flood, and big winged insects with triangular heads, grotesque as archbishops in uniform. They passed a green snake with a yellow belly sleepily sunning itself in a bare patch of sunshine. Dan did not bother to kill it. One more or less made no difference. When one searches for the death that may have come, one is very careful not to take life needlessly.

From antagonism Mary had passed into a mingled state of anxiety and affection. The remembrance of his wooing the night before had come warmly into her again. She could now not bear the slightest delay in finding him. Every time she thought he would be near the next bush or behind the next patch of grass or bare ground and he wasn't, she got more agitated.

They were travelling back, but at the angle at which Hero had wandered on his night feeding, towards the scene of the stampede. The tracks were crossed with cattle tracks.

When she thought she could bear it no longer they came on him. He was lying unconscious behind a log under a tree that threw a little spindly shadow over his body. There were the hoof marks of cattle all about, terrible mementoes of what had happened.

As they came close to him a huge eagle hawk, the biggest Mary had ever seen, rose from a short broken spar of dead tree near the fallen man. Before unfolding his wings he looked as big as a boy, as a decrepit old gold-spectacled doctor in formal frock coat in attendance on the dying. He rose like a bomber taking off, heavy-bellied, his streamlined wingspan eight feet across.

They all dismounted and Bill investigated with the slow care of the man who has seen this sort of thing before. He slit up Sinbad's pullover. Mary and Dan waited.

"He's alive," said Bill, "but badly hurt. Broken leg and fractured arm. Maybe some ribs too. He's had a bad crushing. Don't know what has gone beside. He's got a lump as big as an egg on the side of his head. Maybe that's fractured too. There's no sign of haemorrhage, which is a good thing. We'll soon know from the pain if he's bleeding inside."

"The aeroplane!" exclaimed Mary.

Without waiting for any say-so she dashed straight for camp. All the risks Sinbad had taken in the dark the night before she took now, but racing heedless, with no thought of danger. She had taken Dan's big horse, Socks, the best pacer. She dodged trees, scrub and fire-eaten old logs that were real foot-twisters, her mouth grimacing involuntarily, urging the horse ahead with every mental device she was capable of. "Make it, come on Socks, make it. Hurry up, hurry up."

She was not to the plain yet. From a long distance she heard a low, mumbling roar. It could be a tiny insect in her ear. It could be an aeroplane warming up. She brushed a hand over her ear and the noise stopped. A few minutes later it started again. It was the aeroplane! Warming up. That took time. How much time did she have? Time to save Sinbad's life? She rode faster, harder than she had ever ridden in her life before or was ever likely to again. She didn't have to goad Socks. He had caught the crisis of her need.

*   *   *   *

"Good-bye, then," said Mr. Gosport. "Thanks for every-thing, Mrs. Parsons. What about letters? Didn't that big daughter of yours have some love letters she wanted to post?"

"I wouldn't worry about that," said Ma.

The engines of the big plane turned over. They continued turning over while Helen ate another piece of bread and jam. The pilot was aboard and the navigator and Mr. Gosport. All the shaking hands was done. The pilot revved the engines up, paused, gave them another burst, then another. The mechanic pulled the chocks from the wheels and threw them inside the plane. Then he went and pulled off the tail lock, ran back, his clothes flapping, and was aboard slamming the big doors. With the engines now roaring the plane turned and taxi-ed.

"I wonder," said Helen, "if they'll make it? The navigator was dead scared."

The danger to others besides her own came suddenly to Ma. She watched the machine lumber, faster and faster, the roar unbelievable, like a clumsy earth-walking monster, down the runway the boys had been working on since they arrived. She held her breath, praying. Then it was off, like a ball that bounced once, and slanting, it moved heavily up. Higher it rose and turned, passing low over the camp.

"Well, I'm glad," said Ma, "they haven't got to do that too often. My heart was in my mouth."

"They didn't like the touch-down either," said Helen, also waving. "They wished us to billy-oh."

Mary came shooting past them on Socks, waving frantically, calling as if they in the aeroplane could hear her, "Sinbad. Sinbad's hurt. Come back, come back."

She could see, quite distinctly, someone inside the transparent nose of the machine waving back.

The aeroplane flew on.

"I knew it," said Ma. "I knew something was wrong. I ought to have let them wait." She saw again the untouched tucker tin by the fire. Who knows how circuitously, by an amalgam of irritating trifles, human judgments are shaped? "I made a mistake," said Ma. "If that boy dies, it'll be my fault."

She walked up to the girl standing staring at the aeroplane vanishing like a hawk out of sight. Socks was panting, blood dripping from his nose. He was all in.

"Mary," said Ma gently, "how bad is Sinbad hurt?"

*   *   *   *

Pa and Dan made Sinbad comfortable, gave him a drink and wiped his face. Dan sent Jacky for an axe to shape splints and for other necessaries. They heard the plane coming and watched it drone over and climb away, further and further, till it was out of sight.

"She didn't make it in time," said Bill.

The two men, on the same impulse, walked a little distance away from the prostrate Sinbad.

"We'll have to get him to hospital, Bill."

"The nearest station where there's a pedal wireless."

"That would be—?"

"Naracoota, I think."

"It's all in a hundred miles."

"That would be round by both stock routes."

"He'd die before he gets there. It's the fever that sets in."

"There's the old track out to the mica fields and then cut across from there."

"Hasn't been used for donkey's years has it?"

"It would cut off forty-odd miles."

"Think the waggon would make it?"

"Have to."

"There's the cattle. They haven't been watered for a day and a half, and it's another day to the next bore."

"Ma can manage the waggon."

"Up that track?"

"She'll manage."

"We'll have to lighten the waggon and give her all the water we can spare. She'll only have that one soak on the way, and it may be dry."

"Helen can go with her and look after Sinbad."

"Bad luck, poor chap."

"He was a trier, anyway, give him that in."

They spoke as men speak of the dead.

"Wouldn't it be better to send Mary? In case he needs her," Dan asked.

"We need her more. We can't flog those cattle along without her. There's nothing she could do that Helen can't," said Pa. "She's a good little stayer, that one. Never gets tired. Look, you go on with the cattle. Pick out the camp like you were going to. I'll keep Jacky and Mary and bring up Ma and the waggon as close as we can and pack-saddle all the stores except what they need, and make a litter and set his leg and arm as well as I'm able. We'll have something to eat, and when he's comfortable I'll get them going and then the three of us will come back and pick you up. They can send out a messenger from the station as soon as they arrive and have got in touch with the flying doctor."

*   *   *   *

It took several hours before everything was ready. Dan wouldn't leave till he saw the waggon right and tight for the hazardous journey.

In preparing the patient, Bill hastened with care. He had set men's legs before, and this fracture was not as bad as some he'd seen—the skin had not been broken. It was a mercy that Sinbad had been unconscious so long or had lapsed and relapsed into unconsciousness during his long wait, because it meant that he hadn't tried to move. "The knock on the head, probably," thought Bill. The bone ends grated under his hands as he fixed the limb. Sinbad was conscious now and he screamed with pain. Ma gave him brandy. Helen found Mary at the back of the waggon, her face in her hands, sobbing. She couldn't remember ever seeing her sister cry before; not this way. When they had bandaged and padded the broken limb on its improvised splint and done the same to the arm, and washed and bandaged the injured head and put a wide strapping across upwards supporting his crushed side, Bill said that was the best he could do, and the rest was up to God and the doctor. "And you—" he said to Sinbad, stroking his knuckles on the cheek of the sailor, "—you keep your heart up and you'll be all right." He smiled with the tenderness of a father towards the son he had never had.

"I'm sorry I bellowed," said the younger man, his lips twisting."

"If you hadn't," said Bill gruffly, "I wouldn't have known I was doing all right. Everyone bellows."

They lifted him on the low cornsack stretcher into the back of the waggon. "Gently does it."

Helen jumped up and squatted beside him. Only she noticed that it was the same bit of sacking on which the foal Wild Goose had travelled. She knew what to do. She had the vinegar and the leaf fan and the brandy and water. Dan leaned over the waggon. "Hold him over the bumps, little 'un," he said. "Hold him tight and don't let him go." When he's thirsty give it to him just a sip at a time. Doesn't matter how often, but just a little. He's a very sick man."

She nodded vigorously, her plaits swinging. He smiled. He had the same confidence in her that he had had the night of the brumby catching. "You're a good little mate," he said. "I'll marry you when you grow up." She grinned back. The joke reassured her for the journey. She mustn't let Dan down.

He went round to Sinbad's side of the waggon.

"I'm not much of a cattleman, Dan," said Sinbad miserably.

"You're coming on," said Dan. "It's the first leg hurts most. When you come out of hospital I'll sign you up again

—but at full rates, 'thoroughly experienced'." His face had the toughness and the dependability of well-worn leather, his thin smile stretched in cynical good-will. He finished rolling a cigarette. "You'll make it, chappie. You were game as Ned Kelly to ride that horse the way you did last night. Cheerio. See you in Sydney."

"See you in Moscow," said Sinbad faintly, and gave his first smile since the accident.

"The kid might make it," said Dan to Bill quietly.

Mary said good-bye. The sailor's eyes were heavy; he felt tired and drowsy again. He saw she was crying.

"Did you turn the cattle, Mary?"

"Yes, Sinbad."

"That's good."

"You were very brave," she said.

He moved his head a fraction to say "no," but his lips were pleased.

She held his unbandaged hand and squeezed it. "I would have come with you, Sinbad, but I have to help Dan; he needs me for the cattle."

"I'll look after him," said Helen, cheerily.

"I'm sure you will," said Mary. Then she bent over from her perch on the wheel and kissed Sinbad's lips. For a moment all the pain was sweet.

Then Dan said, "Right, you're all set, Ma."

Bill gave his last private word to Ma. "Don't spare the horses, Ma." She nodded at him, knowing what he meant, and cracked her whip. The horses, shouted at, took the strain, pulled in the first confusion of getting going, and turned their heads into the dusty track. The waggon that had once been a coach, gay with paint and with Her Majesty's coat of arms in gilt on the side, rolled back over the ground the catttle had already covered. The bull dust cushioned the jolts, the hooves struck dully, the waggon, light under its new burden, rode high and easily on its thoroughbraces, the horses stretched their necks and rattled their collars, Sinbad gave a little groan and then clenched his good hand tight and held his teeth hard together.

Chapter XXVIII

MA saw the next day come up, the dawn red as an inflamed eye, the sky blotched with scarlet cloudlets like the skin of a patient with fever. It was cold and a sharp wind lifted dust from the edges of the mountain in front of her and threw it like fine white feathers over the brink of the precipice. The near leader moved restlessly, clinking his traces. She went to him and ran her hand down his nose. The other leaders nuzzled towards her, but the rest of the team were asleep standing. She went to the little fire she had built between two rocks and brought back the bowl of warm mash, flour mixed with water, a little porridge oats and a sprinkle of sugar. She gave a small handful to each horse. In the back of the waggon Helen curled in her clothes under a couple of blankets, fast asleep. The sailor was asleep too. Ma had given him the second of the morphia tablets when she drew up for the night—the short night of rest she had allotted them. She had gone on, plodding after dark along a way lit by moon-light, the slow journeying easier for Sinbad and every extra mile a victory, towards the sharp crest of the ridge where it dipped in a saddle-back as if a giant hand had once leant there and carelessly pressed it down.

She had come on the old mica track before nightfall, which was a piece of good luck because if she hadn't she would have had to wait till daylight; she couldn't have risked the rocks and gutters of the plain close to the mountain by night. The mica track wasn't much of a track. It was years since those fields had been worked. They had closed down after the last war and since then no provision trucks or miners' lorries had rumbled over the winding distance. But the track was still discernible by moonlight, faint like the scraping of dead fingernails against the palm of darkness. The horses sensed the track better than Ma, jolting the waggon between obscuring scrub.

Now Sinbad slept and Helen was asleep and the horses rested, as horses do, on their legs, their heads down, their animal subconscious listening, their respiration regular as waves. Now and then one of them would shiver or twitch. Even though Ma had pulled up in the shelter of a hummock of earth and dodged the worst of the wind, it was still cold.

Ma had not slept. For the second night she had not shut her eyes. She was dog-tired but hardly noticed it. She had too much to do, too much responsibility to rest. She was like a midwife that waits through the long hours of pain for the birth, soothing, comforting, preparing. She had a can of broth and a can of porridge slowly cooking by the fire. During the four hours when the team had rested she had watered the horses from a canvas bucket as they stood harnessed, had made tea, had attended to Sinbad and eased the bandages, taking care not to move the limbs. She had talked to him, giving him hope, but it was clear to her that on this, the second night after his accident, he was in a high fever. She was thankful that the medicine kit had contained the palliatives it did. She would need them all before they made the out-station of N racoota, if they made it in time. She reckoned that they might get there in the afternoon of the next day. With luck. Always with luck.

Now she emptied the second canteen of water into the tea billy. The horses took a lot of water. They could have drunk more than she had allowed them. Next day, over the mountain, was the soak Dan had told her of. When they got there, she would send Helen to scout for it.

She made the tea and drank a pannikin, sugaring it well. The sky was lighter now, the inflamed scarlet of sun-up changing to pink, the colour of galahs' breasts. It was the galahs that had set off the succession of events that had led to Sinbad lying suffering in the waggon behind her. She judged from the clouds it would be a windy day, bad for horses and cattle. She wondered how the cattle were going, but automatically, her main concentration on the needs of her little group.

She poured off some of the tea into two quart pots and stood them near the warmth of the fire. She did not want the tea to stew on the leaves. Sinbad and Helen were still asleep. Let them sleep as long as they could. Then she went forward along the track, seeing what it was like and how she might best take it.

It was bad, worse than Dan and Bill could have known.

The track, scrub-grown and boulder-strewn, went up and down over steep humps and into gullies, gradually climbing

to the main ridge by the saddleback. She couldn't see that
part of it. What she could see of it, guessing by the contours
rather than seeing, was a sharp zigzagging up inclines of one
in four. Even when the road had been used, it had never been
graded. It was just one of those come-by-chance roads made
by the needs of voyagers in Central Australia. The team
would take it hard on the turns, they were so sharp. She
would have to get a pace up to make the hill at all, and she
would have to watch that they didn't get off the road on the
swing and fall down the mountainside, steep and littered with
big boulders. If the leaders went over it was good-night
nurse to the rest of the outfit. The wind whipped at her face
coming round a corner. She turned back, her hair blown out
of its bun and straggling over her cheeks. She could only do
her best, as Bill had done. Trust in providence lay like a sedi-
ment at the bottom of her heart. The exercise and the tea
had made her warm. She hurried back, fearful lest anything
untoward should have occurred in her absence, but refreshed
and confident. The danger to be faced, however terrifying,
would be faced in daylight and with full knowledge.

The sun was half an hour over the horizon when she got
back. "Half-past-six," she told Helen. "Time to get up. S'sh,
don't wake Sinbad."

Helen climbed over the wheel and stretched sleepily. She
drank the tea and ate the porridge her mother gave her. She
fed the horses with the rest of the mash. "Just something to
go on with, dears," she told them. "Now, Blackie, don't be
greedy. You're lucky to get any sort of tucker at all. No
more. All gone." She wiped her hands together and checked
over the harness. Ma put the billy of broth and the warm
tea into the hot-box packed with dry grass that Jacky had
fixed for her on the boot of the waggon.

"Finish the porridge, Helen. I don't think Sinbad will need
any." Helen scraped out the can. There wasn't enough water
to waste washing it.

Ma saw there was nothing left behind and put out the fire,
kicking earth on it with her boots. She climbed up stiffly.
Helen folded a blanket into a cape and put it round herself.
It was still very cold. She tucked the sailor more firmly into

his coverings. "You'll have to hold hard in some places, Helen," said Ma. "The stretcher's lashed, but he may roll over. You'll have to watch he doesn't go over the side on the turns, they're very sharp and I'll have my eyes on the road and won't be able to do anything to help you. He'll probably come to. It'll hurt him a lot, but he'll have to stand it. I won't be able to take it as steady as I'd like to for his sake, but he'll have to stand it. If he shouts or screams don't let it worry you. We have to get him over this mountain. He won't know he's shouting or groaning. That's all just part of a bad accident. Right?"

"O.K.," said Helen.

The horses took up their day reluctantly. Two of them sat back, not pulling. Ma flogged them. They turned out of the shelter of the camp hummock into the wind. The wind lifted their manes and they tried to turn their heads sideways against it. Some curiously-shaped grey rocks loomed high beside the track, their edges blunted by aeons of wind passing over, but standing all the same, aggressively suggesting that the waggon was creaking into a new territory, the land of minerals and miners, not of herds and herdsmen. Ma laid on the whip. She had to get a bit of spirit into the team. A flock of little grey birds flew up from the rocks, twittering, disturbed by their passing. Spinifex, lurid with mocking green and yellow spines, grew between the upthrusts of rock. The team began to cohere, responding to Ma's urging. They had struggled up the first long, steep incline. Helen, watching from the back, saw the plain below widen, marked with configurations and scrawling of rock, earth and scrub.

Before Ma was a dip, a turn and another sharp long climb "Watch out," she said, "I've got to rush this."

The wheels rattled and scraped, the waggon lurched from side to side. It swayed lightly, much too easily. It went over a big stone half embedded in the track and rocked like a board coming down over a breaker. But the speed held. The wheels held the road, the horses made the turn, stretched their necks, settled into the pull, their ears alive to Ma's goading, her harsh and relentless commands. She was standing up to it, her legs braced against the seat, her hands red and cold in

the wind. She gave the horses a breather at the top, then
plodded them on. The worst was still to come. There was a
dip and then a rise and then the worst of the zigzags. Looking
at them from here, with all the elevation they had gained, the
plain spread frighteningly below them, was like looking up
at the wayward scribble of a fool on a high wall. Good
enough for men riding on horseback or trucks going backwards up, in reverse to get more power, but for a woman
driving a waggon and eight horses—! She clucked and gid
'epped. Odd thoughts crossed her mind—that she ought to
have had a swig at the brandy herself before tackling the old
mica road; that this was just the sort of place where Charley's
"horse ghosts" would lie waiting to frighten the team, that
the plain below was like another beautiful safe world, and that
she was in a world of delirium and anaesthesia, that she would
re-visit in dreams for the rest of her life; that anyway it had
to be done; that the third stage of labour was beginning and
it had to be gone through. This was it. "Hang on, Helen.
Keep his head steady. It's rough, but it won't be much longer.
This is the worst."

Sinbad groaned. The groan hurt his ribs and the pain was
like rockets firing. His leg was a fiery darting agony, his head
thumped like a drum going in and out, his arm was a tightness
that pulsated. He broke into heavy perspiration. The drop-
lets ran between the stiff stalks of his unshaven chin. Helen
wiped his face and put the medicine dropper of fluid she had
ready between his lips. He groaned again, louder, the grey
moan of deep pain. The waggon bounced and their bodies
jolted jerkily to and fro like dice in a tight box. He opened
his bloodshot eyes, recognised Helen, and said. "I'm not
brave."

"This is the worst bit," said Helen. "We're nearly there.
You're very brave. Howl as loud as you like. I like it."

"The ruts," thought Ma, driving, "God, what big ruts."
They were eighteen inches deep and she wasn't in them. "If
I get in them we'll capsize and if I don't get in them we'll
capsize. The wheels slewed in to the ruts, but it was a soft
patch and they didn't capsize. A sponge of filtered dust
absorbed the shock. The zigzag came just then and Ma didn't

know afterwards how they made it. They plunged down for an instant and in that instant when the verge of the road was slipping from ·under the leaders' hooves Sinbad howled with the full and unrestrained sudden grief of a child. Ma was sure afterwards it helped frighten the horses back on to the track. The worst turn was over. They climbed out of the last zigzag into a steady slogging pull. Above them rose the saddleback. Seen closer it was a place where the spine of rock was crushed into two perpendicular walls. Ma halted the team at a convenient place on the inner edge of the road and pulled on the awkward iron brake into its last ratchet.

"How is he, Helen?"

"Doing all right," said Helen. She wiped away the tell-tale tears with the sweat and felt the sudden dignity of womanhood. If being an equestrienne in a circus was out of the question, nursing mightn't be a bad idea. "You're all right, aren't you, Sinbad?" She gave his hand a very professional pat.

"Yes," said that poor wretch and went swooning into his own lost world of pain.

"Phew," said Ma, mopping her own face, "I thought we were a goner then."

"I didn't see," said Helen. "I didn't have time to look over."

"Just as well," said Ma. She took a drop of the medicinal brandy and smiled at thinking what Corky would say if he saw her at the bottle.

They made the last careful grade to the saddleback and came down in easy stretches to the foothills on the other side. They kept a good look-out and saw a few cattle round the tiny soak Dan had spoken of.

They watered the horses, spelled them for an hour and went on. Time mattered now. A few miles along, when they were wondering which direction to strike out in, they met a stockman who galloped back to the outstation and got word through to Naracoota. There they just caught the evening listening-in session and relayed Ma's message: "Stockman with broken leg, broken arm, probable concussion, and broken

ribs, high fever . . ." The pedal wireless had caught the
doctor. He would land on the emergency strip in the morning.
Ma rested while other hands tended Sinbad.

There is no kindness like kindness in the outback, where
all travellers are the children of chance and where accident
and death are the common lot of man. If in those vast areas
need raises its despairing voice, then pity, like a magnetic
component, rushes all its resources to the lonely cry. Even
the waggon was sheltered and mended.

CHAPTER XXIX

IT was ten days before the outfit learnt that Ma had arrived
safely at Naracoota with Sinbad.

A stockman called Jim Drysdale, more familiarly Jimmy
Dry, brought the news. Jim was the same sort of drover as
Charley, but without Charley's extraterritoriality of blood. A
thin, sly, rather malicious type, always on the look-out to take
a rise out of someone, but good company if you weren't
depending on him for anything. He travelled along with
them for half a day and didn't realise till supper that Mary
was not another stockman. Nipper was now cooking and the
meal Jimmy Dry sat down to didn't warrant staying longer
with the plant, even if he'd had the time to spare. The salt
beef seemed tougher than usual.

Jimmy said they'd taken Sinbad to the hospital at Charle-
ville. Ma had gone with him and Helen was to get a lift by
army plane a fortnight later. The doctor had praised Bill's
leg setting, but they would have to wait for the X-ray before
knowing for sure that everything was jake. Sinbad had had
a bad shaking on the journey, but all things considered he'd
stood it well. The doctor thought he had a good chance of
pulling through. "Seems to have a pretty good constitution,
that bloke," said Jimmy. "They tell me he was a sailor once
and got blown up twice at sea. Must have had plenty of
guts to take on a trip like yours."

Dan's outfit sat like a family hearing one of its sons praised.
What Jimmy Dry said could be considered as the verdict of
the outback. Sailor had made good.

"And your Missus, too," Jimmy said to Bill, "she done a good job. There's not many women could have done what she done."

Ma got a lot of bouquets later, but that first one was the one Bill valued most.

They were now in the most critical stage of the drove. The beasts were poor and the route, as the stranger Carter had told them way back at Anthony's Lagoon, had been pretty well eaten out. The mob had to spread so far to feed that travelling was slowed up just when they needed to make most haste. For miles round each bore there wasn't a clump of grass, nothing that a bullock could get its tongue around. The windmill driven bores were full enough because there had been plenty of wind, but a couple of others, power driven, made very slowly and watering took longer. Even the most skilful drover could do nothing against that sort of thing. The men huddled into their wind jackets round the camp fire with mittens on their hands and balaclavas and ear muffs keeping the cold out. They talked endlessly on and on about what the government should and shouldn't do to shorten and improve the route. They had liked Mr. Gosport because he knew his job, innoculating the cattle, but they didn't think he was strong enough to stand up for what ought to be done against men in the government who didn't know what was required as well as he did. "You want an expert with the gift of the gab, and a bit of push to get anything through," grumbled Dan.

"It doesn't matter if he isn't such an expert," said Bill, "as long as he knows what's right to do and has enough character to stand up for what's the best thing."

Corky listened attentively. Since Dan had torn up his prospectus about the exploitation of the north he'd not come out into the open with any new get-rich-quick schemes. It took him all his time to get through the day's work. He'd led a softer life than Dan or Bill and now his age was beginning to tell. He missed Ma. His bad teeth played up in the cruel cold winds. She'd always taken the trouble to give him a tender bit of steak or make a special stew for him. Sometimes just before they killed, when the corned junk was a bit too tough for Corky, she'd make what she called "sop" or "poor man's soup" especially for him. It was damper, seasoned with pepper, salt and sauce, broken down with hot water and a lump of fat in it. Nipper didn't have the skill or the time to do that for Corky. He still had to get the horses in while Mary made the porridge and the tea. Corky was game, but he knew he wouldn't be able to make many more trips under such conditions. He'd have to think out a new line of work to keep himself going.

Every night when the cattle were bedded down, the drovers told what they'd noticed about particular beasts; there were some well-known identities among the cattle that they all recognised, old Crumple Horn and old Bally and old Sore Eye and old Black Ear and old Joe with the moustache and Send-it-down-Hughey and Whitey and Limpy and Wally and the Spearhorn with the Double Slit, and so on. Mary often came in after the others. She had the job of watching the weakening cattle that fell to the tail of the mob. Often, if she could get them to the camp, they would bed down with the others and be able to make the track in the morning, but if they didn't then they would be lost to the mob. If they found water on their own they might survive and be picked up by the next mob, but if not it was a perish for them. Dan had picked up a few mickeys like this and in his turn had lost a few.

There was a mob close behind Dan—a couple of days' travel is close—and he couldn't get in an extra day at any bore to rest his beasts or to travel them out and back to get a bit of good feed. He had to keep on. This was the biggest obstacle, apart from the normal hazards of hardship, starvation, thirst and disease, that cropped up in the scheme for overlanding so many cattle from the north at the same time in a poor season. On the earlier dry stretches when Dan had been worried and forced to seek native wells and soaks because of the absence of surface water, the cattle hadn't fared so badly as they did now. Then there had been no mob behind and a fair bit of the desert succulent about, parakelia, a low-growing, tough-looking, blue-grey plant with a little flower, on a stalk sticking sideways. This plant, like most succulents,

stored water and from its fibres the cattle got good nourishment and kept up their condition. Now, beyond the natural
botanical range of the parakelia, in country that normally
would have been much better grassed than other stretches
they had been through, Dan was up against it. After the next
seventy miles the country improved; a few more weeks on
the track and they would be at the railhead and, after trucking, in the first of the fattening paddocks. After a spell there,
the cattle, when they had picked up enough, would go to the
rich coastal areas for their final fattening. Dan, riding round
the mob, almost exhorted them. "If you make it, you beggars,
you'll have a year of plenty. Green grass up to your bellies,
over your backs. More than you can eat in a thousand years!"

"This is the last throw in the gamble," thought Corky as
he lay, full of toothache and what he called a touch of neuritis,
back to the fire and wrapped in all his blankets and with all
his underwear on, trying to keep the cold out of his bones.
He was in that reckless gambler's mood, win or lose, winner
take all, and be damned to it.

Bill had seen steadier men than Dan lose all on a chance
like this. He knew too much to work it out, as Dan did so
constantly, on so many miles a day. "The unforseen always
happens, if you do that," was his rather dour motto. He had
another that was almost as bad: "Hope for the worst and
you'll never be disappointed." He kept quiet about that,
however. Dan would have slung a boot at him if he'd talked
that way at this time.

An aborigine stockboy brought up letters that had come a
roundabout way from Avon Downs. What Mr. Gosport had
told Dan about the bonus was now confirmed in writing.
Corky was a little cheered by it. "I'll keep counting their
bloody noses," he said, "till we get there."

Mary had a letter from her admirer, Bart Wells, but though
she had angled for it and dreamt about getting it for months,
it now meant nothing to her, except the pride of having him
write to her. "Isn't there any word of Ma?" she asked
impatiently.

Pa wasn't deceived. He had seen that last kiss. "Sinbad's
still in danger," he said, "but doing as well as can be

expected." It was a wireless from Ma, transmitted by courtesy and by this time eight or nine days old.

"By the time we get there," said Corky grimly, lining one of his worn boots with a bit of soft hide, "he'll be well enough for the wedding."

"What nonsense you talk, Corky!" But the sudden sharp blush betrayed her.

"As a man who's been married three times," said Corky, "I'm against marriage"—he caught her quick antagonistic frown—"except in special cases—Sinbad's one of them."

Her brow cleared, but she said, "That was a hundred to one shot in the dark, Corky. You didn't catch me. You'll be calling your hunch 'Sinbad's folly' soon. But I can tell you it's a rank outsider."

"I'd take shorter odds. All men are fools," said Corky. She tossed her head as young girls do and went out on her solitary watch. They were short-handed in earnest now.

*   *   *   *

For days they travelled slowly, the route parallel with the border range that sank very old into the plain, like the tired vertebrae of an extinct animal turned to stone and soil. The wind had stopped and the midday suns were hot, but the air was as dry as a sucked sponge so the drovers' lips and fingers cracked and chapped.

A cattleman sees scenery differently from other people; he sees it not as a spectacle but as land to be traversed, as country of good, bad or indifferent feed, as devil country or high lands without water, as so much surface of gibber or sand or salt pan or pasture to be got over. His measure of time is the drovers' six o'clock to six o'clock of sunrise and sunset and his estimate of distance is based on the rate of travelling stock, the slow progress of hooves across a continent. For him there is nothing romantic about scenery except as it seeps into him and affects his disposition like a climate of the soul to which his body grows used so that his nature desires always change and movement; periods of intense activity and periods of drowsing rest and inactivity with the continual refreshment of being alone, away from his fellow man for hours at a time like a hermit or a priest at his devotions.

So, often, through spectacles of supreme interest to the poet or geologist or artist, he rides like a blind man, knowing only the essentials that are important to him, water and grass, and letting the rest go by in a sort of dream, taking notice of each in its course but vaguely; forgetting, when he leaves the forest, what a rain forest looks like; forgetting, when he leaves the semi-desert, the elements that made it so dreary, so numbing to his recollection; forgetting, till he sees and recognises it again, the familiar pattern of long grass waving under wind and dying out under scorching sun; forgetting, till he endures it again, the horror of parched earth and pant-ing beasts. While he is in one type of country it is as if he had been in it all his life, so habituated do his senses become to it. Only when he moves suddenly from one sort of country to the next does his mind react with the excitement a sailor has, making a new landfall. For the rest, it is all journey.

Now danger keyed up the tempo of their travel. Even Corky sometimes walked to spare his horse. Often the song "Hardships" was on his lips, but wearily, like a ritual to goodfellowship long gone by.

Nipper rode out to water the horses at the next bore. The condamine bells clanged and jingled and in the still, dry air the sound came back from the half-circle of mountains, as if another mob was coming in to water from the opposite direction. The horses clattered ahead to the windmill with the straight line of troughing stretching out from the turkey tank. A turkey tank is a bore with a storage tank strengthened by piled-up earth, so that the bore from a distance looks like a big brush turkey's nest. Nipper turned on the water cock and the water gushed into the troughing. The horses put their noses in and drank thirstily. Nipper had a drink himself. The water was cold and refreshing. He filled the water bags and the two big canteens that remained. While he was screwing on the caps the water failed and turned to a trickle. The horses sucked in the water at the bottom of the troughs. Nipper juggled with the water cock but no more water came out. The trickle became a drip. The horses, licking at the vanishing water, moved closer in to the tank. Nipper climbed up the earthen walls of the turkey tank and looked over. Only a slimy surface at the bottom reflected the morning sky. He looked up at the windmill, its large metal vanes still and black against the sky. There was no wind now, but if he connected the pump, wind, later in the day, might send the big blades twirling, their shadows moving sickle-shaped round and round like corroboree dancers, changing the spot of ground they danced on as the sun shifted and the shadow legs of the windmill grew shorter and then longer again as night fell. Then Nipper saw that the windmill would not move until it had been mended. The main shaft to the pump was broken clean through. Some freak of pressure or strain, some too-sudden change of temperature had found out a flaw and it was broken. It could not have been long done.

"What's up now?" asked Dan. Nipper had ridden back but was loath to break the bad news.

"It's no use taking the cattle on," said Bill. "We can't mend that. Even if we did mend it there mightn't be wind for another two or three days. Looks like we're in for a clear spell."

"We can't go back," said Dan. "That other mob will be reaching Red Bore to-night. How far's Argardargarda?"

"Three days at least."

"No good. It's water in two days or there'll be no mob. Just a thousand stinking carcases. We'll have to take them over the top." He nodded to the ridge of the hills, couched like a monster asleep, blind and tranquil and immense.

"They'll never do it," said Bill. He was aware of all the unspoken steps of the other man's reasoning. "They're bullocks, not goats."

"They're Kimberley bullocks," said Dan. "They've climbed hills before."

"When they were full of water and grass and hadn't twelve hundred miles behind them."

"They'll climb or die," said Dan, "if they're thirsty enough."

"If they'd been better-bred cattle," said Bill gloomily, "their legs and their stomachs would have given out before this. They might do it."

That was one thing about Bill, thought Dan, he was old, but he'd take a crack at anything.

Corky groaned and grizzled a bit about the bonus. "They won't need tombstones," he said, "their horns will mark the track." He couldn't see the cattle getting there.

They sent Jacky back to warn the mob behind and drove straight for the mountains. Dan had the idea that there was an old track that used to be used before New Bore, the one whose shaft had gone, was put down. He sent Nipper ahead to find this out and got the cattle going himself, estimating their chances. They were thirsty already, but not to the groaning stage. Then he went ahead to join up with Nipper and arranged how he would signal back to Bill.

Bill and Mary finally got them to the low foothills of the range by the noonday halt. Mary's eyes were puffy with fatigue. It had been hard work. Dan had lit a beacon of dry spinifex to guide them. The fire burnt a patch on the hillside like a cigarette stub on a green baize tablecloth. There was little smoke after the first puff of catching, no more than when a match is struck, but the intense heat ran like a glaze in front of that part of the mountain. Dan came down to get tea at Mary's fire. "Who was that bloke in the history book who took steers over the Alps?" he asked her.

"I don't know," she said.

"Someone I've read about," he said. "All snow and ice and throwing stones at some other bloke's army underneath them. Nobody thought he could get the animals over but he did and that's how he won the battle."

Mary still didn't know.

"Well, it's like that," said Dan, "except that it's us and it's not in a history book."

There was an old camel pad over the range and they used that. It was narrow and the cattle could only get up one at a time or two or three pushing together. In places there were nasty drops into dry ravines and any bullock that went over would be killed or injured. "What we've got to do," said Dan, "is to stop them bunching. Just keep them stringing along as quietly as possible."

The most difficult job was to get the cattle moving up the steep, narrow camel pad. Three or four times they bunched and rushed at the base of the ascent, breaking back down the way they had come, leaping over rocks and into patches of spinifex, hazarding their legs, their necks and Corky's bonus. There were really too few drovers to hold them from break-ing back and to get them moving forward up a track that their instinct told them was too hard. "Senseless beasts," said Corky.

"Mary," called Dan, "you take the lead. Quietly. They may follow you." With pressure behind that was what the bullocks ultimately did. "Whitey and Straighthorn," said Dan, noticing the leaders.

The whips and the curses of the drovers forced the bullocks on. They wound unwillingly up the hillside like a brown trickle of water transcending the laws of gravity. Plug, plug, plug, went their hooves. Out of crevices sun-warmed in the rocks, big 'roos started, bounding always upwards, away from the rising noise, stopping when they thought they were out of danger, balancing on their heavy tails, their tiny fore-paws hanging lady-like, their ears cocked against the violent com-motion. Then they were on their way again, leaping nimbly round and down, ten feet or more at a time.

Corky embellished his opinion of the bullocks with a few well-strung-together adjectives. "I'd change you all into flaming kangaroos," he said. The din of stockwhips and bellowing echoed back from the mountainside.

"Just as well these aren't the Alps, Dan," he said. "You'd have an avalanche down on us."

Dan looked at the rounded rocks sleeping in their pin cushions of green spinifex. They looked firm enough, but if the cattle ahead started any it would be a bad lookout for those underneath. "Couldn't have been cattle," he thought, "that bloke on the Alps, must have been camels."

The ridge they were breasting was twice as old as the Alps. It was a mountain range in decomposition, old as rotting teeth in the skull of Time. The rocks were wind-slippery with tempests that had travelled during millions of years head on, west to east, non-stop, faster than locomotives across the vast plains, the deserts and savannahs of the continent.

A man, helped by a horse, could have been to the top in an hour. A man on foot would have done it in under two, going from one rounded hummock to the next higher one over flat little tabletops formed by the detritus of ages. The cattle did it in four hours up and two down, and that was a magnificent effort. It was much worse coming down. A few beasts slipped down the smooth surfaces and were killed instantly. Dan had to push over a couple that were exhausted and fell, blocking the track. A few more could not be flogged up.

"It's for your own good," said Dan, laying it on. "Cruel to be kind." He hated taking it out of his beasts like this. Some drovers get to be unconscious sadists, but never Dan. His arm ached and his heart ached and time and again he was tempted to call a halt, to give it up, but there would have been no sense in that. Perseverance was the only merit. The cattle were really suffering now; their saliva no longer drool-ing but dried up saltily and their mouths beginning to smell foul, their eyes following Dan reproachfully, their breathing turned to moaning when they paused.

Corky no longer mentioned his bonus. His fat old face crinkled into a sort of dry crying with pity.

Bill, of course, counted their blessings in a sort of negative hoping for the best, snatching consolation from all their reverses. "Just as well Ma isn't here, we'd have had to abandon the waggon anyway."

"Just as well Sinbad isn't here, he couldn't have stood this." "Just as well Nipper got a drink in for the horses first . . ." and so on.

They camped at the very foot of the mountains, the last cattle coming down in the dusk.

"Lucky to make it," said Dan.

They ate stale damper and cold meat and there was not much of anything, not even tea. There was no wood and no wind and little enough water. Nipper lit the dry spinifex and it went up crackling, turning the side of the mountain into brief glory and then dying out. "No more of that," said Dan. "We don't want to frighten them. They've had as much as they can stand. It's water to-morrow or else—."

Nipper hobbled the horses. He offered to ride out seeking water, but Dan said the dawn would do. The broken-in brumbies were very restless. "Don't want to take any chances on them," said Dan.

They used their own water sparingly and gave a half bucket to each horse. There was no talk round the fire. Each fell asleep without turning, bone-tired. The stars were large and pale as water lilies in a dark pond. The cattle lifted their noses, trying to smell out the distant pond in which the stars floated. They moaned all night, a veterinary ward full of pain.

They had lost eighteen beasts.

CHAPTER XXX

THEY went on after a few hours' spell-up, from long before dawn till near noon, the cattle staggering. Now their tongues had begun to swell and they moaned walking, their frames sunk in sudden emaciation, the red-rimmed dull eyes staring from large sockets. None had passed urine for twenty-four hours. Normally a bullock can drink from ten to twelve gallons on a hot day when thirsty. It was their fourth day without water.

Mary had no tears to cry. Compared with the animals' pain tears were a human luxury. She had never seen cattle like this before. She had to urge the stragglers on, and there were so many stragglers. Sometimes a beast would not rise. She left it. If night restored its strength it might yet come to water.

They were making for a line of trees so far on the horizon that for a long time Mary thought it was a mirage, floating double with the trees and the water upside down. But they were real trees and it was real water under them—a billabong that had not dried out yet.

Dan and Bill inspected it. It was quite a large boomerang-shaped stretch of water between crumbling high banks of what had once been a river, a river that might flow only once in fifteen years. The water was brown and muddy and there were the marks of many birds and animals round it. Their horses floundered in mud past the fetlocks as they drank at the edge. The half-rotted carcase of a steer lay swollen and stuck in the mud. Crows and eagle hawks flew up into the branches

"If they rush here," said Dan, "we might as well have left them to rot on the other side."

"It's a bad place," replied Bill. "We could lose nearly the lot here."

"We must water them in fifties, as soon as we can, and take our time about it," said Dan. "Lucky there's no wind. If there was a wind they'd smell it and there'd be no holding them."

"I saw that happen once," said Bill, "after a three days' dry."

They rode back to the mob resting. The drovers were asleep on their horses. "Plenty of water," Bill told Corky, "just like beer, nice and brown with plenty of body in it."

"The old brew," chuckled Corky. "Can't beat it, can you? Nature's best." He had got back his spirit and his optimism on the news of water. He and Mary rode to fill the water-bottles. Sweat and dust caked their faces. Mary splashed the water over her face and wrists in a corner as far away as she could from the dead steer. It was so hot on the plain, but here, under the trees, by this cats' cradle of leaf-decked liquid mud, coolness hung like the memory of all cool things, ice and rain and rivers in flood and brimming waterholes in the Wet.

"Lovely!" said Mary. This pool to her was the epitome of all things precious and rare. Now the cattle could drink.

Then there was a shiver that they did not notice in the leaves, a quivering that was not strong enough to be a breeze, a draught of cool air outwards sucked by the sponge of heat over the plain, a message of moving air that, passing under a door in a quiet household, would not disturb anybody, but enough to reach the cattle. How they smelt it Dan never knew. He saw them raise their tired heads, heavy with great fatigue; he saw them rise sideways to their knees and on to their feet; he saw a wave of disturbance pass through the mob like a thought, and knew then that this was it. This was where he lost his life and the cattle, or saved the cattle and his life didn't matter. That moment had come to Ma on the old mica road, and it came to him now.

Before they had swung into the rush he was among them, boring in, laying on with the stockwhip, turning them back, yelling to the others to stop them.

He turned them and they broke and came on again. He rode clear and was out on the wing with Nipper riding fast to the other wing and Nipper and he turned them again and the lead milled to the centre, and the sides broke out and the mob got away again with new leaders. Then Bill and Jacky got out and rode the lead down and turned them; but every rush took the mob nearer the water and what had been only suspicion of drinking before now became in their intelligence a fixed certainty. So weakness was transformed into strength. The mob found the heart to bellow their need and their frustration and the frustration was sending them mad. Out of their hidden reservoir of strength they summoned another effort and the four drovers couldn't hold them. The fear of the man and the horse and the whip was no longer enough. They were not fast and they were not yet in the last madness of the cavalry charge that waves sabres like horns and plunges into battle like a dying steer into a deep pool. That last madness would come when they saw the water and then nothing would save them.

Mary and Corky heard the thunder of hooves than which there is nothing more frightening to the first tamer of beasts —Man. In the very recesses of every man's being this fear vibrates and echoes like sound in a cave when every instinct shouts, "Run. Run for your life."

They ran for their horses, springing on them and clambering up the yielding, crumbly bank.

Lumbering across the plain with a tread like a circus with elephants, the broken mob streamed in stampede right towards them. The drovers on horseback were still clinging to them, their small figures wistfully impotent. Mary and Corky rode out to meet the charge. It was hopeless, of course it was hopeless from the start, but they rode out and Dan rode to help them and the mob paused with its collective head lowered and its breathing coming from lungs burning like fires and its flanks heaving and a bellow like a spear transfixed in its throat. To hold them by riding was to hold a paper bag full of water in the hand and expect it not to burst.

"Get off your horses," yelled Dan. "It's the only way. Get off and face them." His face was contorted with the agony that looks out of the painted faces in a thousand battlepieces. He sprang out of the saddle and thrust the reins to Mary standing. "Take the horses and get over there out of the way." His arm indicated trees beyond the water.

"But Dan—"

"Do as you're damn well told."

Now the four men stood facing the mob left without restraint, the heads of the cattle down, their pause momentary, their hesitation seeking a new channel, their thirst a burning torture, a thickening of the blood in madness, their dull brains functionless, and only one sense left sharp—the scent of water

The men stood between the water and the cattle.

The cattle came on.

They came slowly at first, then in a short rush and the men did not move, these strange half-beasts with two legs did not move. The frightened cattle paused again.

"The whites of their eyes," muttered Corky, "the whites of their eyes." He had his stockwhip held sticking out like a musket at the ready.

The cattle rushed again, but not so far. The ones in the centre were milling. The leaders hesitated again. An eye to eye battle was on, will against will. It is an old trick that toreadors have in the ring in Spain, to vanquish a bull with the eyes, to vanquish him before the last long sword-thrust into the throat and the brain, the bull falling without another movement. It is the most famous kill of all, and it sometimes comes off, in the big fiestas at Easter with the most celebrated toreadors. Without witnesses the four Australians did that now. They vanquished the mob in that eye-to-eye measuring of strength. Only those who have seen it know that it can be done.

"Now," said Dan in the first instant of the mass will giving way.

The four stockmen moved out from the billabong, on foot, their whips cracking with the savage old magic of command. They moved up on the leaders and the leaders pressed backwards, their four legs each obstinate in refusal to budge, and then they felt the pressure harder and yielded, turning, exhaustion in their throats and only death ahead of them. The mob milled but it was held. It was held as Jacky galloped up and rode a bunch off and as Mary brought back the horses. It was held as brown dead leaves are held together in a whirl of centripetal wind.

*   *   *   *

They finished the watering by midnight. Each animal took a long time to drink and some of them stuck in the mud with weakness and had to be towed out by the horns. As the breeze of evening freshened it brought in stragglers. They tottered to the water and were saved.

The drovers needed meat, but they didn't kill. They used the tins given them by the troops and saved for emergency. At the camp fire Dan made what he thought was a profound remark, "Elephants. That's what they were. And the fella's name was Hannibal."

Bill lifted his eyebrows. "The man's mad," he said. "It's been too much for him. Cannibals and elephants. He's delirious. Put him to bed."

They put him to bed. Nobody stayed up with the cattle. "If they're not b—— well tired they ought to be," said Corky. He had got round again to wondering how many were lost and how big the bonus was likely to be.

"The stunt came off," said Bill, "but it nearly didn't. Dan was lucky they were so dead beat he could show them who was master." He kicked off his boots and rolled into his blankets groaning.

"They were dead-beat crazy," said Corky. "I laid myself ten to one against. There was that big white-faced steer with one polled horn gave me a very dirty look. I thought he had my number. Mary!" he called out into the darkness, "Are you all right?"

"Yes, Corky," she answered.

"Sleep well, there's a good girl," he called back. "After this it's just like a stroll through a park."

"I hope so," she said. Then they heard her giggling— giggling in the sort of way Helen giggled.

"What's so funny?"

She put her head under the blanket. Two hundred miles to the railhead and he called it a stroll through a park!

"Tell you. to-morrow!" It seemed extraordinarily funny to her. She was a bit light-headed.

CHAPTER XXXI

WHEN Dan drew his cheque it was a big one. He sauntered down from the Commonwealth building and people looked sideways up at him as he passed. Six feet six and brown and seasoned as a good stockwhip, he was different from everybody else around. The clothes he wore were ordinary enough, chosen to be inconspicuous and comfortable, but the unconscious disdain with which he wore them, the buoyancy of his step, and more than anything else his height and his natural calm impressed people. Often they turned round to take another look. He didn't like it.

Corky was waiting for him on the steps of the old-fashioned family hotel where the Parsons, like all the other stock and station people in town, were putting up. "Hullo, Dan. Did you get it?"

Dan nodded. Corky was dressed up to the nines in a sombrero style hat, a checked lumber jacket, a gold whip for a tie-pin, and a super-colossal false diamond in a new large ring. He looked a cross between a millionaire mineowner of the eighteen nineties who had struck gold in Kalgoorlie, and the proprietor of a profitable divertissement at the Sydney Royal Agricultural Show. He was excited and anxious to get his hands on his share of Dan's cheque.

With one look Dan indicated the pleasant stranger Corky had just been chatting to and Corky said, "Quite so, old boy, quite so." Before Dan gave that look Corky hadn't had the thought of a confidence man in his mind. Now he walked into the vestibule like an errant steer that has just been heeled back into the mob. "Pa has a big suite no less," he told Dan. "Doing Ma and the girls proud. Says they won't have long in town, so they might as well enjoy it."

"Quite right, too," said Dan. "I'll be glad to get out, myself. Town chokes me after four days."

"It was grand getting a ride down in that aeroplane," said Corky.

"That's the way we'll travel back," said Dan, "to Cloncurry."

"You don't say!" Corky was impressed.

"They seem to think we did a good job," said Dan, "and there's more cattle to be brought down, so we're going back. Bullocks are more important than bullets—you've heard it before. The Parsons are all coming with me. I don't know about Helen—there's some talk of putting her to school. How about you?"

"Well—" said Corky. "When do you think you'll start?"

"In about a fortnight."

Corky's face fell. "That's not long, is it?" He wiped his mouth with the back of his hand. "Let me think it over will you, Dan? It's not that I'm not anxious to go with you, but there's just a chance—. I've heard they're making some new appointments to the Stock Board, and I've put in for it. Of course, if I don't get it I'll be with you with my ears back, but if it comes off—. You don't mind, do you?"

"Not at all," said Dan. "If you can fall into Easy Street all the best to you. You can let me know right up to the last minute if the job doesn't come off and you still want to come."

"That's decent of you, Dan. I appreciate it. You know I'm giving a radio talk on the trip?"

"I heard."

"Might help me get that job."

"Could do."

"By the way, what's Sinbad going to do?"

"He's with Ma now. His arm's still bound up, and he's got to have a few more weeks' treatment, but after that he's coming too."

"The whole gang, eh? Nipper and Jacky?"

"Yes, I'll be taking them back."

They went into the lift, a dazzling hotel blonde in stilt heels just ahead of Corky. When they came to the floor where the Parsons's suite was Dan got out, but Corky said, "See you later, old boy," and continued the journey.

Ma's sitting room was gay with flowers. The girls had new dresses. So did Ma. Pa had the same old hat, but he had his town clothes on, fresh from the cleaners, with creases down the front. Sinbad was pale and convalescent. He was brushed and spruce with a new hair-cut, and he looked as happy as the proverbial sandboy. Ma was being interviewed by a lady reporter who was dragging the words out of her. "Well, yes," admitted Ma, "I did have tea brought to my bed this morning, but I can't see how that could possibly interest your readers. As a matter of fact I was awake three hours waiting for it. It would be much simpler to get up and boil the billy. I've been thinking of buying one of those little spirit stove gadgets— but it might be against the rules. A beauty treatment? What-ever for? Do I need one? Oh, just for the fun of it? Something to remember when we go outback again? There might be something in what you say. I might try it. One of the new dust-facials? I hardly think that would be new for us. You see . . ."

The reporter lady took a few notes and then selected Helen as her next victim. "How old are you, Helen?"

Dan had a word with Ma and Pa and settled down to write out cheques.

"Excuse us," said Mary.

"We're going shopping," said Sinbad.

They escaped.

Helen was giving the reporter lady a pageful. "These cattle," she said, "they were so wild that stampeding at night over rough country their hooves struck up sparks from the flints so bright you could nearly read a newspaper by it . . ."

Ma looked at Pa. "Corky," she said softly.

Pa said, "Maybe she'd better go to school."

"Little 'un," said Dan, warningly, "are you still my sweet-heart? Then lay off!"

The lady reporter gathered up her purse and her pencil. "Do you mind, Mrs. Parsons, if I gave your little girl a really special double banana ice cream sundae? We could talk better alone. I'll bring her back." She swept out. Helen winked as she got through the door. Dan said softly, "Gutsache!"

Ma held Dan's hands. "You look fine, Dan. Was everything all right?"

"Sweet," said Dan. "They seemed to think fifty-three not much of a loss on a thousand head travelling fifteen hundred miles in eight months of a bad season."

"I'll say," said Bill warmly. "Let them try to do it."

"Ready for the track again, Ma?"

"Any time you say, Dan. I'm not much of a one for towns."

"We'll be leaving," said Dan, "in about a fortnight."

"Might as well," said Bill.

Corky popped his head in the door, all excitement. "Dan," he said, "Dan, they're waiting for you on the roof."

"Who's waiting?"

"The newsreel men. They want you to say a few words. They want to know about the Northern Territory. Everybody wants to know about the Northern Territory."

"Couldn't you tell them?"

"They want you, Dan."

The laugh was against Corky. Dan rose with a grin. At the end of the corridor he could see the blonde waiting. "How about," enquired Corky, "a little of the ready on account, Dan?"

Dan dug his hand in his pocket. "You'll be back on the track in a fortnight," he prophesied.

Pa wandered restlessly round the hotel sitting room. "That spirit stove, Ma. It might be a good idea. A cup of tea wouldn't go bad."

"There's an electric point," said Ma, comfortably, "and I've borrowed an electric jug." She rose to make tea.

"Ma," said Pa, "you're wonderful."

She gave him a look.

"What do you think," he asked, a little humbled, "Sinbad and Mary might be buying?"

"Might be a ring," she said. "I didn't ask them."

"A real engagement ring, eh? How do you like the idea, Ma?"

She sipped her tea. The two of them were sitting down on the couch.

"He's a good lad," she said. "Steady, but not too tame. He ought to suit Mary."

"Is that how you like them, Ma? Steady but not too tame?"

"You ought to know," said Ma.

"Between them they could work Glenrichard," said Pa, thoughtfully. "Build it up again proper."

"That's a long way off," said Ma tartly. "There's a lot more cattle to come down first."

"All right, Ma. Give us a kiss, will you?" Their lips met in the loving-kindness of being twenty-odd years married.

"I guess we're still overlanders," said Pa.

AFTERWORD

I do not think Harry Watt could have written the script and produced the film *The Overlanders* without the help, inspiration and loyalty of the little band of Australians who helped him from the moment of his arrival in Australia. I certainly could not have written the book without being in that group and being on location in the team that accompanied him while he was filming the Australian epic. The film is in fact a record of a real cattle trek that occurred in the Second World War. It was the Minister for Food in the Australian Commonwealth Government of the time who suggested that a film should be made to publicise this great feat. He may not have heard of Napolean's dictum that "an army travels on its stomach". His slogan was "Bully Beef not bullets."

At that time Singapore had fallen to the Japanese. They had conquered all the islands of the Dutch East Indies, now Irian Jaya, and had dropped a few bombs on Darwin, in the Northern Territory. It looked as if Australia might be next to fall. Even Sydney, New South Wales, had many apprehensions and two real frights. The Americans came to help us.

Many people moved out of Sydney to what they thought was a safer area to the west, the Blue Mountains. When the battle of the Coral Sea was imminent, my friend Doreen Martin and I, with my son Jarrah, aged two, were evacuated to a sheep station near Canberra which had been prepared for a last ditch stand. It even had a secret Aboriginal cave with provisions and arms in it. On the way, at a railway crossing, we saw wheat trucks going north, soldiers in uniform filled them. They were going to what was then called the Brisbane Line. But in fact, it turned out to be New Guinea and the Kokoda Trail.

A few weeks later, after the victory of the battle of the Coral Sea, Doreen and I returned to Sydney. My condition and Doreen's nine months later was due to the exuberance of our respective husbands on our return. Doreen's husband was a state cabinet minister. My husband Bert was a writer and a political journalist. We had just bought a house in Kirkoswald Avenue, Balmoral Beach, which at that time was protected from possible invasion by huge round pointed pillars of concrete, locally called tanktraps. Balmoral is directly opposite Sydney Heads and therefore very vulnerable for an invasion. I was sitting cosy before a gas fire in the living room when the air raid siren sounded. A shattering impact of sound and then a desolate whine, like a wolf in Russia waiting for the sleigh to break down. Nothing more happened for ten minutes. Then the door bell rang. A tall man was there.

"I am the air raid warden. Are your black-outs all in place?"

"Yes."

He looked me over.

"I'm supposed to have a baby tonight," I said. It was an apology.

"Where's your husband?"

"At work."

"Where's the hospital?"

"St Luke's Maternity Hospital in Elizabeth Bay."

"You can't get there. The Harbour Bridge is closed." Silence. "You had better go next door." He jerked his hands uphill.

"But I don't know them!"

"They'll take you in. Tell them I sent you."

I put on a coat and did what he said. They took me in. They played the piano and started to sing. About two o'clock the "all clear" sounded. I went home. Bert came much later, excited.

"The Japs," he said. "They shelled Bondi and then sank a freighter in the Harbour. Then the submarines were detected. Radar from Middle Head. Something scientific and quite new." That was the War in Australia in 1943.

Richard Kanga Birtles was twenty-two months old when I started working for Harry Watt in February, 1944. I had met him very casually in London in 1935 at a long Indian film about peasants and poverty. It was the "Left Review" magazine period. I had a flat in Marchmont Street, Bloomsbury, and was writing fashion articles. Harry was smart, very good-looking, in a black three-quarter length coat, and I wrote a send-up, a funny article about men's fashions. I was wearing a brown leather coat that had seen hard wear on a motor trip around Europe with my sister Vera Cable and two other Australian women. Such a trip was unusual then, the Australian flag flying jauntily above our Austin radiator. That trip was a political education for me: Hitler in Germany, the burning of the books, a bottle thrown against the car in the Spanish town of Burgos. I had seen a middle-aged nicely-dressed woman spat on outside a shop in Frankfurt, Germany, that said, "Jews Forbidden". In Berlin the Nazis were insultingly arrogant, there was intellectual and political tension in Vienna, and marked apprehension in Hungary. Out of work Welsh miners sang hymns in the streets of London.

When he came to Australia, Harry had read my husband's book *Exiles in the Aegean*, about politics in Greece under Metaxas. We were the first Australians to live in and write about Greece in 1935. He had also read my *North-West by North*, a sailing adventure. He asked me to do the research for *The Overlanders*. We met again at a small party. Harry had considerable flair and he was then tossing up about making a film of Eureka — the gold-miners' rebellion about the high cost of the miner's right to dig for gold against the government of the day in the 1840s. The alternative idea Harry had was a contemporary theme, a film that would enshrine the scorched earth policy in Australia. At that time the Russians, retreating from the German eastern offensive were said to be destroying what they could not carry with them. It was Napoleon's retreat from Moscow that the Russians were said to be emulating in reverse. "Take what you can. Destroy the rest." Patriots in Sydney were very fond of Russia in those days. Two of our friends called a magnificent tabby cat of theirs, "Timoshenko" after the marvellous defence of Stalingrad. There was also Mrs Jessie Street's "Sheepskins for Russia", a charity to keep the besieged or fleeing Russians warm and leave nothing for the Germans.

Harry turned to what he had really come out for, the film that the government wanted, about the cattle drive. I researched all the droving of cattle from the Kimberleys in the Northern Territory to Rockhampton in Queensland, and all I could find of other trips on the long stock routes. Harry now had to work out his plot. Find his actors. Establish a base and employ technicians and make arrangements for buying cattle, five hundred of them, and horses. Unpaid actors with no trade unions except the cruelty to animals legislation and the strong natural habits of their own.

Arch Spiers bought the cattle. (Ultimately as prices went up in the War Ealing Studios made a profit.) We used two separate mobs of mixed cattle, not specially-bred herds, just all we could get. One mob was used at Narwetooma, about thirty miles from Alice Springs and another on the Roper at the famous Elsey Station. Narwetooma was close enough to the Alice to make communication with Sydney possible and also for food and other necessary supplies. The cattle rush was done there, done in daylight with filters so as to get the effect of night, which was in fact the time when cattle would be grazing and nervous, and when rushes most frequently occur. For me and all the hands it was physically the most tiring time. Even Harry was puzzled. It was the highlight of the plot. He talked to me. The cattle had to rush in daylight. How to work it?

In Madrid I had gone with my sister and two other Australian girls to the most prestigious bull-fight of the year. The head waiter took us and told me all the fine points of this heroic sport. Man against bull, and death the joker in the pack. At the end when the matador has to die or conquer, it has to be a real victory. He has to conquer the will of the bull. The man's eyes, and sword, against the bull armed with his murderous horns and kicking hooves. Fantastic, exaggerated as it may sound, I saw it happen. The best bull in Spain. The best matador. Silence, fighting, skirmishing, the bull getting the better of it. The matador escaping, again and again. The bull angry. Then the slowness, the wariness of each. Both tired. Narrower margins of escape. The crowd absolutely silent. And then the face to face. The flash of the sword. I saw it. Slowly, slowly the bull went down, not a shiver or quiver or a kick left in him. The eye and the sword. But Harry's actors had to control a stampede with no swords and a terrible lot of bulls without balls and what about all those expensive horses? Horses are well loved, the public wouldn't stand that. Nor he, or the cast. It was in the script.

My research as well as my persuasion had done it. I remembered that cattle are usually controlled by men on horses, no dogs. That a Jewish pedlar pushing a barrow from Adelaide to the gold fields had made his way through a big mob of cattle like the crossing of the Red Sea by the Isralites in the Bible. That men without swords had caught, bridled and broken-in horses, that horses in medieval times and the First World War had died for their loved masters, in tournaments and in war. That men on foot could catch wild brumbies. OK give it a go. No women though in that lively sequence, and the actors had to agree to it. At Narwetooma we went through it time and again. No water, plenty of takes. Plenty of hoof marks on the same patch of sandy soil. I and others smoothing them out on hands and knees. My hands and back had long got used to hard work. There were enough takes to satisfy the perfection Watt demanded. We got sick of it and so did the beasts. We had to shout behind them and make other threatening noises to make their protesting legs rush.

Then there were the actors to choose. Chips Rafferty, the six-foot-six hero of Charles Chauvel's film, *Forty Thousand Horsemen* was a natural, an ideal hero. He did all the hard riding himself except the breaking in of the brumbies. Stunt men did that because Harry could not risk his star actor being injured.

The role of the heroine was more difficult but Harry, by lucky chance, found a beautiful girl, not an actress but an A.M.W.S., Daphne Campbell, who was on leave from North Queensland where there was a military hospital. Her people lived at Orange, New South Wales, and an army mate had asked her to deliver an educational film back to Film House, Sydney. The girl at the desk asked Daphne, "Can you ride a horse?" She could indeed ride and had ridden since childhood. Daphne rode in Centennial Park and had screen tests in the studio. Three days later she was offered, and accepted, the leading female role, Mary. Daphne was given leave without pay from the army and a salary of ten pounds a week from Ealing Studios. Chips got twenty five pounds a week. And Daphne recently laughingly said, "I went from one low paid job to another. I got three shillings and four pence a day in the army and ten pounds a week from Ealing." I know I got ten pounds a fortnight for a weekly article I wrote in the Sydney *Sunday Sun* called "Other People's Lives". It lasted from 1944 to 1945 and was very popular.

I had had a lot of trouble convincing Harry Watt that Australian women always went outback with their husbands, that the bush could not do without women, that girls grew up in the bush, that like my friend Miles Franklin, they could be well-educated, marvellous in the saddle and beautiful like Daphne. Then I found in a contemporary Queensland paper a small item about an overland cattle drive with a family bringing cattle over to Rockhampton. Henry Watt was then convinced that Australian outback women did go on cattle drives. The Parsons family were now integrated into the script.

Jean Blue who played the other important female role, Ma Parsons, was a nursing sister and a great actress in the left wing New Theatre in Kings Cross. Harry saw her in Ibsen's *Ghosts*. She was a quiet steady woman with a rather concealed sense of fun. There was an air of rectitude about her, a moral integrity and dignity that everyone felt and respected. I think I gave her the credibility of the role she played in the film, the language, the attitudes, the abilities, the understanding and feelings of the bush mother — the women of our old Australian outback. John Nugent Haywood played the part of the father, Bill Parsons. John was a seasoned actor, well cast. He had a private passion, gold mining. He knew all about Lasseter's Reef and took likely samples of ore from here and there on our various locations. Helen Greives, the little girl with the foal, was the daughter of one of Harry's friends and, with Ma and Pa Parsons and Mary, made up the Parsons' family. Helen was fresh, a charming little girl, we all loved her.

After all these years my respect for the job we all did grows. I suppose Harry was the magnet that drew all these talents up like metal filings to his genius. We had to be iron-hard to get by sometimes. Maybe it was hardest for Peter Pagan. I had chosen him when I was doing some of the casting. He was my character. I wanted a foil for Chips, someone fair, a new chum, Harry saw him as the love interest, if he had to have women and a pretty girl, Peter Pagan, who spoke with an English accent, would do. Harry had an instinct at that time to give in to Dora, have women, for plot. The cattle trek was the theme, well, a bit grudgingly, embroider it with a love interest.

I had now graduated from researcher to script conferences and casting, after insisting on women being in the film. Several weeks later I went to Alice Springs. In wartime one had to get permits to travel. I had high priority, a great privilege. In the bus going out to Mascot airport there was an officer with plenty of red on his tabs. At the airport there was a Japanese prisoner of war, miserable, sitting on the floor, guarded. He was going to interrogation and prison camp. Our credentials were taken, our priorities checked. There were also a lot of soldiers, ordinary ranks. I was told to go aboard. The high ranking officer was not. He scowled at me. He had not liked the look of me. Solid shoes, felt riding hat, heavy drill trousers from the sailing days. He felt his rank insulted. Meekly I got on board. I was the only woman. No seats. We sat on small canvas slides close together, our bottoms almost on the floor. There was a lot of heavy machinery in the back of the plane. It was a D.C.2. Soldiers crammed into the other slides aft of me and a whole line opposite. I suppose there were about twenty or so.

We took off with a roar and a whiz. Then it happened. We hadn't made height. There was a bang and a crash. Heavy metal and men slid down on me. Quick as lightning soldiers had the exit doors opposite swung open, men leapt down. I was squashed by the sliding cargo but I got out quick. It was thirty feet to drop. They held out their multiple hands far below. I jumped. Last out. They caught me as I fell. "God" said a man, "if it had been a Lockheed Lightning we would have gone up in a flash." They ran away from the plane, caught high on the perimeter fence of the airfield, the back of the plane cocked up high, the men, dusting themselves, running well away. Me too, limping, my left side hurting but walking, safe.

"Come tomorrow" the Airport people said, "Same time. Different plane."

Next day I flew safely to Melbourne. In the morning I saw a specialist. "You've got two ribs cracked," he said. "I don't think they are out of place. If you take it very carefully you'll be alright. If you have any trouble see a doctor at once. Be careful." He put two wide elastic bandages round the left half of my rib cage. Next day to Adelaide and then on the "the Alice". I had never been so far before by air. It was enchanting. Sunshine, scenery. We flew easily, my own country below me. Wonderful to be free, to have a job, extra fine that Harry wanted me to stay with the crew. I soon found out why. Publicity. Now we were on the job, Daineschefsky at Ealing in London wanted news. Soon we should be moving out to Mataranka, and on to the unworked pastoral country at the foot of the McDonnell Ranges.

The army were very good to us at Alice Springs and had prepared a special camp on an army reserve not far from the military airfield. The Alice was a small place at that time. One hotel, some shops, the post office, the police station, the hospital, the Todd river dry as a bone. Mrs Jenkins, the old-timer with her shop of opals, her native weapons in a barrel in the backyard and lots of good stories and good humour. Her husband worked his gold mine out at the Olgas. At Alice Springs we had a party. It was crowded, very merry, late in the afternoon. Local women came too but most had gone south. Darwin was barred to white women after the Japanese attack on it. Only the policeman's wife at Mataranka stayed.

From Alice Springs we went to Narwetooma. Now it was hard work and discomfort. The Englishmen must have found it strange, uncomfortably demanding and very difficult. Tents, cold, work started early. Up at six o'clock and on the go at eight. No water closets. Hot showers — sometimes — but mostly cold. Dust, fine as powder getting in your hair, your ears, eyes and nose. Stinging your face. Then transcendentally beautiful short sunsets, night coming down like a blanket. A couple of Aboriginal families outside the camp, a few fires glowing, sleepers with blankets or curled up in hollows they find or make. A magnificent Aboriginal warrior, majestic, a wonderful king among his own people stood by the pile of our camp-logs and tree trunks swinging his heavy axe insolently, lazily, reluctantly, hating the instrument, us and his job. Chopping wood for the stupid white man's big stoves and fires.

Syd Gresham was worried about the expense of going back to Wyndham to get authenticity for the embarkation scene. Because of my sailing experience I saved Ealing an enormous amount of money, quite simply. When I heard of the difficulty I said, "Quarantine station on North Head. It has bush and beach and there is a Navy wharf at Obelisk Bay you might use." So a steamship was hired for the day. Our children, their mothers, their friends, and everyone we could rustle up were extras. Camden airport was also used later for the aeroplane shots of the departure from Wyndham. The outback shanty hotel scenes of Anthony's Lagoon were shot at the old Telegraph Station in Alice Springs. There were some Aboriginal children there and I spent a day with them. Having been a teacher and now a mother, it was delightful. They taught me, laughing easily at my ignorance and stupidity. The sand was their blackboard. I couldn't recognise their bare footprints in the sand. They showed me the tracks of birds and animals with their little knuckles pressed in the sand, and how to find widgety grubs and how to eat them.

We had our own spectacular conclusion. VJ Day when the Emperor of Japan capitulated after the bombing of Hiroshima. The army at Mataranka requested our presence to celebrate the event. "The four women of *The Overlanders* must go" Harry said. I put on a pretty blue cotton dress with lots of little frills. There was only room for two women and the driver in the front seat of the army truck. Gallantly and foolishly I stood up in the back of the truck. We went for miles and miles of deep red rutty road, me holding on to the top of the cabin. Outside at Mataranka Officers were waiting for us. The girls got out. Hands were held out for me. I jumped. There was a roar of laughter. Nobody could help it. Whatever was the matter? I was red dust from head to foot, face, frills, petticoat, everything. I was taken in to an officer's quarters, given an army uniform they thought would fit me and left to shower. The hut had slatted sides, the shower no shower curtain. I got the unmistakable feeling that eyes were looking at me through the slats. When I emerged the soldiers told me I looked better in uniform. In the big open-air picture theatre speeches were being given. The girls and chaps were on the stage with the big brass. They got a wonderful reception.

The camp on the Roper River was a job, except for the heat, the flies and so on. Jack Hickson the stills photographer from the *Daily Telegraph* came up especially, he went up a tree and took magnificent pictures. I was below him holding equipment and bracing my heels to avoid slipping in and being accidentally in frame. One of his shots got a double page spread in an American newspaper and a coveted prize for best action photograph of the year. The main actor, the crocodile, was off stage in Taronga Zoo. The crossing of the river sequence was most difficult and exciting of all. The local tribe gave us a farewell corroboree. It was the best I ever saw, and I had seen quite a few before. They were in no hurry. Preparations had taken a long time and it was getting late on a dark night. When they were ready they lit small fires, a row of them, yet they had never seen stage lights. I realised that this was pure theatre. We were the audience, they the players, the dancers be-daubed with white and red on shining black skins, their make-up complete and impressive and their entry dramatic. They burst out of the surrounding bush with a war cry. It sent a shiver down the spine. This was for real, it was important for them as for us. No women in the dance. A digeridoo and hand-clapping on skin for sound, the imitation of animal noises as well as gestures. It went on a long time and when we left it continued far into the night.

Our work was over. The indoor scenes would be shot in the Pagewood Studios in Sydney. We travelled for the last time to Mataranka loaded with the booty we had acquired, spears, shields with kills notched on them, one burn mark meant one enemy slain. A coolamon for me. We flew back to Sydney in the largest troop transport plane the army had. Home life began again. Publicity rolled in. Shrewd Syd Gresham suggested I write the book *The Overlanders*. I sat in my study upstairs and wrote it quickly. It flowed. I had lived it, helped mould and make it. I was part of Harry Watt's team. He went back to England to finish the film. I never saw him again.

The book had a great success. Ten editions. I got a station wagon, one of the first six in Australia, out of it. No more bicycling. Now I don't even drive. "It's not your eyesight Mum, it's your reflexes," said our two boys. A fellow in a high-ranking sports car had knocked into me. So now I've lost my transport freedom. I'm getting old. But when I can't run on the beach or for a bus I shall be really old. We have six grandchildren. I am just another granny.

Very recently I had the pleasure, after all these years, of seeing *The Overlanders* on the small screen in black and white – there was no colour in our time. The sound was very good – Ted Hunter had battled to get results. What was exceptionally marvellous was the music. Ealing spent a lot of money on the music composed by John Ireland. They had a full orchestra and it was really wonderful. It swept along powerfully, combining the mood with the action. It was a man's film; women or no women, it had the unmistakable stamp of masculinity and adventure. What was more remarkable was the idiom, our Australian phraseology. We had to teach Harry that. He was a good listener. The language is authentically Australian of the period. Slang and usage change. My idiom is out of date now and I know it.

War breeds a strange state of mind. There is all the anxiety, the fear, the dread, the burdens of being alive and keeping going and the sudden need of pleasure, of real friendships, of hilarity. In that climate we made *The Overlanders*, a film that was a world-wide winner. It brought in a lot of money for Australia and was the *Crocodile Dundee* of its time.

Dora Birtles, Sydney, 1986